ALSO BY
ALEX ESPINOZA

Cruising: An Intimate
History of a Radical Pastime

The Five Acts of Diego León

Still Water Saints

THE
SONS
OF
EL REY

A NOVEL

ALEX ESPINOZA

SIMON & SCHUSTER

New York London Toronto Sydney New Delhi

1230 Avenue of the Americas
New York, NY 10020

An excerpt from a previous version of the novel was
published in *Air/Light* Magazine.

First Simon & Schuster hardcover edition June 2024

SIMON & SCHUSTER and colophon are registered
trademarks of Simon & Schuster, LLC

Simon & Schuster: Celebrating 100 Years of Publishing in 2024

For information about special discounts for bulk purchases,
please contact Simon & Schuster Special Sales at
1-866-506-1949 or business@simonandschuster.com.

The Simon & Schuster Speakers Bureau can bring authors to
your live event. For more information or to book an event,
contact the Simon & Schuster Speakers Bureau at
1-866-248-3049 or visit our website at www.simonspeakers.com.

Interior design by Lewelin Polanco

Manufactured in the United States of America

1   3   5   7   9   10   8   6   4   2

Library of Congress Cataloging-in-Publication Data
has been applied for.

ISBN 978-1-6680-3278-7
ISBN 978-1-6680-3280-0 (ebook)

For Kyle

Thank you for teaching me how to love with force
and without regret.
I remain forever with you in this struggle.

In the ring, and even in the depths of their voluntary ignominy, wrestlers remain gods because they are, for a few moments, the key which opens Nature, the pure gesture which separates Good from Evil, and unveils the form of a Justice which is at last intelligible.

—ROLAND BARTHES

ERNESTO VEGA

A friend once told me the dead tell the best lies. I will try to be honest even though I never learned how.

No, I wasn't born a luchador. I was shaped into one by circumstance, by a life lived without tenderness or sympathy, by my father's beatings when I was a boy, his constant attempts to toughen me up, to make me a man. *Un hombre valiente*, he'd say. El Rey Coyote was my lucha libre persona. The long and flowing cape with its wide shoulder pads and furry collar, the spandex tights, the boots, and the mask, bright white fabric inlaid with thick gold borders outlining the eyes, nose, and mouth . . . it was an act and I got lost in it. I can't be blamed, though. I only wanted to be seen and recognized. And I got my wish; all over Mexico, throngs of people packed those vast stadiums. They stood on their seats, raised their voices. They cheered for him, for me, and I was truly loved. But I didn't choose to become El Rey Coyote. When I moved to Mexico City with my wife, he found me. We were destined for each other. Either good guy técnicos or bad boy rudos, we do it for la gloria, for the honor, for the sacrifice.

The punches to the stomach, the chest, the groin. The smacks on the back from an opponent or the mat as I leapt from the top cord, pivoting in the air, then falling so hard the sensation sent shocks like bursts of lightning from the base of my spine, up and down the column, from my fingers to my toes. The choke holds. Broken noses. Head injuries. Busted lips. Black eyes. Cracked fingers. Snapped wrists. Pulled tendons. Hands yanking my hair and twisting my arms. Legs wrapping around my neck, crushing my larynx, nearly suffocating me. Boot soles stomping my face. Scratch. Punch. Pound. Break. Blood running. Always the blood running.

Yes, the feuds are scripted, penned to hype up the drama, to get the audiences invested in our characters, to keep them coming back. And even though the fights are choreographed to avoid injuries, they still happen. Some think it's all fake, but they're wrong. You just need to look to our bodies for proof.

Like me, it was circumstance that led my son, Alfredo, to follow in my footsteps and become a luchador. Unlike me, it was his choice to do so. This was the 1980s, so all everyone talked about besides nuclear war with the Rusos was Satanic messages hidden in songs, cocaine, and teen suicide. After his mother died back when he was in high school, he started drinking, smoking mota, getting into car wrecks, and nearly killing himself.

Something needed to be done, so I got him into the ring and trained him in the tradition of lucha libre. That changed him, and he surpassed even my expectations. He followed in my footsteps, donned boots, tights, and a cape with bright colored stones. He covered his identity in a mask of shiny fabric adorned with jewels and beads, flashier than mine. As it is in our tradition, he took my name. Alfredo became El Rey Coyote Jr., the toughest luchador in all of Los Angeles. My grandson, Julián, was born to wage a different kind of battle, born to don a different type of mask.

I want to tell them I know how divine it can be, all that fame and adoration, all the ways they crave bodies like ours. But this can also ruin us, lead to our demise.

My children, Alfredo and Mercedes.

Julián.

Elena, my wife, my only real love.

Even him, that other me, El Rey Coyote.

I want them to know I understand now. I see what parts of us are forever lost in all this beautiful chaos. But I'm more dead than alive at this moment, so it's too late for me anyway.

FREDDY VEGA

It was taken before I was born. He's a different person from the old man currently dying inside a drab hospice room, eyes barely open, unable to speak. In this photo, my father defies gravity. Behind him there's a truck; the sides are banged up and dented, the paint chipped. The bed's stacked with bricks three and four high. He holds one in each hand, his fingers dusted with rust-red chalk. He's growling, though my mom used to say he was laughing. To me, it's a growl, and there's a wild look in his eyes. He's in the air, having leapt off the back of the truck. His knees are tucked against his chest. Whoever took the photograph managed to snap it at the right angle so that it looks like he's suspended, not hurtling back down to the ground, but floating.

I've memorized every detail: his tights and white boots; the fabric of his cape billowing out behind him; the *Bohemia* beer sign hanging from the side of a crumbling building in downtown Mexico City; a little girl in a green coat darting across the street, blurred and ghostly. To my father's right there's a shadow stretching over the concrete sidewalk. It's small, and anyone else would miss it because it looks like nothing more than a smudge, a flaw in the film. But it's my mother's frame. She's pregnant with me.

In that moment, I'm just a shadow, something far away and distant.

I'll have my own son one day; he'll arrive on a rainy morning in February, his cries so loud they'll drown out the thunder shaking the skies above us. We'll give him my middle name, Julian, and I'll try to be a good father just like his abuelo had been for me. But I'll fail epically. I know he's moved on, let the past be the past. I haven't though; I've doomed us all. In that picture, my mother and I are incomplete, but my father's not. He's whole. There he is. Right there. This is the memory of him that I hold close to me, that I always have. Ernesto Vega leaping out of the bed of a truck, holding a brick in each hand.

For as long as I can remember it's been nailed to the same spot on the wall inside the office, right next to the door leading out to the weight room, slightly crooked, the frame a dull silver. When I remove it, the color of the cheap wood paneling behind it is lighter, not dingy or sticky from grime like the rest of the room. A crooked screw pokes out from the surface. The frame falls apart; the glass tumbles to the ground and shatters. The shards cover the carpet so worn away in spots that it's patched together with strips of electrical tape. That's been the only thing holding this photo up all these years. A tiny nail. Thin as a baby bird's bones. Thin and just as frail.

In the mid-1980s, when I was still in high school, my father left his factory job. He took all his money and rented out this space: a run-down, one-thousand-square-foot warehouse in an industrial area located on Mission between First and Meyers, east of the Los Angeles River bordering the railroad tracks. This was right after my mother died. I remember my sister, Mercy, and I thinking he was nuts. Maybe he was in shock? How could we convince him it was a bad idea, not worth the risk? But he converted this dilapidated place into something special. People from all over LA flocked here to work out, to spar in the ring, to train for weightlifting competitions. In the early '90s, when that WWE shit became popular and they started running it every Saturday night on Channel 13, he decided to start offering classes in the art of lucha libre. He'd been a luchador in Mexico during the '60s and '70s. His name was El Rey Coyote, and he sported white tights, shiny lace-up boots with thick heels, and a long cape with a fur collar.

Then there was his máscara, the thing that gives every luchador their powers and abilities. Bright white with gold outlining his mouth, nose, and eyes, it fit over his face so tight it was a second layer of skin. He was a tried-and-true good guy técnico who traveled all over the republic battling rudos from Tijuana, Veracruz, and Monterey. He even held bouts in El Paso and San Diego, taught these gabacho wrestlers a thing or two, and starred in some low-budget films where he fought mobsters and space aliens. After high school, I joined the operation, working first as a trainer's assistant, then, once I debuted as El Rey Coyote Jr., a bona fide lucha libre star and coach in my own right. But that was a lifetime ago. When I felt invincible. Like I could have it all. The overworked hospice nurses and the short doctor with the oily hair say there's not much left to do to try saving him. All we can do is stand on the sideline and watch. Now, here inside the gym he founded, the place he fought so hard to keep, I feel him in every corner and cold pocket.

Bands of sunlight break through the plated windows facing the gravel parking lot. Like many small businesses, the lockdowns royally fucked us. And now that we're past all that upheaval, I learn about the big-shot developer buying up properties around here. Little by little, the junkyards, auto detailing shops, and warehouses are being replaced by art galleries, trendy bars, and expensive lofts only guys in skinny jeans and handlebar mustaches and their hipster friends can afford. Even though we're heading into summer and things are kicking up again, going back to something resembling normal, something resembling life before the entire coronavirus desmadre, our gym members have moved on, forgotten about us. These days it's only the loyal clients who trickle in to lift weights or use the outdated treadmills that somehow still work. There hasn't been a single new customer for as long as I can remember. All the others have just let their accounts lapse, so I've been forced to cancel them. Not much to do around here these days, so I'm using the downtime to organize, clear things out, and keep my head occupied so that I don't go crazy thinking about my dad, about all the ways I've failed him. They're saying it could be months or days until he passes. My wife, Grace, packed me a couple of sandwiches. I have a thermos full of café de olla, hot clove and cinnamon so strong it cuts through the smell of rubber and metal and the layers and layers of sweat and sacrifice this old gym still holds.

"I have some sick days," Grace said to me this morning. "I'll go down with you and help." During the lockdowns, she got promoted to lead cashier because she was able to remain calm during all the chaos, her boss said.

"We can't afford it. You go to work."

"Okay." She folded a damp dish towel and draped it over the edge of the sink. "I'll call Julian. He doesn't start teaching again until the end of the month, and you two need—"

"No," I interrupted. "Just . . . let me do this."

She turned, looked at me, brows glistening with sweat, the box fan on the dining table blowing strands of hair in her face. "Stop being such a damned macho. I'm calling him and that's that."

Terca. That's the word my father would use to describe Grace. And my mother. *Mujeres tercas.* He'd throw his head back, laugh. *They always keep us honest.*

There's so much here. Punching bags. Racks full of weights. Bench presses. The mats. Medicine balls. None of it being used. Everything silent and still. And then there's this cramped office where my father managed the whole operation with the help of his buddy Hugo. The crazy dude with shrapnel in his leg courtesy of the Vietnam War. He always wore so much aftershave his fingers left everything perfumed, a lingering combination of flowers and baby powder. Hugo took a shot of tequila every morning and once stabbed a guy who was trying to rob a prostitute. He and my dad worked together for years—balancing books, filling out forms, renting out the ring, keeping careful track of everything. Once the news about the spread of the pandemic started hitting, Hugo was one of the first to pack all his shit up and head for the mountains, some secluded cabin in Big Bear. I haven't heard from him since.

I'm determined to sort through all of it, trashing what's no longer needed, keeping what calls to me. There's a big metal desk in the office, its drawers crammed with receipts and ledgers, its surface scratched and scored. In the far corner, pushed up against the wood-paneled wall, is an old filing cabinet. Inside, more forms, more receipts, more invoices, more envelopes stuffed with letters and contracts, names and addresses of businesses we'd worked with, places that are permanently gone. It's all suddenly lost its meaning. His life's work no longer has a place. It doesn't belong anywhere anymore. It's just an inconvenience, and perhaps that's the most tragic thing about all of this. I want to throw my hands up, say fuck it, torch the building, and call it a day.

But I can't. I won't.

Outside, a few garbage trucks and semis rumble down Mission. For a Monday, it should be busier. I should be seeing the short man on the corner of First setting up his little stand, firing up the burner where he cooks his famous breakfast burritos stuffed with scrambled eggs, chorizo, bacon, cheese, and huitlacoche. I should see the cooler wide open, the glass necks of Mexican Coke, orange Fanta, and the apple-flavored Sidral Julian used to love so much as a kid poking out from the ice.

Where did everyone go?

At around ten thirty, there comes the sound of a car approaching outside. A door slamming shut. Julian strolls through the front entrance. Baggy sweats. A dark hoodie. High-top Nikes unlaced. I remember what it was like for our family during the lockdowns, when we were forced to stay apart. He'd drive by the house and sit out on the porch, Grace and I talking to him through the dusty screen door. He started shaving his head when the barber shops closed, and now that they're open, it looks like he's not planning on growing his hair out. Stubble sprouts from his chin, along the edges of his sharp jawline.

"What's up?" I toss the two trash bags full of old invoices and binders from the office by the door.

He shoves his car keys in his pocket. "Mom said you might need a hand."

"I'm good. Don't worry about it."

He sighs. "Let me help."

"No," I insist. "You've got your own shit to deal with. This is something I gotta do. For your abuelo. He left me in charge."

"Dad, come on. Don't do this." He takes a step forward.

To him, I'm being stubborn. To him, I'm playing the macho card, acting all tough. But if only he knew the truth, what it's like right now. I've been defeated. Everything's spiraling out of control. The depression I felt after his abuela died all those years ago has returned and is settling in, making itself real warm and cozy inside me. The thought of the sandwiches Grace packed turn my stomach. I can't sleep. Even when I take the pills.

"Go on, Son." I raise my voice, widen my stance. "It's fine."

He shakes his head, sighs, and mutters, "This is all *so* fucked up," before turning around and taking off. I want to say I know it is. But why bother now?

As El Rey Coyote Jr., I was raised to fight. I carried on my father's legacy, inside and outside the ring. But I failed. Because these things I can't battle. All around me, the whole world has stopped fucking spinning and been turned upside down. And what's left is the madness that silence brings. The absence of all these memories, of lives with nothing left, shouting in protest, resisting, refusing to go quietly.

JULIAN VEGA

He doesn't think I get it, but I do. The men of my father's generation aren't the best communicators. They were taught to stay
quiet, were raised on a crap ton of testosterone and aggression.
Violence and poverty were their norm. Asking for help was seen as
a sign of weakness. It's all such macho bullshit, a total act that's almost laughable. He's always been bad, but he's gotten worse since
we've been forced to face the truth that Abuelo's dying.

I race out of the gym's parking lot, kicking up dust and gravel,
my father's silhouette moving back and forth inside the derelict
building.

He doesn't want my help? Fine. Fuck it.

* *

They still make you put a mask on when you visit the hospice. They
got signs up, too. *Don't enter if you have a fever or a cough. Wash
your hands with soap and water for twenty seconds.* Shit we already
know, but I follow the rules. I need to be with my abuelito today.

Some think these places are depressing. Drab walls. Outdated
furniture. Faded green carpet. Old people shoved inside tiny rooms
that smell of stale pee and latex, all of them just waiting to die. Call
me weird, but they're anything but sad to me. It's quiet in here,
like a church.

Since they admitted Abuelo a few weeks ago, I've made it a habit to stop by on a regular basis, especially now that I'm between classes; I won't start teaching summer school until later this month. Even though they're both only basic English writing sections, I feel lucky to have nabbed the two classes. But the pay's absolute shit, and I don't know how far I can make my money stretch until fall without dipping into what little's in my savings account. It's June now, right before the official start of summer. I've got to make it to September somehow. Three damn months.

Graduate school didn't prepare me for this kind of financial vulnerability.

Too much to think about right now, so I push it aside as I make my way down the hallway, past the front desk where an orderly in aqua-blue scrubs is talking to a nurse sporting a billowy smock.

"Good morning," a male receptionist announces as I stroll by. His name tag reads *Randy Bravo*. He's tall with smooth skin, cherry-red lips, firm thighs, and nice arms. Totally my type.

"Hey." I raise an eyebrow, letting my gaze linger, placing my mask on after I've passed.

He smiles at me and reaches for the telephone, its ring rude and shrill. "East LA Hospice and Palliative Care. This is Randy."

Every day I bring Abuelo the same bottle of chocolate Yoo-hoo, his favorite drink. I set it down on the side table near his bed and adjust the blinds so that the room isn't so dark and morose, so he could know the sun's out, that he's still alive, still with us. His eyes mostly remain closed, though every now and again they flutter open, and he peers around, his look both amazed and terrified, like he's seeing the world for the first time. There's so much about Abuelo Ernesto that remains a mystery, obscured by secrets and time, a long life lived decades before I was even a thought. I reach out, hold his weathered hand, his fingers twisted as dried grapewood branches. My grandfather doesn't respond, though. He's too far out of reach now.

Even my dad doesn't know for sure why my grandparents left Mexico right before he was born, why they landed in LA with nothing but a few boxes of clothes and pictures, having driven all the way from the capital in Abuelo's shiny Impala with its gold rims, the spokes glinting like a queen's crown. He asked my grandmother once when he was a kid why they came here, but she got all quiet and serious.

"I think something bad happened to them," he told me. "Something that made them so sad."

He and Tía Mercy knew not to ask about their lives in that other country, the one they only knew about through photos and old magazine clippings of Abuelo's escapades as a luchador. This is how it is for most of us with parents or grandparents who leave the poverty and political upheaval behind. We try to tease information out of them, try understanding what could motivate them to risk everything to come here. So often our questions about why and when and who are answered by more questions: *Why not? Who knows when? A smuggler helped us, I guess?* Or vague replies that only heighten the mystery even more: *It was terrible there. Be grateful that you live here. If you only knew what we went through.*

Imagine trying to sift through endless fragments of your history. Imagine not knowing what year your grandfather was born, where your grandmother went to school. Imagine knowing you have family somewhere in Mexico or Guatemala that you'll probably never meet. In elementary school, my teacher gave each student in our fourth-grade class a sheet of paper with a drawing of a tree. Next to each branch was a blank spot. *You're going to fill out your own family tree*, she explained.

Someone asked why.

"So that we could know who we are and where we come from," she replied.

Someone else asked why.

"Knowing where we come from helps us understand ourselves better."

I knew a lot about my maternal grandparents, Steve and Patricia Mata, my mother's mom and dad. Grandma Patty baked me birthday cakes and decorated these with squiggly drawings of fire trucks and plastic action figures of Spider-man or Superman, and they'd sometimes fall over and get frosting stuck to their outfits. Grandpa Steve worked in an insurance office and read books about war and political sabotage. He had a library, and I wasn't allowed to go in there. Ever.

"That man has never seen a day of hard labor in his life," Abuelo once said to my father. "You can tell by his hands. No calluses."

They were never Abuelo and Abuela. They were always Grandpa Steve and Grandma Patty.

Grandma Patty's parents fled Mexico in the 1930s and immigrated to Southern California. Her father drank himself to death, leaving his wife to raise all seven kids, including Grandma Patty, by herself.

My mother was the awkward middle child who had dreams of becoming a nurse after she read a biography about Florence Nightingale. Back in the mid-1990s, her life took a different turn when she met my father. Around that time, there was a crazy guy going around assaulting young girls, and my mother and her friends from community college heard about the self-defense classes being offered at Abuelo's gym.

"I was exaggerating some that day," she confessed. "I was more interested in getting close to your father than anything. I'd seen him once before when I stopped in. He was cute, and I wanted him to ask me out."

They fell in love. She made him mixtapes of all her favorite songs recorded from the radio. She kept these in a cardboard shoebox, and sometimes I'd play them, laugh at the cheesy music and silly lyrics.

My mother's older brother, Uncle Danny, had been a "wild child," Grandma Patty told me. Very unconventional. He listened to punk rock in high school, sported a mohawk, and wore safety pins pierced through his earlobes. Tío Danny lived in a trailer in northeast Utah, near the Uintah and Ouray Reservation. He sent me birthday cards that carried the scent of patchouli oil. Those cards came every year without fail. The brown envelopes, his neat writing. Inside he'd include pencil sketches of flowers, hawks in flight, a pack of coyotes perched atop a boulder. Sometimes he'd send these little booklets with writing that looked as though it had been printed using an old typewriter.

They were handmade, the thin pages stapled or tied together with twine, full of the strange paranormal accounts of the region and of a place called Skinwalker Ranch. Some of the booklets included illustrations of objects in the sky or shadowy humanlike figures lurking behind thickets of trees. He'd write in the margins, *Julian, I saw one of these*, followed by the date of the alleged encounter. My mom's younger sister, Aunt Cathy, was a born-again Christian who liked to post news stories about conspiracy theories and Covid-19 signaling the second coming of Jesus Christ to my social media feeds. She'd leave comments, too: *Repent, mijo. The Lord loves you and will forgive you. Let HIM into your heart!*

I had to add her to my list of blocked profiles.

I could say with certainty that, of all the relatives, none had more of a direct impact on my life than Abuelo Ernesto. Without his decision to get up and go, to leave it all behind and start up again, I wouldn't be here to tell you this.

The only times I ever got close to livestock were the trips we took as a kid to the Los Angeles County Fair in Pomona. There are pictures of me petting sheep, sitting on top of a donkey, and feeding stalks of grass to a goat. Abuelo went with us a couple of times, and when we got to the section with the pigs, he used to tell me about the different breeds. The golden red ones called Duroc were used to make lard, he'd explain. Then there were the Hampshires with their black-and-white coats and ears that always stuck straight up. This made them very alert and good at grazing. Hampshires were the most common in the United States and raised for their meat. His favorites were the ones called Yorkshire pigs, because their meat was lean and the sows of this breed produced many piglets.

From pig farmer to luchador. When I was younger, he loved to show off his old clippings, the posters advertising his fights, Polaroids of him standing in the middle of a crowded bar, arms extended out, muscles oiled and flexed, surrounded by women with puffy hair and too much makeup. He wore his mask like a second skin, braided around the back of his skull by a series of thick laces. The gold borders outlining his eyes and mouth were thick, defined, and even though he was one of the good guys, the thing always made him look sinister to me.

In some of the pictures, there's my grandmother Elena in her polyester jackets with wide collars, her hair in a beehive bun, fake eyelashes fuzzy as moth wings. She's holding a wooden spoon up to Abuelo's mouth, and he stands beside her in a brown-and-orange checkered shirt, chains hanging from his thick neck, his lucha mask over his face because, like all luchadores, he kept his identity a secret from his fans.

She's smiling, but there's something faraway about her expression. In some of the images, though, when he embraces her, it's like there's something between them, an unseen barrier.

Abuelo Ernesto is all grins under his mask.

But if I looked long enough, my abuela Elena's face would speak to me, would tell me, *I'm lost. How do I find my way out?*

I try to stay here in this moment with him, because he's slipping from us one breath at a time. A nurse comes in and tells me I need to step out of the room for a while.

"We have to suction him," she explains. "You can come back in about an hour."

It's not a pleasant thing to experience, the gurgling sound of junk being pulled from his lungs.

"Yeah, I should head out anyway," I reply, grabbing the warm bottle of chocolate milk and shoving it in my pocket.

I make my way towards the front entrance of the hospice. An old man in a hospital gown speckled with red stars sits in a wheelchair near the double doors. He lifts a finger as I pass, pointing to the bottle of chocolate milk.

"Yoo-hoo." He sings it. "Yoo-hoo. Yoo-hoo. Yoo-hoo." He grins, the inside of his mouth all gums, pink and slick.

I lean over and place the bottle in his lap and don't take off my mask until I'm inside my car, away from the specters and memories tugging and tugging at me.

Tomorrow, I think. *We have tomorrow. For now.*

Elena Vega

What he said isn't the truth. I wasn't Ernesto's only real love. But here's what *is* true: I wasn't all that content living in La Peña. Sure, we had our little house with its shiny metal roof and its sturdy brick walls painted bluer than the sky. We had two small rooms. There was a bed with a soft mattress and pillows and warm quilts. The house was on a large plot of land that once belonged to his father. Wide green fields. Soil rich in minerals. There was even a little brook that ran a few feet behind the barn. How I loved the trickle of water skidding over the slick silver rocks.

Each morning, after he'd leave to tend the pigs, I'd boil water and sit out back, smoke a cigarette and sip my coffee and watch the cornstalks sway in the breeze. We had chickens, and they grew fat and healthy, and they laid eggs and I fed these to him, swimming in red salsa. We had money. Not a lot, but enough, first for the refrigerator and then the television. We placed it on top of an old wooden drum. He fiddled with the dials and the antenna, until the fuzzy picture cleared and, just like that, the world entered my house. I had my comadres. On Saturdays, we went shopping in the markets, bought lipstick and false eyelashes, ate lunch, drank beers and gossiped. There was church on Sunday, eating toasted peanuts on metal park benches in the zocalo, strolling under shaded porticos.

But I knew of a bigger world, one with more shine, more luster, thanks to our television and all those *Buenhogar* magazines I would thumb through at the newsstands scattered along the broken and narrow sidewalks of our town. The glossy photos showed blond-haired gabachas modeling pleated miniskirts and leather boots. There were advertisements for shampoo, perfume, cigarettes (*Her lips love Regal Slims!*), and makeup.

I loved our town. Don't get me wrong. But I also found myself yearning for something more. That's part of the reason why I followed them. I could just hear our daughter Mercy's reaction: *A man shouldn't control your destiny. You don't have to go where he goes, do what he says. You are your own person.* He left me no other choice; I'd do whatever it took to preserve my family because he had his eyes elsewhere. He expected me to agree to stay behind and wait, but I had my own plans. I wasn't some pendeja from the campo. I knew things, even back then.

I had something to prove too.

El Rey Coyote

Let's get one thing straight, ¡cabrones y cabronas! I'm not like her, the wife. She's a ghost. I'm something more, something ancient, powerful. Both the old man and not. I extend beyond life and past death. I am a force of nature not to be toyed with.

But this isn't about me. It's about them. And about what they did to that poor man, their friend. They betrayed him and their entire country, turning their backs on us after everything we gave them. Cowards. Too ashamed to admit what they set in motion. Too embarrassed to face the ruin they caused. They ran away, tried shedding that former life, tried burying it. But the lies, the deceit, the mierda, it ALWAYS has a way of resurfacing.

¡Eso es la verdad!

ERNESTO VEGA

Why does he bring that bottle of chocolate milk each time he visits?
It's like a taunt, a sad reminder that I can't drink anymore because
I got a giant fucking tube sticking out of my throat. Hijo de la
chingada. Screw the chocolate milk. I need a shot of tequila.

It might sound like I'm not taking this whole dying business
seriously even as the nurse jabs the thin tube into the hole and then
turns the machine over my head on to slurp all that green fluid out
of my lungs. Who knew my body was still capable of producing so
much? Rest assured that I know this is serious. There's a sadness
that extends beyond the basic definition of that word, too. It's
something transcendent, like the lamentations of monks and saints,
a mourning that cuts right through flesh and bone and straight to
the soul. When one is so close to departing, no grand thoughts
fill the mind. Instead, it's the madness of insignificant things you
focus on. Like the nurse's freckled arms, the scent of coffee on her
breath, the sound of a child whining out in the hallway.

But I can barely feel anything even though I know that I'm
still inside this body. These arms and legs. These bones. Brittle and
weakening. These ears can still hear. And there are my eyes. Still
my eyes. Clouded over, shadowed edges, the dim silhouettes of my
family when they stop by, but these eyes still *see*. Like wearing a pair
of sunglasses at dusk. Overhead, there are fluorescent yellow tubes

encased in plastic. The darkness beyond my bed intensifies, circles closer, and it's as though I'm being stalked by a vicious animal, an unseen predator. And the mind. This mind. My mind. It still holds on to memories. Are they the last to go? Rattling around like seeds inside the hollowed-out rind of a cantaloupe.

Then I see it, hovering at the foot of my bed. It comes into focus. The figure of a man. He's dressed in my boots, the tights I wore, my flowing cape with its fur collar. A silver glow speckled with flecks of gold encircles him. It's me. Another version of me, and everything about him is normal. He has two arms and two legs, a torso, broad shoulders, a fleshy neck. It's my own body, up and about, swirling over me. There's his head, my head, but it's as bald as a newborn's. There are my two ears. There's my chin, scoured with scars. But my eyes, my mouth, my nose? They're missing. There's only skin, pulled tight like elastic, over the whole of my non-face.

—Are you going to take me away? I ask.

—No, he replies.

—Then why are you here?

—To remind you.

—Of what?

—¡Ya sabes, cobarde!

—Stop, I insist. Please leave. I'm trying to die.

The nurse is wrapping up the suction tubes. Can she see him? I try asking, but gravity seizes my tongue. It's nothing but a dry, swollen thing rolling around in my mouth. Nothing works anymore. Then, just above her right shoulder as she leans over to adjust the IV drip, coiling it under my blanket, I notice something penetrate the haze around her. First there is a pattern I remember. Blue with tiny yellow flowers. Her dress. The one we buried her in. Elena, my dead wife, materializes before me. Transparent at first, she slowly takes form until she's solid, standing so close to the bed that I can feel the heat from her body pass through my dying skin, reviving the blood still inside my frail veins.

—Ernesto? She looks at me, puzzled. Where are you? Who is this woman?

—I'm dying, I reply. They've brought me here.

—Who did?

—Alfredo and his wife, la Grace. Our mija, Mercedes. Our grandson; you died before you could meet him.

—Do I look dead now? She lifts both arms above her head, making fists with her hands.

—No. You look alive. It's amazing.

—You can't go yet. You must talk. Keep thinking. Keep remembering.

—But I can't. It's impossible. So much has vanished.

—It's still there. I'll help you find it.

—But what if I don't want to? I can't face the truth.

—You must, she implores. You simply must.

And then there it is. A thought. A memory's left behind, the residue of a life once lived, like patterns on the side of a mountain that mark the remnants of extinct oceans. My friend. A boy I once knew and cared for very much. There he remains in the folds of my brain, refusing to be forgotten.

* *

There was music playing inside the cantina that day. Then a voice said hello; Julián Tamez circled the room, greeting everyone. He reached into the pockets of his bell-bottoms and pulled out a wad of pesos, told the bartender to get everyone in the room whatever they wanted.

"Mira este." Israel Navarette, another hog farmer, turned to me, chuckling, as Julián went from table to table, slapping each man on the back. "Regresa muy catrín."

He flashed a ring at us. Around his neck he wore a heavy gold chain with a large crucifix. Some of the men mumbled and nodded. We gathered around Julián, drinking cold Victorias, and he told us all about his life in the capital. There were skyscrapers, he went on. Rascacielos, they called them, tall buildings that touched the clouds. There were wide avenues and plazas and fine restaurants that you could get to by using the new metro subway lines connecting the city. He talked about Chapultepec Park, about museums that housed the artifacts of our ancestors. He talked about fancy cars and houses so big that everyone in our entire pueblo could live inside of one and there'd still be more than enough room. Many of the men stumbled home by the time he finished, but I remained, mesmerized by his tales. It was a Sunday. Elena was out with her friends. I had the whole day to myself.

"Ernesto," he said, cupping his hand over my left shoulder. "The last time I saw you we were still silly boys pretending to be men." He whistled through his teeth. "Híjole."

I shook my head. "It's good to see you again, old friend."

We sipped our beers, and he asked me what I did for a living.

"I raise hogs. On what's left of my father's ranch. He died. So did my mother."

"Did you marry?"

"Yes. Elena Pimentel."

Julián nodded. "I remember her."

When I asked if he ever thought about coming back to La Peña, he laughed. "Shit no."

"But your mother's here."

Once, during a fight with her, his father poured lye into Carmen Tamez's eyes, blinding her for life. He then went to jail, leaving his wife with a teenaged boy, two young girls, and a small plot of land, which was sold, the money used to buy a house closer to the center of town, near the one medical clinic in La Peña. Carmen was cared for by Julián's sisters, twins named Teresa and Tomása. Their only job was to keep constant watch over their mother. When Carmen Tamez needed to use the bathroom, Teresa and Tomása each held their mother by an arm and escorted her, Carmen taking small steps, inch by inch, towards the toilet.

"The money I make in the city helps here," Julián explained. "If I return, what would I do? Raise pigs to try and sell? No offense."

The countryside was no place for young men like us, he believed, because we belonged in the cities, working and moving and making money to support our families, wherever they may be. He looked around the cantina; only a few other men sat at the low wooden tables playing dominos and drinking pulque out of tornillos made from dull green glass. There was confidence in his stare, in the way he carried himself. He wasn't strong or broad shouldered like the rest of us. He was slender, he wore his hair long and shaggy, not clean cut the way men of the campo did during that time. His plaid shirt was unbuttoned, revealing a tan chest dotted with moles. My memories took me to that hot afternoon by the rio. Swimming in the cool water, our legs brushing against each other as we kicked and splashed, laughing, our mouths open as we looked up at the sky. We splayed out on the rocks, naked. I tried not looking at his body, the tender skin, his flaccid penis slick from river water. Julián had his eyes closed. I gritted my teeth to hide the excitement, cupped my hand over my groin when I felt the blood rushing there, swelling me up.

Julián shook his head and sighed now. "Look at these poor bastards. Tired. Wasting away. There's nothing here except ghosts and los espíritus, the dead, they tell the best lies. You must stop listening to them, mano, get out while you can. Before the children come. Because mocosos make everything more difficult."

"Do you have a wife there in the capital? Children?" I asked.

He whistled at the bartender who was reading the newspaper. The man set it down, grabbed two more bottles of beer, and placed them next to us. "No, hombre. I'm not the type who's going to do that."

"I was thinking about going to the United States. Like my brother," I said. "Just for a while. To make enough money to start a savings account."

I had been contemplating it for some time but never mentioned anything to anyone, not even Elena. It was a relief to hear myself utter it out loud, breathing my ambitions to life. Julián flicked his hand and told me the United States was a waste of time because everyone was going there. All the good jobs were taken. In Mexico City it was easy to find chamba, he called it, without even trying. The capital was where I stood a better chance of getting work that was going to pay me well so that I could start saving, maybe even buy Elena nice things.

"Have you heard from Heriberto?" he asked.

"No."

The last thing we received from my brother was a wire transfer five years earlier. It was money to help with the burial cost for our mother, who passed away after our father did. *I'm sorry I can't be there*, he wrote. Another man who had left with him returned to La Peña and said Heriberto was caught up in an immigration sweep at a factory in Chicago where they both worked.

"They put him on one of the other buses," this man recounted. "But when we arrived in Juárez, I didn't see him. I bet he snuck back."

Julián took a long sip of his beer. "They say you'll die if you go there."

I didn't want to die, but I was looking for something else.

He then lowered his voice. "Do you believe in fate, brother?"

I shrugged my shoulders.

"You know? Since before I came back here, I've been thinking of you. You came to me in a dream. A premonition. Then today, just as I was out and about, something pulled me in here, into this pit of a cantina where I find you. It's as if we were meant to meet up. To go on a great adventure together."

I laughed, then finished my beer and said goodbye.

I tried making it work. But it was slow in the countryside and those little towns were scarred with the legacy of war and revolution. And it stared at you in the face every single day. You heard it stirring in the wind when it rushed through the branches of the huizaches or across the empty cornfields. Wailing. It never stopped. It was in the ripples of water, in the crow of a rooster, and in the stone faces of the mountainsides. There were wounds of sadness all around. And in that way war never ended. It just went on, distorting light, bending time. It made you remember when all you wanted to do was forget. Then there was the memory of my father, a man who only knew spite and never-ending work, a man who forced us to labor in the fields alongside him, from sunup to sundown, as soon as we were old enough to hold a hoe and plow a field. He pulled Heriberto out of school when he was nine. Thanks to our mother's intervention, I lasted until I was thirteen, but eventually joined them.

If we ever complained about the backbreaking work, if we were sick or wanted to do something else, it was his fists or his belt we would answer to. My two sisters married men as soon as they were old enough and left La Peña, left my father's tyranny and endless rage. Heriberto set his sights north once the crops got bad and our father lost the will and strength to work the fields. In his final days, his spirit was shattered, and all he could do was sit around and cry while my mother prayed to her saints and angels. I couldn't abandon them like my brother and sisters had, so I stayed behind and continued working the land. I watched over them and the animals as I went from growing corn to raising pigs. Then he died from a heart attack. My mother said it was his rage that did it, a rage so heavy and toxic it poisoned his blood, made him bitter for reasons she never knew. After he passed, it was as though a massive weight had been lifted from her shoulders—mine as well—and she felt free to talk about him in ways she never dared to when he was alive.

"He wasn't the most attractive, but I remember it was his gentleness that I liked," she told me once. "Men that kind were rare back then. When the revolution happened, so many of them returned damaged by all the things they'd done, all the people they'd been forced to kill." She shook her head. "Afterward, there was a darkness inside him, and no matter how hard I tried, no matter how much I opened myself to him, it never went away."

The years following his death were the happiest of my mother's life. She carried herself with a lightness I'd never witnessed before. She became a young girl all over again. Her constant laugh melted away the wrinkles my father's presence had brought on, and there was a calm energy wherever she went, a love that radiated from her body, warm and serene. My mother passed in her sleep. I found her early one morning. The sun was barely rising, and she lay there in the cold predawn stillness, her thick gray braid a rope tangled among the blankets. She clutched a rosary in both hands, and a smile, slight as a whisper, stretched across her lips.

I was alone then, alone in the house my father built, alone on that remote patch of land passed down from great-grandfather to grandfather, to father, to me. My brother was lost somewhere in el norte, maybe even dead, and my sisters were scattered to different corners of the republic and raising families of their own, their children strangers to me.

This was around the time I first met Elena, and she reminded me so much of my mother. She moved into the house with me soon after we married. She painted the walls bright colors, sewed curtains and pillows with embroidered patterns of hummingbirds and flowers. She tried tempering the anger and the resentment I held against my father for his punches and insults, at my mother for dying, at my siblings for abandoning me. Still, though, it wasn't enough to eliminate it completely, and I yearned for something, anything, else. There developed a restless energy inside me, an urge that kept me awake at night as I spent hours in bed imagining the life I could be living instead of the one I was forced into.

When Julián Tamez appeared that day, something was reignited.

I raised the hogs, fattened them up, and sold them to buyers who slaughtered them for food. That's all I did. Season after season. It was always the same thing. It never changed.

I wasn't surprised when Julián came to see me a few days after we talked at the cantina. I was tending to my hogs, up to my knees in shit.

"I'd forgotten how a pigsty smells." He circled the perimeter of the large pen I'd constructed myself. It was sturdy, made of thick wooden beams held together by posts jammed into the ground. Inside, the ground was muddy because pigs weren't happy unless they were rolling around in dirt. I'd also made a feeding trough where every day my pigs gathered to eat their slop—a mixture of grains and table scraps we saved in a bucket.

I removed my straw hat and wiped sweat off my brow. "Bienvenido."

Julián hopped up on one of the horizontal beams, swinging his legs around, his feet dangling. A few pigs strolled over, sniffed his boots, then walked away. "Friendly animals you have here. Too bad they'll be butchered."

We both laughed.

He pulled a pack of cigarettes from his pocket and lit one.

"I'm serious about what I mentioned the other day, hermano. You should come back to la capital with me."

"Elena would kill me. I don't know."

"You want to live the rest of your life here?" He whistled and flicked his cigarette into the pen. "You're meant for more, Ernesto. We both are. There's only misery here. Ghosts. The dead tell the best lies in order to keep you in this place. You should come with me, hermano. What have you got to lose?"

And there I stood, panting, sweating, caked in mud and shit. "But Elena. I can't just—"

"Even if it's only for a few months," he insisted. "There's no harm in that, is there?"

* *

Later that day, she was silent when I told her about my conversation with Julián. The idea didn't sit well with her. She stood outside, her back to me, tossing bits of grain at the hens flocking at her feet.

"You'd just go?" she asked.

"Why not? Julián says there's work in the capital."

She pointed to the chickens, to the pigs. "There's work here. Why do you think you have to look elsewhere for something? There's plenty all around us."

"But not the kind that pays. Not the kind I'm interested in."

"Your father was a farmer. So was your grandfather."

"So that means I must be one as well? Stay here. I'll send money."

"Are you crazy? I'm not going to sit around like some burra. Last week, Luz Calvo hopped on a train for Tijuana with her kids. She got tired of waiting for Felipe."

"What are you saying?" I asked.

She stopped feeding the hens, folded her arms, and turned to me. "I'm going too."

"But you—"

She interrupted me: "I'm packing and going."

She glanced around the yard before walking past me and into our house. Inside, we stood in the kitchen. It was tiny with a cast-iron cookstove, a cupboard where we kept our dry goods, and an old light-blue GE refrigerator. We were one of a handful of people in La Peña who owned one and were the envy of the whole neighborhood.

"No," I insisted. "You will stay here, and you will wait for me."

"I won't."

"Elena, listen to me. I'm the man of this house. You do what I say."

"Or else what?" She chuckled. "I'm not going to let you abandon me. I'm not stupid."

I told her the journey would be by bus, and that it would be long and uncomfortable. Doesn't matter, she replied. We'd probably have no place to sleep when we got there, I insisted. Doesn't matter, she repeated. Nothing swayed her.

Preparing for the trip a few days later, I said Julián ate rats when he first got to the city. It was, of course, a lie. She shook her head as she placed our belongings into a suitcase we'd bought from a vendor named Pancha Serrato who sewed rebozos to sell to tourists passing through La Peña on their way to Pátzcuaro, to the lake, to the butterfly sanctuary where the monarchs went to rest under the warm canopies of fir and oak trees.

"Then I guess I'll have to eat rat tacos." When she finished packing, she sat on the edge of our bed, her small hands gripping each knee, and said absolutely nothing.

Elena Vega

I came from a long line of female fighters, soldaderas who took up arms just like their maridos during the revolution. My abuela Azucena once told me how all the men in her village left to join one of the many battalions roaming the countryside.

"We weren't safe from the soldiers who'd raid the pueblos, eat our food, have their way with us, then leave only for another group to come a few weeks later and do the same thing," she recounted. "Can you imagine? We were fed up, so we got together and taught ourselves how to shoot rifles. We had our babies to protect. The next time those guerrilleros showed up on horseback, we were ready. We fired at them, and they retreated. We fought back, kept fighting back, until word spread of a group of women with pistolas defending their ranchitos and their children. Nobody fucked with us again."

According to Abuela, that itch, that impulse most men were born with to dominate their women was bullshit. She would spit on the ground, raise a finger, and tell me not to be fooled. "No te dejes engañar, mi chiquita."

I remember as a little girl laughing when she cursed and spat and gave me her consejos. I had no idea how true her words would ring, and what they'd ultimately cause, but I learned to be loyal to my family, to honor the blood that binds us, and to never back down from a challenge.

My parents had a strong marriage, a union built on trust and communication. My mother was not subservient to my father, and he never raised a hand to her, never tried controlling her life. They were equals, and that's what I wanted when I met Ernesto. That's what I was fighting for, what I was striving to preserve. A perfect balance between two opposing forces. I thought he could give this this to me. How wrong I was.

Pero tengo ojos. I knew back then. Hell, I knew it on the day we married. Ernesto Vega wasn't interested in a woman like me. It wasn't the traditional love between a husband and wife that kept us together. What pulled us to one another was convenience. Back then, being single was something unorthodox, abnormal. You had to marry, even if you didn't want to. It was my stubbornness, my need to see the world beyond what I already knew. I deserved that. I wouldn't be swayed. Julián was polite the day he came over and sat in the kitchen with us, drinking black coffee and smoking his American cigarettes.

He smiled, cleared his throat, and glanced at Ernesto. "So, you're joining us, huh?"

I folded my arms and nodded. "Wherever my marido goes, I go."

"But, Elena, it's—" he continued.

I interjected, looked him square in the face, and replied, "You'd be a fool to try and stop me."

* *

We sold the pigs, the chickens and the goat, then the television and refrigerator, so there was money. I locked the door to the house that last morning and left the keys with Leonardo Medina and his wife Irma, who lived across the street.

"Take care of our house," I said.

"Of course," they replied, hugging both of us.

"Please sweep the front step now and again," I reminded Irma.

"I will," she told me. Then my friend clutched my arm and whispered, "Elena. You can always wait for the men to get settled, then you can follow. The city . . . tanto mal."

Ernesto bit his lip. Julián sighed and glanced away.

"No." I took her hand and squeezed it. "I'll be fine."

* *

I wore my best outfit—a tangerine polyester skirt with my only pair of nylons and my church shoes, the ones with gold buckles. My green sweater itched; I was hot and uncomfortable. I reached into my purse, searching until I found the handkerchief I'd placed there the night before, and dabbed some of the sweat from my face, careful not to smear my makeup. All of me was trembling. The buses gathered in an empty dirt lot on the outskirts of town, next to the cemetery where my parents and Ernesto's parents were buried.

La Peña wasn't much, but it was home. I watched it pass before us as we gazed out the window, the bus lumbering down the uneven road. I waved goodbye to the children on the curb. They waved back, smiling, giggling. Julián sat behind us, his straw hat pulled down low, the brim covering his eyes. He slept the whole way; even over the hum of the bus engine as we started down the highway, we could hear his snores.

* *

Eight hours later my throat tickled from all that automobile exhaust. I marveled at the lights and the billboards inside the terminal. It smelled terrible. And it was noisy. I missed my kitchen, the skirts and blouses I didn't have room to bring. Two soldiers in green fatigues stood guard near the bus terminal's main entrance. Beside them, atop a strip of cardboard, sat a woman in a thin dress. Her braid was frayed, nearly undone, her hair coarse and dry, and she wore no shoes. The soles of her feet were shiny, like plastic. Her face was smeared with grease and dirt; she held a single hand out and stared at us through a pair of brown, watery eyes.

"Limosna," she pleaded as we passed. "¿Señora? Por favor."

I stopped, but Julián snatched my hand. "¡Deja de eso, mujer!"

He pointed across the street. Gathered near the base of a ragged palm tree—its trunk scarred with initials and names and coated in exhaust and fumes—was a group of beggars. Men, women, even children. They all stood there, the same weathered looks on their faces, eyes glassy and vacant of emotion.

"It's endless," Julián explained. "You give to one and then another and another. Pretty soon you'll find yourself with nothing left."

"See?" Ernesto responded. "The city is no place for a lady. I should have been firmer with you."

I laughed. "You couldn't even if you wanted to. Ernesto, you have no idea what I'm capable of."

He called me "terca."

Fine, I thought. *That's me. Stubborn woman.*

FREDDY VEGA

Not a single customer came in to use the gym today.

Not one. I remember when this building was alive with activity. Now there's no movement, the air uninterrupted. When I turn the overhead lights off, two rats scurry behind some boxes. *Fuck,* I think. *Just what I need.*

My eyes fall on the wall calendar on a pile of old papers. The image drawn on it is called *La patria y el niño.* A woman wears a flowing white dress. In one hand, she holds a wooden pole. Behind her, the Mexican flag unfurls, tumbling out in massive mounds of green and red, the eagle and serpent emblazoned in bright gold across the flag's center band, the same white as the woman's dress. Her eyes are closed, her hair braided in two thick trenzas black as licorice. A laurel leaf crown decorates the sides of her head. Her other hand clasps that of a young boy in tan boots and blue jeans that are rolled up above his ankles. He clutches something in his arm—a book, a satchel. It's hard to make out now because the image is faded. Behind them is a ring of tall mountains covered in snow. The woman and the boy lean forward, both marching onward. Below this is the name of the butcher shop in bold red letters, *Carnicería La Michoacána*, and the street address. This was back when Avenida César Chávez was called Brooklyn Avenue.

* *

My parents arrived from Mexico just after I was born and rented that dark one-bedroom apartment above *La Michoacána*. Then Mercy was born, when I was around three. My memories of that place come to me in quick, scattered images: a kitchen with a patch of mold growing in the corner of the wall, gray and menacing; a fire escape where I'd sit, watching people on the sidewalk below; a boy my age named Victor who lived down the hall. Victor wore metal braces on both legs, and he only spoke Spanish. Once, when his father overheard me trying to teach him some English, he shook his head.

"Nosotros hablamos el español," he said. "Only Spanish speak here."

I never played with Victor again.

It was cramped, and the building manager never fixed any of the busted pipes or the broken locks. The main door leading onto the street was always left wide open, and homeless people used the entryway to sleep, addicts left used needles, and once a cholo high on PCP broke into the mailboxes and stole everyone's letters and bills, bank statements and paychecks. But it was the robbery in 1980 that did it for my father. Burglars climbed up the fire escape and tore the place apart while we were at church one Sunday morning. My mother's gold necklaces and medallas from Mexico City were taken. Our television and record player and speakers were gone. My father kept an envelope of cash sewn into the thick lining of a coat he never wore. It hung in the closet. We found it on the bedroom floor, ripped apart. They left the envelope behind.

"Whoever did this knew where to look," my father insisted. "We're not staying here. Someone's got eyes on us."

The following year, in 1981, we left that apartment. My mother took the calendar because she said it was always important to have something with you when you leave a place, even if that something might seem worthless and insignificant. I remember her rolling it up and placing it in a box with her frying pan and comal.

We moved into a three-bedroom house on Verona Street, south of Whittier Boulevard. It had wall-to-wall shag carpeting, Formica countertops, and popcorn ceilings dusted with specks of glitter that would fall off and land in my cereal and on my superhero action figures. Verona Street was wider, with shaded sidewalks where we could play. My mother bought Mercy a big bucket full of multicolored chalks, and she spent our first afternoon there scribbling our names and drawing flowers, squares, and rainbows on the broken concrete. Our neighbors had roosters, chickens, and even goats. An older woman who lived on the corner, who everyone referred to simply as La Susana, showed up a few days after we were all settled. Susana presented us with a tray of chicken enchiladas and Spanish rice packed inside a plastic margarine tub. Her husband had died the year before.

"El diabetis." She blessed herself.

My mother set the food down and massaged Susana's shoulder. "Que dios lo tenga en su gloria."

Susana was what they called una Guadalupana, a devout follower of Our Lady of Guadalupe. Every year during the Virgen's feast day of December 12, Susana erected a shrine in her backyard with the help of some of the other neighborhood señoras and their husbands and families. They brought out a statue of Our Lady that Susana said had been blessed by many priests, and they set it on a platform surrounded by fresh roses all the ladies grew in their yards. They lit candles and strung Christmas lights from the lemon and guayaba trees, and everyone from the neighborhood flocked to La Susana's to sing and eat and celebrate the Virgen's day.

* *

My mother used to say, "America is the land of unlimited opportunity."

"And what is Mexico?" I asked one time.

"The land of unlimited misery."

"Why?"

"Because it is," she said, her tone defiant. "I never want to go back there. Bury me here when I die."

The thing I remember most about my mother during this time was the way she threw herself head-on into all things American. She learned how to make hamburgers and grilled cheese. Despite his protests, she forced my father to teach her how to drive, and soon she was running errands by herself or picking me up from school, honking at cars and trucks that cut her off on the freeways, speeding through intersections. She perfected her English by spending afternoons watching soap operas like *Ryan's Hope*, *All My Children*, and *General Hospital*. Her favorites, though, were the evening ones, especially *Dynasty*. She'd sit in front of the television, repeating lines of dialogue from the show: *And that, my darling, is how it's done; How dare you!; You're not angry that I'm involved, are you?*

"That Alexis is venenosa," my father said one night to the television. "Que culebra."

"Maybe she is," my mother responded. "¿Pero mira? She gets what she wants. I wish I could be like that."

"Estás loca," he responded.

I watched how my mother glared at him when he said this. There was pure spite in her look. And with her hair pulled back and away from her face and the heavy mascara and eyeliner she wore, her skin shining white against the television's glow, my mother and Alexis Colby could have been mistaken for twins.

* *

Whatever needed doing, you went down to Whittier Boulevard to do it. Wire money back to the rancho in Mexico. Pay off bills. Borrow cash. Order a wedding cake. Put a down payment on a car. Buy a tea to calm your nerves. A candle to ward off bad spirits. Get a new mattress. A living room set. A big table with matching chairs. Piñatas in all shapes and sizes. And the food stalls. Tacos de asada, lengua, cesos. Churros. Piping-hot tamales stuffed with shredded pork, raisins, or corn. Banana- and chocolate-flavored licuados. Cubes of fresh fruit swimming in lime juice and sprinkled with Tajín. On Friday and Saturday nights, lowriders cruised up and down the street—Impalas, Chevys, El Caminos with bright whitewall tires the people called "sneakers." An empty storefront didn't remain so for long. Another taqueria, barber shop, mercadito, panaderia, or carniceria would swoop in, set up shop, and that was it.

Like our neighbors, we'd stroll up and down the boulevard on Sunday afternoons, Mercy in her pigtails and pleated navy skirts, me in my tie and stiff-collared shirt. One day, my father stood out in the middle of the sidewalk as my mother walked a few feet ahead of us; she was headed towards the beauty salon for a curl tamer and Sun-In hair lightener. When my father asked her why she wanted these things, she ignored him, grabbed her purse, and said to all of us, "Let's go."

But I knew. She wanted to change her hairstyle to resemble the glamorous actresses on *Dynasty* with their flawless makeup and exaggerated shoulder pads.

Standing on the crowded sidewalk, my dad looked at the nearby trash can overflowing with sticky Styrofoam cups and greasy bags. All around us, the air smelled of gasoline and bread, cigarette smoke and warm tortillas.

He shook his head. "You know what this place needs, Elena?"

My mother held Mercy's hand, my sister guiding her through

the crowd towards a display window where portable radios were arranged on a shelf.

"What did you say?" she asked as my sister tugged at her arm. "Mija, no. First the beauty salon, okay?"

"A gym," my father shouted into the roaring traffic and to the pedestrians. "A place to burn off all the fat." He turned to my mom. "Elena?"

But she'd already led Mercy far enough away that his voice was nothing more than a weak whisper. I saw her black head of hair moving fast and determined towards the front door of Emporio Belleza.

Back then, he worked at a mannequin factory. He took me with him once, and I remember the smell of hot plastic and varnish he said made you dizzy and stoned if you breathed it in too long. He led me through a large room full of machines, and I watched the bald heads of the dummies parade past, their lifeless eyes looking up at me. There were pink arms and legs swaying from hooks above. Men stood in front of long conveyor belts, sorting through limbs and torsos, their arms thick and sweaty, maneuvering around the gears and levers of machines, their sharp teeth just itching for the chance to take a finger or even a whole hand.

I heard them talking one night. My father was complaining about one of his supervisors, a skinny guy with thick-framed glasses and oily skin named Castro. He was telling my mother that Castro was unqualified for his position and the only reason he landed the position over my father was because the guy was engaged to the lead floor manager's daughter.

"That baboso doesn't know mierda. Nobody on the line respects him," he explained. "Today I found out how much he's making. It's criminal. I'm doing my job and his, and he's raking in all the money."

I could hear my mother placing dishes in the cupboards. "Ask them for a raise, then."

My father laughed. "You think they're going to give me one because I ask? They're gabachos. They'll just fire me and hire someone off the street. Pay them even less."

He was fed up, he went on. Tired all the time. The job was monotonous. A waste of energy. He'd have to wait ten years before being promoted.

"I've gained weight. I'm out of shape. Look at me," he told her. "I should go back to the mat. Back to lucha libre."

"Are you crazy?" My mother's voice was louder now. "That's not a job. It's a hobby."

"It was a job in Mexico."

"That was there. It's different here."

"I was good at it, made more money. People respected me."

"We agreed to leave it behind." Then she slammed the kitchen drawer shut, the utensils rattling inside. "I'm fine with the boxes of photos and articles, with the outfit, even. But the rest? Better to forget it all. For the sake of our children. I'm never going back to that place."

"I was happy," my father said.

"I wasn't. I was miserable. I never want to be that person again. If we'd stayed, you would have left me and chased after him, after Julián. You promised things would be different here, said you'd change, said you'd control yourself. Or have you already forgotten?"

There was anger in that voice. She didn't sound like my mother anymore.

Still, he began hating that job more and more. He grew quiet, withdrawn; after dinner, instead of hanging out in the living room with me and Mercy as we did our homework and listened to the radio, he'd go to their bedroom, close the door, and watch television until he fell asleep. The next morning, he'd rise early, dress, and be out the door by six, come home in the late afternoon, eat, and retire to the bedroom again.

"What's wrong with Papa?" Mercy asked our mother one day.

She shrugged her shoulders. "It's nothing. Work is just making him tired and sad."

Mercy drew him a picture—fluffy clouds, a rainbow, the sun peeking out from behind a mountain. She folded it and asked my mother to place it inside his lunch box. When he came home the next evening, he hugged her and said it cheered him up.

"Why are you sad?" she asked him.

"It's hard to explain," he went on. "Someday you'll understand."

He folded her drawing and placed it in his wallet.

A few weeks after that, we sat around the dinner table: Mercy studying for a vocabulary test; my mother eating with one hand, the other leafing through a sale circular; my father at the head of the table, freshly showered after his shift, taking sips of a cold beer between forkfuls of food. He'd be off the next day, which was Friday, and the Monday that followed. A four-day rest from the hard labor of the factory, but my mother had already decided she would take advantage of this; there were plenty of things she needed done around the house. My mother rattled off a list of tasks that demanded his immediate attention: screws that needed tightening, hinges that needed oil, leaky faucets that needed plugging, burned-out bulbs that needed changing. Friday mornings in my classroom were always "show-and-tell" time, and I mentioned this to my father and asked if he could give me something of his to take with me. When he asked what, I said, "I don't know. Your lucha libre mask or a picture of you in your costume."

He looked over at me, then glanced at my mother. "How about

I dress up? The whole thing. Boots and cape and mask and every-thing. And you can take me."

"Ernesto," my mother protested. "What are you doing?"

"It's for him, for our boy."

She sighed, shook her head, rose, and went to the kitchen.

Mercy looked up from her book. "Why's Mom all mad?"

"She's just . . ." My father's voice trailed off. Then he rose and went after our mother.

I thought that was it. I thought the next day I'd wake up to find him sleeping in, happy not to have to roll out of bed and change into a pair of grimy pants and heavy boots that were hot and uncomfortable and blistered his feet. Instead, he was sitting at the breakfast table, his mask on, making faces at Mercy, who tried repeatedly to yank it off. When we walked into the classroom and he sat next to me, the other students stared wide-eyed at him.

"Freddy has brought a very special guest with him to show-and-tell this morning," Mrs. Ashlynn told our class when it was our turn.

"This is my father," I said. "He's a luchador."

"What's that?" Samantha Rojas asked.

"A wrestler," I replied. "He was a champion in Mexico. He fought bad guys and made movies and everyone loved him." The kids gasped some more. My father flexed and posed. He crouched and paced back and forth in front of the rows of chairs we sat in and let me do the talking. They wanted to know everything: if the fur around his collar was from a real wolf; how old he was when he had his first fight, why he wore a mask.

"Does he ever take it off?" they asked.

"Never," I said, even though it was a lie.

"At the dinner table?" they asked.

"No."

"When he sleeps?"

"No."

"What about when he showers?"

"No," I repeated.

All they could say was "Wow!"

* *

Late last night we got a call from one of the evening nurses at the hospice. His blood pressure had dropped, depleting his already overworked organs of oxygen.

"So, what's it mean?" I replied.

Grace was standing in the doorway, a tube of toothpaste in her hand. "Oh God," she muttered.

I put the nurse on speakerphone. I asked again. "What does that mean? Is it time? Should I head over? We're less than ten minutes away."

There was a slight pause that lasted an eternity. Then she spoke. "It's fine. They're telling me he's stabilized. He's out of the woods for now."

For now? I went to bed thinking: *And what about later?*

* *

It's early evening when I reach the facility. The air smells of cafeteria food and flowers. *Lilies? Roses?* The front desk clerk reminds me to secure my mask and asks me to raise my palm up to the wall-mounted sensor to take my temperature. A note taped to the side of the machine reads, *Give us your best Iron Man pose,* and there's a picture of the superhero standing with his arm extended out.

He's lying still, but he's in there. I can feel it. My mind wanders back to that day in elementary school. When the bell rang for morning recess, my classmates gathered around my father. They touched his cape, his boots, and he bent down and let them run their fingers over the smooth fabric of his mask. Outside on the blacktop, he ran around with them, and all the other students from all the other classes stood and watched and marveled at this man in a shiny outfit, in a long silky cape that flapped and spread out like one massive wing as he chased them around and around, and they laughed and giggled when he picked up a little girl whose name I didn't know, lifted her up on his shoulder and strutted around with her. I watched him then, towering over that mass of tiny bodies chasing after him, shouting. I imagined those children rushing home at the end of the day to tell their own mothers and fathers about the visit from this mythical being. I couldn't understand why my mother had such a problem with any of it. In that outfit, in that disguise, my father was transformed into something else entirely.

Grace shows up a while later, freshly showered. Her damp hair smells like the green apple conditioner she uses. She's in cutoff jeans and my old LA Dodgers jersey.

"Where'd you find that?" I ask.

"Left work a little early. Did some rearranging of my own around the house."

A reusable grocery bag printed with drawings of fruits and vegetables is hooked over her arm. *Freshness guaranteed* is written across the bottom. She reaches inside and pulls out some old images of my father during the height of his lucha popularity back in Mexico. She hands me a picture of my parents on their wedding day, so tattered and thin it feels like it'll disintegrate. "I thought maybe we could tape these to the wall. Make it feel . . . familiar? I also got him this."

It's one of those fleece blankets they sell at indoor swap meets emblazoned with pictures of eagles and white tigers and lions. The internet calls them *Mexican cobijas*. This one has a picture of a wolf.

"That's not a coyote," I say.

"Duh. But it was this or an elephant. I figured it was close enough."

Mercy's texting to let me know she'll be flying in from Berkeley. *Tell him to hang on a little longer*, she wrote. *For me. Tell him. Okay, bro?*

I'll tell him, but can he even hear me now?

After she finishes taping the picture up against the wall, Grace unfurls the blanket and uses it to shroud his body. No longer a coyote. A wolf. Un lobo. He's transforming again right before our eyes, and this will be his last evolution.

El Rey Coyote

You're stubborn, I'll give you that, ¡viejo! It's admirable. The way you keep fighting, breathing all labored, eyes two blank sockets, lips desiccated and dusted with dried sweat. Alfredo and his wife are here today. He dabs your forehead with a white towel and whispers to you.

Mercy's coming soon, Pops. Hold on, okay? He leans in close, his breath rippling the hair covering your ears.

Watching your family treat you with such . . . honor. It's a joke. If I could only tell them who you really were. What you hid. Do you think they'd still be going on like this? ¡N'ombre!

—Stop. The ghost wife floats out from the walls, all mad, hands balled into fists. Stop it. This isn't how we'll get him to cooperate. You're such a . . . a sangrón.

I try taking swings, but my arms cut through the mist of her body. Smoke, she's just smoke. Just like you'll be. Soon. So very soon.

JULIAN VEGA

I only know what I've managed to piece together from my own research. The lucha libre we're familiar with today started with a dude down in Mexico City called Salvador Lutteroth. This guy was living near the Texas/Mexico border and would go to El Paso and watch some of the wrestling matches on the weekends. He became so obsessed with it that he quit his job and moved his whole family back to the capital where he began the first lucha libre syndicate, the Empresa Mexicana de Lucha Libre, or the EMLL. But people didn't give a shit about wrestling because boxing was everyone's jam. So, he invited this white guy whose gimmick was to disguise his face behind a simple leather mask for some weird reason. The trick worked, and that's when they all started wearing them.

Then came El Santo, who (everyone agrees on this) was the biggest and most celebrated luchador that ever lived. El Santo starred in all those cheesy movies. Even Abuelo, I'm told, made his own, but there's no trace of them anywhere, not even on the internet.

Lucha grew in the 1970s and '80s and crossed the border to the United States and even Japan, where it's apparently huge. Now there are multiple lucha syndicates all over the world. There's lucha libre reality television shows, cartoons, craft beers, socks, shirts, greeting cards, blankets, action figures, Halloween costumes, wrapping paper, Christmas tree ornaments, candles, lollipops, soda, protein powder, stuffed toys, light switch covers, posters, enve-lopes, tattoos, murals. I even once saw a fucking lucha libre con-dom wrapper. There are women, little people, and men in drag like my nina Scarlet Santos, who baptized me when I was a baby. They're called exoticos, and they, like all the others, can kick some serious ass.

Abuelo's reintroduction to lucha libre on this side of the bor-der happened by accident, right after Abuela Elena passed away. He met the owner of Taco Macho, a chain of restaurants that serves greasy Mexican food. There's only one of them left since the company got sued in 2015 when a man slipped at the location on Avenida César Chávez. Supposedly the place used to be good back in the day. The owner paid Abuelo to dress up in his lucha getup and entertain customers, then he starred in a few local commercials and was a little bit of a celebrity around the neighborhood. Like a social media influencer before that was even a thing.

Anyway, Abuelo was so good at it, and the commercials were hits, so he took his savings and signed a long-term lease on a shabby building and started a gym on an industrial street lined with auto body shops and scrapyards. It became a place where people from all around Boyle Heights, East LA, even some of the hardcore old-school gangbangers from fucking Hazard and Ramona Gardens, came to pump iron and, of course, watch my abuelo duke it out with rudos inside the ring on weekends during the 1980s and into the '90s. His flips and acrobatics were legendary, I'm told. It was like he could fly. His feet never touched the ground, I hear.

My father was a badass fighter himself, but he got hurt all the time. My mom told me she used to ice his injuries after big bouts in the years before I was born. She talked about bandages soaked in rubbing alcohol, the smell of ointments and oils waft-ing through the house on Saturday evenings. She remembers my father's grunts, a litany of injuries she could list off the top of her head, even now: bruised ribs, torn tendons, sprained hamstrings, cracked fingers and wrists. There was always a lot of blood, apparently. I can't stand the sight of it. Far away, sure. Up close? That's another thing.

"I wanted to be a nurse. Guess I got my wish," she'd say.

My father and Abuelo put their bodies through so much just to survive.

As soon as I was young enough to stand, I was going to the gimnacio with my dad. Abuelo was always there. His friend Hugo, the guy who'd helped him set the place up, told me to call him Tío. He'd put boxing gloves on my small hands and stand me in the middle of the ring.

"Ándale, mijo," he'd shout. "Left. Right. Dale. Dale."

Abuelo would get a real kick out of that and call me El Rey Coyote Jr. Jr.

There are pictures of me inside the cramped office where they conducted business, sitting on the desk chair, the old-school phone's giant receiver pressed to my ear, hitting the punching bag, riding on my father's shoulders. He's in full costume as El Rey Coyote Jr., that magnificent cape of his extending down to the ground, that beautiful gold-and-white mask covering his face, broad bare chest tanned and oiled.

When they dressed for a bout, my father and grandfather were transformed. And that's one of the many things that makes the sport of lucha libre so unique. Donning those costumes, you literally become someone else entirely. I imagine it's the same thing actors go through when they take on a new role, or professional drag queens in wigs and sequined gowns. My father and Abuelo walked differently. Their voices carried a different tone, and every word they uttered—even simple commands—took on an air of reverence and respect.

I used to love trying to identify the moment when my father

went from Alfredo Julián Vega to El Rey Coyote Jr. And the marvelous acrobatics and flips and somersaults they could do inside the ring. Such a fast, dizzying spectacle. It was easy to be convinced that they were superhuman. But the most amazing thing about it all was that they were just ordinary men and women. Then there were crowds. Let me tell you about the crowds. The energy and ear-splitting shouts and roars. The curses and insults hurled at the rudos, even at the técnicos for rooting for the bad guys, because there are spectators who do.

All throughout elementary school, my birthday parties were held at the gym. My parents covered folding tables with colorful vinyl tablecloths, hung streamers and balloons. One year, Grandma Patty found a set of tiny plastic figures dressed as luchadores. She drew a wrestling mat out of red piping and jabbed four toothpicks in each corner and connected these with string. Then she arranged the luchadores around and inside so that it re-created an actual match. My father, Abuelo, and a couple of the other luchadores working with them at the time would stage fights, and I'd sit with all my closest friends around the ring, and we'd watch. Then there'd be pizza, cake and ice cream, and music. All my friends knew that I always threw the best birthday parties.

And if I would have been asked back then if I wanted to be like my father and grandfather, if I wanted to carry on the family tradition, I would have said yes. But that didn't happen. So, the legacy ends with me. That's just the way it is. It was everything to them. It even meant the world to him. My first boyfriend. Phillip.

* *

He was an accident. The furthest thing from my mind when I started college. I wasn't looking for a boyfriend. But then there he was one day. This cute Black guy with eyes the color of new pennies. When he smiled, something inside me released, a flood of chemicals coursing through my body all warm and soothing that made me want to get dangerous with a guy like him.

We were both on the third floor of Stonebrook, a low brick building on the north end of our campus. The dorm rooms were bare and always cold. At the end of each hall there were communal bathrooms and a lounge with chairs, tables, a television, a pool table, and a microwave. I'd first noticed him on move-in day. My parents had followed me because I couldn't fit everything in my car. My dad parked his truck in one of the loading zones, threw on the hazards, and we hauled boxes of my stuff while my mom was inside making up the bed with the new sheets and blankets we'd bought. During one of the trips back down the stairs, we ran into Phillip, lugging an overstuffed duffel bag. One of the straps had broken, and he was holding it from the bottom, cursing and swearing.

My father tossed me the keys to the truck then turned around, grabbed the other end of the duffel bag, and said to Phillip, "I got this side."

"Thank you, sir," he replied. "I appreciate it."

"No problem." I watched them heave it up the short flight of steps and walk down the hall, past my dorm's open door, and into his room towards the back of the hall.

My roommate was a Chinese American guy from South Pasadena named Brian. He showed up with his parents just as mine were taking off. They only stayed long enough to look around our room and drop off a few things.

"I'm good," Brian told them. "I got it."

Once they left, he rolled his eyes. "Parents, man." Then he changed into a pair of shorts and a tank top and said he was going to look for the gym. "Want to come?"

"No. I need a nap."

Later that day, we walked around campus and ended up eating

burgers and fries at a restaurant in the food court near the main library. He was an engineering major.

"English," I said when he asked me.

"Jealous," he replied. "I've always liked reading. If I had my way, I'd study history or philosophy, but my folks don't think that's practical." Brian shook his head.

"Parents, man." I finished my milkshake.

"Yup." He pumped a fist in the air. Brian was looking forward to rush week and couldn't wait to join a fraternity so that he could get out of the dorm. "Are you gonna pledge?"

I shrugged my shoulders. "Hadn't thought of it."

"Come on, man," he said as we left the restaurant. "It's college. You're, like, supposed to party and hook up."

I smirked. "I guess."

Standing outside the university bookstore, we trailed behind a group of girls laughing and drinking bobas from clear tumblers with fat plastic straws. Brian whistled and asked which one of them I thought was *hot*.

I tried being cool. "All of them?"

He walked a few steps ahead, caught up to the girls, muttered a few words, and they all turned around, looked at me, and chuckled.

When he waved me over, I shouted, "I forgot something back at the restaurant," then turned and left.

"Dude," I could hear him shouting behind me. "Hurry!"

I ended up back at the dorm, showered, and lay in bed, listening to the constant shuffling feet and voices out in the hallway. It was late when I heard Brian come in.

I pretended to be sleeping.

The next day, during freshman orientation, I saw him in the breakfast line. He held a paper plate loaded up with mini blueberry and banana muffins, slices of fruit, and sugary Danishes with neon-red jam pressed into their centers. He was talking to a guy and girl when I approached.

"What happened to you yesterday?" he asked.

"I got sick. Must have been the burger."

The girl was named Sunny and the guy was Neil. They were all friends from high school and invited me to sit with them.

"Where are you from?" Sunny asked.

"East LA. You?"

She smiled. "San Marino."

I remembered an incident. Driving through there with my parents once when I was a sophomore. We'd exited the 210 free-way because there was an accident, and all lanes were at a complete standstill. My father was lost, and we found ourselves driving through a residential neighborhood with giant houses set behind wide green lawns. At a stop sign a cop on a motorcycle pulled us over, asked to see my father's license, and wanted to know what we were doing. My father explained about the backup on the freeway and how we were trying to get home using surface streets. The officer asked where home was, and when my father told him, he smirked, handed back the license, and said we were lucky because he wasn't going to ticket us for driving at dusk without headlights on. As we pulled away, my father gritted his teeth, mumbled, *That skinny fucker wouldn't last a minute in the ring with me. Racist honkey.* I remember my mother breathed a long sigh of relief once we were back home, safely parked in our driveway.

I told Sunny, "Oh yeah. San Marino."

Neil replied, "Man, East LA's, like, the hood."

I rolled my eyes.

Sunny shook her head at this. "You're so ignorant," and punched him in the arm.

"Just ignore him," she said to me. "He's stupid."

Neil reached over and patted my back. "I'm sorry. My bad."

The banquet room was big, carpeted, and university caterers darted around carrying trays of dirty coffee cups and empty milk cartons. Glass fishbowls full of index cards were placed at the center of each table. Staff members from the university's student life office paced around the room, all of them dressed in identical polo shirts the same shade of blue as our school's colors, the university's logo over the right pocket. They wore headsets and went around introducing themselves to us.

The place we were in was called the Silver Ballroom. I thought about my abuelo and my father, about the ways we assign meaning to colors and symbols throughout our lives. How different would my life be compared to theirs? All those years of hard labor, years of fighting both inside and outside the wrestling ring. There I was, a college freshman nervous and uncomfortable in a room full of my peers, all of us sweaty and jumpy and desperate to shed the awkwardness and insecurities that had mired our high school years. Who would I become over the next few years? I knew who I'd been—shy, insecure, uncomfortable, unsure about my place in the world, unable to connect with the tradition of lucha I'd inherited. My father and Abuelo knew with absolute certainty who they would become at moments like these. But me? I was fucking clueless.

And petrified.

Even though Sunny was nice and charming, I was annoyed by Brian and Neil and their constant chatter about frats and keg parties, so I told them I was going to use the restroom and I'd be back in a bit.

Brian said, "Don't disappear again."

"We'll save you a seat," Sunny replied as I turned and left.

All the banquet tables were filling up fast, and as I was scanning the room looking for a place to sit, one of the organizers took the stage up front and announced we'd be starting soon. Through the loud murmuring of voices, the constant clatter of dishes and shuffling chairs and feet, I heard someone say my name.

"Julian, right? It's Julian?" I looked behind me to see him standing there holding a blueberry bagel.

It was the guy from the day before, the one my father had helped.

"Yeah. You're—"

"Phillip," he interjected. "Your dad told me your name."

"Cool." I smiled.

He glanced around. "You know anyone here? Because I don't. My roommate is kind of a prick. Wanna sit together?"

I chuckled. "Don't get me started on my roommate, man. Yeah. Let's do it."

One of the staff members working our side of the room instructed everyone at our table to take turns fishing an index card out of the glass bowl and reading it to the person sitting next to them.

On mine was written, *Where are you from?*

Philadelphia, he said. "Phil from Philly. Easy to remember. Though nobody calls me Phil. Not even my folks."

He was the only child of his parents, though his father remarried, and his new wife had three daughters. The girls were nice, but he had little in common with them. Things were tense between him and his father, and they remained so when Phillip decided to come out here for school.

"He wanted me to attend Penn so I could stay nearby. My mom told me to ignore him. So here I am."

"Your turn." I pointed to his index card.

Tell me something surprising about you.

I thought about it for a minute before replying, "I come from a family of professional wrestlers."

"For real?" he asked.

"Yup. My grandfather was a wrestler, and my father still gets in the ring now and again."

"So, like WWF?"

"Not quite. Mexican style. Lucha libre."

I was surprised when he didn't scrunch up his face, when he didn't pause or throw an awkward smile and pretend to know what I was talking about.

"You know it?" I asked.

He took a bite of his bagel. "You sound surprised."

I admitted that I was. It wasn't exactly common. What he said next, though, really blew my mind.

"Were they técnicos or rudos?" He pronounced each word in perfect Spanish.

"So you—" I began before he interrupted me.

"Speak Spanish? A little. Afro Panamanian on my mom's side. I watched lucha libre with my abuelo. He loved the sport. I learned everything about it from him."

He was studying anthropology because he was fascinated with the past, with understanding where people like him came from, with bones and fossils, with memory and time. He didn't have a clue what he would end up doing with a degree in anthropology, he admitted, but it was what he liked, and he wanted to study something that made him happy.

"My dad still hopes I'll change my mind and become a hotshot attorney like him, but that ain't happening."

It turned out we were enrolled in the same English Composition class. Phillip had already scouted out the library for a good, hidden spot to study. We didn't have to keep pulling stupid index cards out of the fishbowl. We didn't hear the presentations on good note-taking techniques, on sexual harassment. We carried on a conversation all by ourselves and didn't even notice when everyone got up from their tables and shuffled out.

ERNESTO VEGA

The ceiling tiles. Off-white. Each square pocked with little holes. That's all I can see when my eyes manage to open. The boredom is enough that I try counting them, but my mind strays. Now here's a nurse, her hands wrapped in latex gloves. Eyes behind thick glasses peering into my face. *We're going to roll him over and wipe his bum. Grab his right shoulder.* Her voice is muffled by the surgical mask she's wearing. Another pair of hands turn me on my side. *Gently,* she says. *Let's get this heavy blanket off. Try keeping the trach collar as stable as possible.*

A picture there. Taped to the wall. Me in a tuxedo. Elena in a white dress, hair curled. A veil over her face. She's holding a small bouquet of flowers. Easter lilies. Those were her favorites. So fragrant. I can smell them now. Behind us a statue of Christ crucified. Such agony on his face. Such torture and regret.

What was I thinking, mujer?

* *

I didn't express my doubt to Elena. She would have said, *Didn't I tell you? Didn't I say this was a bad idea?* Better to remain confident and assured.

I held her hand and we followed Julián through the crowds of people who were everywhere in the capital, swarming from one place to the next, like a hive of confused bees. The terminal's lobby was massive. Tall windows covered the entire front wall of the building. A large board above the main ticket counter displayed the names of cities, lot numbers, and departure and arrival times. A woman announced over a speaker that the bus due in from Durango was behind schedule and that a child named Angelica Terrazas had been found by herself in the men's bathroom and was with security officers near the front entrance. Beyond the double doors, there was the street. Taxi drivers hovered around the waiting area, holding up signs listing rates to different parts of the city. A toothless old man was shining shoes, whistling the whole time, and a woman in a pink rebozo and leather huaraches sold lottery tickets from the sidewalk.

"No," Julián said to anyone who approached us, offering rides, bruised fruit, and candies wrapped in bright tissue paper.

I gripped Elena's arm when she coughed.

We followed Julián as he led us down restless alleys. Skinny cats with matted fur and sharp claws hissed at us from behind piles of trash. Stray dogs howled in the distance. We paid no attention to any of it, though. According to Julián, if we obeyed the rules, we'd be fine. He guided us down an uneven sidewalk, towards an avenue where a few storefronts and newsstands lined the street.

"Where are we going?" I asked.

"We must board another bus, Ernesto," he replied.

"I thought you lived here."

Julián nodded. "I do, hermano. But in Ajusco. It lies on the outskirts, in a place called Pedregal."

"How much longer? We're tired, compadre."

But he ignored me and continued, his footsteps fast and determined, the tapping of his boot heels loud. We went on and on, past dark houses and shops, through empty parks and dirt lots where men in coats hovered around large bonfires, smoking cigarettes, their faces bathed in a dull orange color. We crossed wide avenues, dodging cars and taxis that honked at us. Slowly, the shimmering glow from the neon signs and automobiles receded into the background as we left it all behind and moved into neighborhoods that grew increasingly darker and emptier.

Left. Then right. Then left again. The road beneath our feet hardened, our breathing ragged. We climbed steadily up and up, towards a single streetlight illuminating a corner. We had traversed one of the many hills cradling the city. We were standing in a maze of twisting dirt roads pounded flat by a multitude of feet, not cars; I could make out the tread marks of hundreds of shoes. Houses sat perched on the edges of steep cliffs where, below, lay a massive garbage dump. The smell of sewage mixed with the scent of chiles and fresh ground corn; a few feet from where we stood, catching our breath, a man was making tacos. I could hear meat sizzling. He was handing people food wrapped in brown butcher paper. We wanted to eat. We were hungry.

Years before, they'd come from the countryside, mainly Michoacán, and found themselves there, among the rubble, among the jagged glass and shards, the thickets of weeds, and the clumps of mud and dirt. Those early migrants built simple shacks out of brick and wire, anything they could find, really. They tilled the soil, planted seeds and fed those seeds water from the nearby river, and those seeds yielded corn and tomatoes and squash. They borrowed from each other, here and there, and before long there was a community. On the southern outskirts of the capital, in a colonia known as Pedregal, Ajusco had no electricity. Simply put, Julián explained, it was never intended to be. He said it was possible because of sheer stubbornness on the part of those early residents who exercised their squatter's rights when the police and city officials tried pushing them off the land. They claimed it as their own and they marched and protested and stood up to those in power, and they won.

We would be among our kind, Julián explained as he led us on. The neighborhood was nothing more than a few simple houses surrounded by fields of volcanic stones; in the dark there were lights flickering behind some of the windows we passed. I heard voices, an old song on a radio. We turned off the main road and wound down a skinny path towards a cluster of trees. Beyond these we saw a simple building painted white with glass windows framed in black metal. Three wooden doors faced the path we walked on.

Julián pointed. "My place is the middle one."

It was dark inside. Julián shuffled about before a match struck; he pressed the bright orange flame to the wick of a candle, and the room lit up. Atop a table there was a set of pots and pans, and on the floor in a corner was a large blue basin full of water. Julián's cot was pushed up against the opposite wall.

"Are you hungry?" he asked us.

We nodded.

"I'll be back, then."

Underneath a pile of Julián's clothing there was a mattress. The padding was very thin, but it was soft and smelled clean. I unrolled it, removed my jacket, folded it, and place this under Elena's head as she lay down. Julián returned with a pack of fresh tortillas, some cheese, butter, and a glass jar of red salsa.

"Did you steal this?" Elena asked.

He rolled his eyes. "No. I'm not a damned thief. I walked down the street to Doña Chelo's house. Everybody borrows from one another in these parts. When somebody doesn't have something, they simply ask. And when you have something to give back, you do. That's how it is."

He had nothing when he arrived. Only the address of a friend of his uncle's. But he was told the man had left for California. Everyone said Julián should just move in.

"He never came back?" I asked.

"No." Julián shrugged his shoulders. "Not to this day. And if he ever does, someone will find him another place. He probably won't, though. When people around here leave for California, they end up staying forever."

We slept so deeply that first evening with Julián, our bellies full, the sounds of the city just beyond the door. The next morning, Julián and I took turns at the plastic tub, splashing cold water on our faces and brushing our teeth. We ate what was left of the previous night's tortillas with coffee that Elena brewed on an electric burner.

She looked at us before we stepped outside. "What am I supposed to do while you're both gone all day?"

Julián gave me a quick glance and shrugged his shoulders. "Don't ask me. You wanted to come."

I gave her a few pesos. "Just be careful. Don't wander off too far."

Outside, we were standing in the middle of a narrow road with a row of low buildings flanking its sides. Overhead, there were no wires crisscrossing the sky, though Julián had told us that everywhere you went in Mexico City there was electricity, more lights than in all the sky. Even this early in the morning, there were people out and about, running to catch buses or trolleys, waving them down, banging on their sides until the drivers either stopped and let them on or gunned their engines, leaving them stranded in rings of smoke. I followed him to the end of the street. Etched into the sides of the hills in the distance were more houses, the flat roads snaking through them like arteries. Farther away was a cluster of tall buildings like square wooden blocks, a thick coat of mist encircling them.

"We missed the first ride into the city," Julián announced. "So we'll catch the next one, okay?"

More buildings far-off in the distance, so many of them perched on the edges of crumbling hills. Some were painted bright blue, pink, yellow, or green. Grouped together like that, they reminded me of a continuous strip of yarn, stretching across the jagged cliffs. An old woman emerged from one of them toting a jug of water. On concrete cinder blocks around the dirt lot in front of her home, someone had placed geraniums in rusted cans. With a shaky hand, she tipped the jug over, and a steady stream of water poured out. She did this for each, one by one, until the container was emptied.

The bus that came for us was an old pickup truck painted orange. We all had to find a way to pile up in the bed. I ended up on the ground, my back pressed against the tire well, the bump jabbing into me each time we rumbled over a dip in the road. We passed paved streets and monuments, museums and cafés. We drove down boulevards flanked on either side by massive buildings, and it was as though we were inside a vast canyon. I looked up; the sky was a single patch of blue. Julián and I were the last passengers, and he tapped on the back window of the truck, and the driver slid the glass open.

"El Zocálo," he directed the man. "Vamos al zocálo."

It wasn't that much farther, Julián assured me. We would arrive very soon, he said. "But get ready."

"For what?" I asked.

"This zocálo is not like the one back home."

The driver made sharp turns. Left then right, flying down narrow streets and alleyways. He drove aggressively, cars honking at us.

"Pinches perros babosos," he yelled at two semis that cut him off. "Chinga tu madre," he screamed to a man in a fancy black car that stopped in the middle of the street. "Cabrón. Hijo de la sociedad."

"This guy's crazy," Julián said.

I was relieved when we finally stopped and hopped out of the truck. We were now in a street crammed with vendors who had set up makeshift tables along the sidewalks. They sold statues of Jesus Christ and Our Lady of Guadalupe, Mexican flags, candies, newspapers and comic books, and wooden toys.

"This way," Julián led us. "The construction site is across the zocálo, next to the pyramid."

"Pyramid?"

"Yes. Now come on. Let's stop sightseeing. You're not a tourist, mano."

We headed through a crowd of people towards a boulevard, crossing busy intersections, and into a wide square laid out in stone. Right in the middle was a single large pole jutting out from the ground, and in the breeze, I watched as one of the largest flags I'd ever seen unfurled slowly, like the tongue of a massive serpent.

"La bandera Mexicana." Julián pointed. "It's big, no?"

I nodded.

There were musicians playing instruments for money, preachers standing on boxes shouting about God and Armageddon, and old women with silver braids and worn huaraches selling woven bracelets. There was an old colonial building with arches and wide columns and a balcony on the second floor. Julián said it was the government palace where the president stood to deliver *el Grito de Dolores* for the Independence Day celebrations on September 16. We continued along, past more vendors, groups of student protestors, past nuns in black habits, and military officers toting rifles. When I asked Julián what the soldiers were there for, he waved his hand and said they were always present.

"You find them here because the government wants order. Absolutely no civil unrest. They'll do anything to stop the smallest mitote. Hijos de puta."

We continued on, past the Basilica of Our Lady of Guadalupe. There, on a hillside where wild cacti bushes grew, just above the threads of telephone and electrical lines, over the tarred rooftops and iron balconies, was the place where the dark-skinned virgin appeared to Juan Diego. I've never been much of a religious man, but even I was caught up by the sight of so many devotees paying their respects.

Julián then led us towards a giant depression in the ground, and I thought, *This must be the construction site where he works.* He pointed at a structure that looked like nothing more than rubble, nothing more than a group of large round stones grouped together near a giant wall reaching down into the ground for several feet.

"Do you know what this is?" he asked.

"Is this where you work?"

He chuckled. "No." Julián swept his arms across his face, like he was conducting a symphony. "That is the remnant of an Aztec pyramid."

We went down another narrow street, through even more mazes of avenues and alleys, past more shops and restaurants where people sipped coffee and ate eggs, and my mouth watered. I had no idea where I was. If I got separated from Julián, I would never find my way back to Elena.

Finally, we stopped.

Behind a simple chain-link fence there were two trucks parked beside a giant pit dug into the ground. Inside, a man wearing rubber boots used a hose to spray the inside of the hole. Scattered about the construction site were pipes and miles of electrical wire. Some of the other men mixed batches of wet cement, while others hauled equipment and drove off in trucks that spewed black exhaust into the chilled morning air.

"What are they building?" I asked as we walk towards a man smoking a cigarette and reading a newspaper.

"An apartment complex," Julián replied. "More housing for all the people streaming into this city on a daily basis."

"Like us?"

He smirked. "I suppose."

The smoking man was the main supervisor on the site, and he was the one we needed to talk to.

"I can't pay you very much," he explained, flicking his cigarette on the ground.

"He's not asking for much," Julián told him.

"No," I insisted. "I'm not. I just need to make some money."

"All right, all right," said the man. "Congratulations. You're hired."

His name was Balderama, but everyone called him *Segundo* because he was second in command to the main boss, the owner of the construction firm, Cuauhtémoc Linares, who sometimes showed up in a long white Cadillac.

"Muy suave, that car," Julián assured me. "You'll know it when you see it."

I was responsible for filling a wheelbarrow with cement that I scooped out of a mixer with a large shovel. I then carried this over to a group of men who used trowels to smooth it out onto the ground. They were making a path that would wrap around the building.

"It's hard to see," said one of them to me, "but once the cement is dry and the building's frame goes up, you'll be able to know what it'll look like."

That's what I did all day. I filled the wheelbarrow with cement, hauled it over to the men, watched as they spread it on the ground, then I went back for more cement. Over and over. By the time the day was done, my arms were so sore and tired it felt as though they'd fall off.

"You'll get fit." Julián massaged my lower back as we ended the day.

"Yes. I suppose you're right."

Segundo whistled at me and walked over. He handed me an envelope with a few pesos inside. "Come back tomorrow."

It was so little for so much work, but more than I would have made back in La Peña, and for that I was grateful. We waited for our ride, and I leaned against the cool brick wall of an old building along the avenue. My back ached, my muscles throbbed, the tendons hot under my clothes and skin. My bones vibrated like filaments pulsing with electrical currents. I jumped when Julián jabbed my side.

"Vámonos."

It was the same driver from the morning, pulling up to the curb, his orange truck dingy and dented along the sides. From the rearview mirror there hung a scapular with the image of Saint Jude, the patron of lost and hopeless causes. Over the honks of cars and buses, he shouted "Súbanle, súbanle" at me and Julián and a handful of other passengers, all of them in uniforms, all of them with tired looks, their skin glistening with sweat. The trip back to Ajusco took longer because we had to stop and pick up more and more passengers. By the time we arrived at Julián's little street, it was nearly dark. All I could think about was eating a good meal, something warm, maybe, and washing my face.

Elena Vega

Yourself, Ernesto. You were thinking of yourself, but I wasn't going to let anything—or anyone—come between us. Like you, I would go to great lengths to keep what was rightfully mine. And you were mine.

Yes, I was, still am, terca. Like my daughter and nuera. All of us women so proud and unintimidated. That's why Julián's words and indifference wouldn't sway me. That's why I followed you. I would dig my heels in, stand my ground, and make the most of our life in Mexico City.

After they left, I took a stroll. I found a small plaza with a dried-up fountain, its stones glowing green with moss. I bought a papaya and a sweet roll from a vendor and sat at a bench and ate. Finished, I grabbed my purse and wandered towards the stalls where people drifted from table to table, buying nuts, herbs, and roasted chiles, their seeds still rattling inside the dried hulls like maracas. I bought bananas, a bag of beans, coffee, needles and threads, a spool of twine, a bar of Jabón Zote. I found a tablecloth and embroidered towels and strips of cotton and lace fabrics. There was so much that I asked a young boy waiting on the corner for the bus to help me carry it all back to Julián's.

Inside, the thin mattress you and I had slept on rested in the patch of yellow sunlight coming in from the room's single window. His place was a filthy and disorganized mess.

I knew the things that made Ernesto happy, that tugged at the nostalgia he carried inside of him. That's what I had over Julián. I knew my husband better than he did.

Next to the electric burner I'd used that morning, I found a radio, turned this on, and fiddled with the dials until I picked a station playing mariachi music. I boiled water and poured it into two plastic jugs. The woman who lived next to Julián saw me, said hello, and asked if I needed anything.

"Do you have a broom? Maybe a mop?" I asked.

"Of course," she replied, grabbing them from her place and handing them to me.

I worked all afternoon, wiping sweat away from my forehead, and turned to see the woman from the next apartment standing in the doorway awhile later.

"I'm Antonia."

I introduced myself and sighed. "I've never seen so much dirt!"

She laughed. "Juliánito's always working. Never has time to clean. The ladies around here keep an eye on him. We know he's a bachelor. Every good man needs a woman."

"Absolutely," I replied, handing her the mop and broom. "They'd fall apart without us."

"Call if you need anything," she said, then reached into the bag she held and placed a mango on the mattress.

I continued picking up. I folded our clothing and rolled the suitcase next to our mattress. I made his bed and ours and spread the cloth out on the table. I wiped down the counter in the kitchen and scrubbed the electric stove's burners until the silver crowns gleamed like new. In a tin box there was a metal mallet and a handful of nails. It wasn't easy pounding them into the flimsy walls without thinking that the whole place would come crashing down on me, but I managed. Unspooling the twine, I tied one end to a nail then stretched it across to the other, pulling it until it was taut. I unpacked some of the thin sheets of fabric I'd brought and strung these up, separating our mattress from Julián's bed, giving us some privacy. Suddenly, that drab place didn't look so drafty and unwelcoming anymore. It's one thing to miss home, but it was necessary to grow and move on to thrive. I would not let fear dictate my life, would not let someone like Julián swoop in and threaten to take away what I'd worked so hard to build.

My abuela Azucena. My mother. The lives they built with their husbands. The families they raised and struggled to protect.

Of course I'd do the same.

* *

The energy in the hospital room changes when she walks in. The air flows with purpose, intention. Everything is charged, electric. This is because she is the perfect balance of the both of us. Your brute strength and valor. My determination and unwavering loyalty.

Aquí viene. Mírala. With those broad shoulders. That powerful stride. My cheekbones. The same look in her eyes whenever you were worried. My head of hair. Thick and black as night. A horse's mane. She's so different from her brother, but we already know this, we already know why.

Hey Pop. She plays with the fur of the thick blanket. *What's on it? An owl?*

Wolf, her brother answers. *They were all out of coyotes.*

Do they even make blankets with coyotes on them? Mercy's eyes are red from crying, swollen from fatigue.

Probably. Alfredo leans forward in the chair, rubs the palms of his hands against his face. *They make them with eagles, tigers. I even saw one with a giraffe on it.* He rises. *I need some air.*

Go, Mercy assures him. *I'll stay with him.*

There are things inside of her, Ernesto, that she wants to say out loud to you, but she can't. She wants to tell you she's sorry for all the times she defied you, for how stubborn she was, that she went out of her way to be obnoxious, unruly. *I could have behaved,* she thinks. *Especially right after Mom died.*

Mercedes sits in the chair, reaches out, holds your moist hand. She knows for certain, though, that she wasn't born to listen to you or to anyone attempting to rule over her life.

I could have tried being the kind of daughter you wanted me to be, but we both know that it never would have happened. And she disobeyed you in the years after I passed, went behind your back, lied to you, had sex with boys in dark places, even kissed a few girls.

If you pushed Alfredo, he'd relent, give in. Trust you.

¿Pero mi niña? She'd push back. Hard.

I hated you. Was jealous of the way you and Freddy bonded when Mom died, jealous that he started training with you, followed in the tradition, began his lucha career. You treated me differently because I was a girl. What bullshit, Dad.

Mercedes wishes now that she had the courage to say this to you while you were alive. Not because she owed it to you to say the truth.

She owed it to herself.

You did, mija, I say to her. *You did.*

FREDDY VEGA

It's something I've dreaded having to do, but there's no way to avoid it. They deserve to know, and I'm the only one left standing, the one whose responsibility it is to give the rest of the crew the word that it's time they move on, that it's best if they look for another side hustle because shit is finished here, and I don't need them anymore.

* *

Hugo was with me right up until the pandemic. Dude came in every morning and opened the doors at seven for the early Zumba classes. By the time I'd roll in an hour or two later, tossing my keys and sunglasses on the desk, chugging down my protein shake, he'd had a full day. Sitting in the office, bright-eyed, the radio tuned to the station playing old Mexican tunes by Rocío Dúrcal and Juan Gabriel, organizing files, harassing anyone who owed us money. He was an essential part of the team. Now I'm not even sure if he's still up there in the mountains. Maybe he ended up moving down to Baja to spend the rest of his days on some secluded beach, smoking cigars and eating fish tacos. Wherever he is, I hope the crazy old fucker is happy.

I dial Paca and Edgar Torres. Our two-person maintenance crew. Both of them a few years older than me. Both undocumented.

Paca handled the janitorial side. In those flowery mandiles with their deep pockets and colorful patterns, she toted a little case crammed with bottles of solvents and rags and went around wiping everything down. She cleaned the women's restroom.

"El de los hombres, yo no entro," she told me their first day on the job, making the sign of the cross and kissing the gold crucifix around her neck.

The men's restroom was Edgar's job. He also replaced burned-out light bulbs, tightened screws, patched up holes in the drywall, changed fuses, repaired pipes. Inside his Toyota van were tackle boxes full of wires and hooks, extension cords and nails, cans of WD-40 and paint, spatulas, and hammers. Everything was neat and labeled. Like a shrine on wheels. It would be tough letting them go. They rented an apartment and used fake social security numbers to hold down jobs. Paca had bad nightmares about ICE and detention centers. She said if they were ever deported back to Nicaragua, Edgar would be killed. Their cell number changed a lot because they used burner phones.

When I dial, there's no answer. Only a persistent ring.

Next is Guadalupe Kimura. Japanese-Mexican girl in her mid-twenties. Strutted in one warm afternoon in a pair of ripped cut-offs and knee pads. Heavy eye makeup and jet-black hair blowing like strands of smoke when she stood in front of the industrial fans. She was short. Muscular legs. Thick thighs. When she blinked, the curtain of bangs draping her forehead quivered.

"Two cholas kicked my ass yesterday as I was walking to my car." She pointed to bruises on her arms. "My father's from Okinawa. They don't just do karate there. They live it. Like a religion. I wanna learn to fight. Like my ancestors. I'm tired of getting beat up."

She folded her arms and stared at me and my father, said she wasn't going to budge until we taught her everything we knew.

She only gave me her home number. When I call, her mom picks up. I leave a message.

Guadalupe fought under the name Kamikaze.

Nobody ever kicked her ass again.

Next is José Madrigal. I thought he was a punk when he first started coming around about five years ago. Arrogant. Cocky. But Hugo convinced me we needed someone like him. Young and flashy. He grew up watching WWE, worshipping payaso fighters like Hulk Hogan and Rowdy Roddy Piper, so the dude had moves. They were sloppy, exaggerated, but he had them. He worked with me for a few months, and in that time I got to know him. He reminded me of myself when I was a teenager, all rebellious and full of shit. He had long hair and pierced ears and a tribal band tattooed across his left bicep. He listened to bad music—Slipknot, Limp Bizkit, Sublime.

He adopted the lucha libre name Volcán, and we advertised him as a rudo. His mask was black with red vinyl piping around the eyes and across the mouth. He wore black tights and thick patent leather boots. By the time he had his first bout, he'd completely done away with the whole WWE influence. He was less theatrical, more serious, refined.

José's in his car driving when I call. "Doing Uber, Lyft, Grubhub . . . you name it, boss. Just trying to survive here. You? How's the gym? We getting back in there or what?"

I tell him about my dad, about the sorry state the whole operation's in.

"Sucks," he says. "Sorry about your pops. He's a good man. Doesn't deserve to go out like that."

"Fuck," I reply. "I wish things were different."

"No sweat, man. You did what you could. Besides, don't worry about me, boss. I got enough to keep my ass busy for now."

I'm on to Scarlet Santos next, our best and baddest exotico.

Scarlet's real name is Marco Antonio Flores, and he was born in Mexicali. He studied hair and makeup and worked in a beauty salon. I caught him in the ring one day, practicing takedowns and choke holds with a flaco teenager in baggy shorts and an oversized T-shirt.

"Yo siempre he sido muy girlie girlie," he told me after he'd finished his warm-ups that day, toweling his face.

"You got solid moves."

He clutched the towel to his chest and smiled. "You and your papa. That tradition. You don't know how proud it makes me to hear that, especially coming from you."

Back in Mexicali, he learned to fight because one of his amigas was in an abusive marriage with a man who beat her. One day, Scarlet watched the man slap his friend and shove her into a puddle of mud.

"¡Esto se acaba hoy!" he shouted to the dude. He'd been working with a few men at a local gym, learning basic self-defense maneuvers. "Zap! Pow! Then I kick him in the nuts." He laughed as he retold the story.

I asked him to join our syndicate, to use the gym whenever he liked, to help us stage and advertise fights, not because I felt sorry for him, but because he had heart. Because he was courageous and didn't give a fuck what anyone thought of his appearance. He wore sequined leotards and gold lamé boots, feathered boas and skirts, and did his makeup—lipstick, blush, fake eyelashes slick as crow wings. Scarlet was a sight to behold, a top-notch fighter, one of our most popular luchadores. Even the hard-core cholos in their muscle shirts and starched baggy Levis, the hyper-Catholic ladies and their paisa husbands in charro hats and thick leather belts, paid to watch men in makeup kick ass with one another and some of the other male fighters like Volcán and Beto.

When we were making plans to baptize Julian, I asked Scarlet to be one of his godparents.

"Godfather or godmother. Your choice."

"Pues, godmother. Of course," Scarlet responded.

When I dial his number, it goes automatically to voice mail. I leave a long message laying everything out. "Call me if you have any questions," I say. "Take care of yourself, Scarlet. Julian asks about you constantly. Maybe you can swing by the house sometime."

Beto answers on the first ring.

"What's up, man?" He's upbeat, tone as optimistic as ever, like the past couple years never even happened.

"I got news, bro."

"Let's hear it."

When I break the bad news and say he shouldn't bother coming in anymore, he cries. There's a long pause.

"You know what, man?" he tells me. "It's gonna be fine. Just wait and see. This is only temporary, bro. We'll be back. Better than before."

Looking around this place, dilapidated and broken and about to fall apart, his words ring hollow in my head.

Still, though, I hope. I hope.

* *

Almost a whole week of tossing things into the dumpster outside and I keep wondering: *How'd this all end up here?* There's junk crammed in a corner of the utility closet, up on a shelf in the bathroom, inside an old desk drawer. It's so random, so accidental. Like I'm on a scavenger hunt. My father's left me clues. I'm supposed to gather these things up and, together, they'll lead me to a profound truth about us, about what I'm supposed to do next.

There are three prayer cards in an envelope inside a supply cabinet. On them is my mother's name and the date of her birth and passing. Below that the Hail Mary. These were given to everyone who showed up to her funeral.

She died in 1987, two days before my sixteenth birthday.

* *

It was a weekend. Early Saturday morning. I woke to the sound of my father calling my name. It wasn't urgent. He just called out to me, over and over. *Alfredo. Alfredo. Come in here, please.* Mercy was standing in the hallway in her pajamas, hair unraveled, eyes puffy from sleep.

"Mom?" she shouted. "What's wrong?"

I could see my father sitting up on the bed, holding my mother's head, and when Mercy tried getting a better look, he shouted at her to stop, to stay back. She went into her room and shut the door; a few seconds later, I heard music coming from the other side of the wall. Madonna sang "Material Girl."

My mother wasn't breathing. Her eyes were wide open. A seizure? Shock? She was stiff. So cold.

I helped my father carry her into the living room, and the nightgown she wore dragged across the carpet, and I stepped on it. The edges tore, strips of soft blue fabric with a pattern of bright yellow chicks trailing behind us. Her head was flung back, her eyes still wide open, taking in those things that only the dying can see. We sat her on the couch, and I reached for the telephone and dialed the operator.

It was a brain aneurysm, and the doctors explained that it must have happened at some point in the middle of the night. My father had slept right beside her. *I didn't hear anything*, he'd said, again and again to the medical examiner. *I didn't hear anything.*

For days he cried.

Mercy didn't eat and refused to leave her room.

I balled my fists up and punched a wall.

In my father I could see myself, the way we would both tilt our heads slightly to the right when something bothered us, how we couldn't stand the taste of cilantro and loved drowning our tacos in lime juice. But in my mother, I struggled to find myself in her, tried identifying the parts of me that resembled her, the traces of the genes that had been handed down from her family to me. I was her son, this I knew, but there were times I wondered how it was that I came from her. Where was I inside my mother?

* *

In the afternoon, I get a call from Mercy. She's already back in Lima, Peru, working with a coalition of Indigenous people fighting against a logging company threatening to encroach on their land.

"These fucking corporations," she rants. "I don't know how much more of this I can take. Anyway, how's Dad doing?"

I sigh, grip my phone, try to push back the sense of dread roiling around inside my stomach as I take in all this . . . junk. "He's hanging in there. He looked good after you left the other day. I think he's going to pull through."

There's a long pause on the other end before she speaks up. "Bro, you're kidding yourself. I saw him. I don't think there's any pulling through this." She says I need to face facts. That everything's coming to an end, that I should close the gym and move on.

"Move on?" I laugh, toss a rubber floor mat across the floor. "Where to? What to?"

"I have no clue. But it's time you stop thinking you can save it all, Freddy. It's time you realize that sometimes it's just better to walk away. For your own sake. Please."

But how, when all I've ever known is this life? This place? These battles.

El Rey Coyote

E rnesto was only playing the part. Ya lo sabes, Elena. You always have.

Julián or no Julián.

You'd never have him all to yourself.

Ernesto Vega, always acting, always masquerading.

JULIAN VEGA

Every morning since I swung by around two weeks ago and offered to help him, I've been texting my dad to see if he needs me. All his messages are the same: *I got it. Don't worry.*

My mom says to ignore him. "When he says that," she instructs me, "you go anyway. You stay there whether he likes it or not."

But I'm not gonna hang out where I'm not wanted. That's what I tell her when she calls me this morning as I grab my duffel bag and head out the door.

* *

I'm at my gym working out—trying to focus on my reps rather than my father's stubbornness—when Tim approaches. I'd seen him in the days before the pandemic—on the rowing machine, doing leg squats, running on the treadmill. He's a nice-looking guy in his late fifties with salt-and-pepper hair that he wears cropped close to his scalp along the sides. He sports a pair of trimmed sideburns, and two pierced nipples poke through the taut fabric of his shirt. A scar running up the entire length of his left forearm's tattooed to resemble a snake, the raised ridges of skin disguised as scales, the tip a rattle curled around the wrist. Beady eyes peer back, floating just above a pair of sharp fangs. He's tall, about my height, muscular, with a firm ass that sits high up on his thighs like a trophy. It's the kind of ass that demands to be seen, that preaches when it walks by. *Hallelujah!* There's a swagger to him, and when he smiles, the left side of his mouth curls up so that it looks more like a pout. I'm there doing bench presses when he strolls over. I sit up, toweling my face.

"You survived," he says, then offers to spot for me.

"What?"

"The shit show that was 2020."

"Huh?"

"The pandemic. You know?" He twirls a finger in front of his face, the skin across his jagged jawline glimmering under the gym's lights.

With everyone all packed together again, sweating, grunting, and the music blasting from the Zumba classes, it's almost as though it didn't even happen, almost as though so many people didn't lose their lives, so many that we stopped counting.

Almost.

"Oh, yeah. All of us, I guess. Cool, right?" I reach my hand out. "Julian."

"We can do this again."

"Huh?"

"Shake hands. Touch. Human contact. Nice, isn't it?" We switch positions on the bench press. "I noticed you here. Before, I mean."

"Is that right?" I stand over him now, my legs slightly apart, his head just below my crotch. His eyes linger there for a long while. "Getting a good look?" I ask.

"Easy, tiger."

Tim grimaces between reps, his face turning beet red, neck muscles bulging as he strains to lift the weights. He's sweating, huffing.

He sits up now. "Yeah. I did get a nice, long look. Appears to be very impressive."

"You have no idea."

"You're cocky. I dig it." That smirk-pout again. "I have a prop-osition."

"Sounds intriguing."

"It's a chance to make some extra money. And you'll have fun doing it."

"And illegal."

"Have dinner with me. I'll tell you more. At least hear me out, okay? If you aren't interested, no biggie."

I shrug my shoulders, flex my muscles in the full-length mirrors lining the gym's walls. It's been so long since I've gone out. Dinner with a relative stranger, a nice, even sometimes awkward conversation with someone I hardly know, a night of raw, intense sex, sounds fucking great.

"Sure," I say. "Let's do it. Let's have dinner, stud."

* *

Like all of us, I spent 2020 and most of 2021 in front my laptop, staring at my countless students, their faces caught in the small electronic tiles that filled the screen. Their cameras would freeze up, their voices cutting in and out. It sometimes felt as though I were talking to myself as I asked them questions about the assigned readings, as I lectured on about thesis statements and misplaced modifiers. There were enough days that convinced me I was losing it. The walls inside my dingy apartment closed in. Even with the ceiling fans on high, the air was hot and still. I'd take long drives through downtown LA and Hollywood, but the endless miles of empty streets, the sidewalks clear of pedestrians and tourists snapping pictures only depressed me more.

I've never been one to sit still, to stay put. I crave movement and contact. Just like my tía Mercy. Her job as a civil rights lawyer had my aunt traveling all over the world—Brazil, Spain, China,

Thailand—until travel restrictions kept her at home in Berkeley during the lockdowns. She'd call me at least once a week during this time, checking in to see how things were going, if I needed anything.

I was teaching six classes for four different community colleges and barely making ends meet. Each section had, on average, thirty students. Before schools shut down, I was spending most of my time stuck in traffic, commuting from one school to the other, grading endless stacks of "compare and contrast" essays or research papers on gun control, climate change, and abortion. Once the state ordered schools to switch to online teaching, I found myself pretty much in the same exact situation. Except I wasn't driving from one end of Southern California to the other. Instead, I was glued to my laptop, teaching session after session, grading papers, and holding virtual office hours. Groceries were delivered weekly by a driver whose face I never saw. Sex was a bottle of lube and gay porn websites or cam-to-cam sessions with men from Canada, Germany, or New Zealand, where we'd watch each other jerk off and then abruptly cut off our feeds once we were finished. We thought it would last a few weeks, maybe three months max, but it went on and on.

I ordered more lube.

If you see me, the first thing you might think is that I'm one of those Mexicans who just crossed over. With the right clothes I can easily be mistaken for a day laborer or a gardener. In baggy jeans, an oversized hoodie, or a baseball cap, I'm a hard-core cholo from El Sereno or Belvedere. My skin's dark, but not too dark. I get this from my father, who got it from Abuelo Ernesto. I have a square jaw; a thin, pointed nose; sharp cheekbones; and dark eyes set deep behind a set of low, heavy black brows. Sometimes I sport a goatee or a stash, sometimes I don't. When it's grown out, my hair's black as oil and just as slick. I keep it buzzed down to the scalp, especially after the pandemic, because shaving it was easier than letting it grow out or learning how to cut it myself.

Exercising is something I take seriously. No matter what. Even during the lockdowns I kept in shape by lifting inside my living room and jogging around the neighborhood. But here's my thing: I don't like being hit, don't like the sight of blood. Ever since I was a kid, when I was six and fell and hit my head on the edge of the bathtub. My dad was with me, was supposed to be supervising me while my mom was in the kitchen. He turned around, and I slipped trying to get out. All I remember are those drops of blood on the smooth porcelain, my eyes clouded; the whole room turned red, and my stomach churned and churned. My dad panicked, grabbed a towel, pressing it against the cut, but it was soaked in a matter of seconds. Next thing I remember, he's cradling me in his arms, and we're running out to the car, my mother trailing behind us. Inside the emergency room lobby, they got into a fight. It was so bad that one of the security guards walked over and asked my mom if everything was okay. The fear of being hurt only grew the older I got. In elementary school, I avoided the blacktop and spent recess leaning up against the brick wall by the drinking fountain. In junior high PE classes, the teachers yelled and pushed me on the basketball court and the football field. Their taunts only made my condition worse, only worked to raise my anxiety. In high school, the only reason I agreed to try out for the wrestling team was so I could get my dad off my back. But my time there didn't last long at all. I walked away. He didn't say so, but I knew my dad was disappointed. I could see it in his eyes; he never looked at me the same again.

Even though I didn't follow in their footsteps by becoming a luchador, I still respect the tradition, still know it. My likes are just different.

Before the pandemic, sex was a full-time job. I've been with guys inside supply closets. Gas station bathrooms. Department store dressing rooms. Empty fields. Along secluded roads. Adult bookstore video arcade booths made of flimsy plywood walls where the stuffy air reeks. Countless hotel rooms. So many hotel rooms. Target bathrooms. Airports. The cab of a big rig truck. The office of a college professor. A locker room. On rooftops. Balconies. Dark movie theaters. With two, three, ten other guys. In swimming pools. Jacuzzis. Tennis courts. Construction sites. The kitchen of a five-star restaurant in Beverly Hills. A funeral. A wedding. A quinceañera. A bris. Yes, a fucking bris. At a major intersection. Inside an elevator. During a lightning storm. In the middle of an earthquake. During a once-in-a-century pandemic out on the front landing of my apartment late one night because I couldn't have him inside just in case he was infected. I tied a bandana around my mouth and nose, and he gripped the railing of the second-story balcony and gritted his teeth. When I penetrated him, he moaned, and I worried my neighbors would hear, would come out and find us there—me half-naked, the guy with his pants around his ankles, his freckled ass so pale, blue veins marbling his skin. It was two in the morning. We were out in plain sight, the chilled air hardening my nipples, and the heat radiating from his body smelled like soap, and in my head, I traveled through the night air up into the sky and watched as a multitude of small lights below me were blown out for good.

* *

The server at the restaurant where I meet Tim points to a little sign on the table that reads *Scan Me* when he asks if we can have some menus.

"Hi-tech, right?" Her name's Kaylee.

Tim smiles from across the table once we're alone. "Our brave new post-pandemic world."

His collared shirt is the same soft green as his eyes. He sports khaki pants and leather sandals, his toes slim and tender-looking. Yellow whisps of hair cover his taut arms. He looks around the restaurant, at the people crowding the bar, at the masked servers darting between tables, carrying trays of food and glasses of water or wine. He apologizes a few times for taking so long to reach out after we ran into each other at the gym; for being slightly late; for Kaylee, who takes a while to return with our drink order.

"It's cool," I say.

"What part?"

"All of it."

We're getting used to being out again, to meeting up at bars or clubs, at parties and social events, I assure him. I've always been good at small talk, at making whoever I'm with comfortable and confident, I say, even when things are awkward.

"I can tell," he replies. "It's one of the reasons I first noticed you."

According to him, there's something magnetic about me, something charming and likeable. I have a vulnerability about me, he asserts, a quality that makes people want to nurture and take care of me. But he senses that, at the same time, I can be rough, shrewd, take control of things.

"Is this a psychic reading?"

He laughs. "You seem to be possessed of many talents."

"The only talent I got right now is the talent for correcting grammar and making a shitty salary."

Apparently, I'm in luck, because he's in the business of finding young men who are not only attractive but smart and able to hold a conversation if need be.

"I recruit people like you," he continues. "Good-looking. Nice bodies. Guys who are versatile and uninhibited."

I take a swig of my beer. "Are you going to offer me a job selling steak knives door-to-door? Because I did something like that in high school, but with candy bars, and I was terrible at it."

"No. Nothing like that."

Kaylee brings our food over; mini chicken tacos for him, a cobb salad for me. We order another round of drinks and eat in silence for a while. The restaurant's more crowded by now, and even though cases have dropped nationally and globally, and the hospitals and emergency rooms aren't overrun, it's still a little unnerving to see so many people packed together so tightly.

"We haven't learned much," Tim says.

I chuckle. "You read my fucking mind. So, this job? It's gay porn, right? I'm a college teacher. I have a master's degree. There's no way I'm doing porn, no matter how much it pays."

He takes a bite of his taco and wipes his face. "Not gay porn."

I'm supposed to think about it like a series of blind dates or parties with different men. They pay me for my time, and whatever I make, he gets a cut of it.

"So, you're a pimp?" I ask.

He places his hand over his heart, mouth agape, taco carnage plastered to his roiling tongue. "I'm so insulted."

"Sorry, but, well, that *is* what you are. In the technical sense."

He smirks. "Kidding. I'm not insulted. Yes, I'm like a pimp. But a classy pimp."

"So, you're offering me a job as a hustler? I'm supposed to have sex with these dudes?"

"Not always. But it's common."

The men he works for are wealthy. They live in Beverly Hills or Malibu or Pacific Palisades or they're in town on business. They're studio execs, lawyers, bankers, oil tycoons from Texas, rich farmers from Iowa, software engineers from Silicon Valley. They have a lot of money, and their sexual proclivities need to be kept secret. Tim's job is to find hot guys who are semiprofessional, educated, drug-free, and screened regularly for STDs.

He wipes his mouth. "I think you've got what it takes to make some very good money. The whole package."

"To be honest, I don't know if I should be flattered or insulted."

He says that's how he first felt when he was approached by his boss. Tim was at a club with a few friends. This guy with a thick pinky ring approached him. He carried wads of cash and kept buying Tim drinks.

"I was flat broke at the time. Hurting," he says. "Marco took me in, fed me, bought me clothes, even paid my rent. And all I had to do was go out with a few men a couple times a month. Dinner. Drinks. Trips to Carmel and San Francisco. Real extravagant shit."

He takes good care of his "boys," he assures me. They are never without the things they need to help them get by.

"And you pimp them out in return?"

"Well, technically yes. I get that you're resistant to the idea. Let me ask you something: Do you like having sex with men?"

"Yeah."

"How often do you do it?"

"As often as I can get it."

"Then why not get paid for it?"

He has me there. Still, the whole idea's unsettling, and all I want to do is finish my meal and leave and never have to think about being propositioned again. Outside the restaurant, Tim gives me an awkward hug and says he hopes to bump into me sometime at the gym.

I'll be doing my best to avoid him.

ERNESTO VEGA

I looked over at the table that she covered with a cloth. She arranged photographs of our parents around a vase filled with water and a single red carnation. Sheets hung from a piece of twine running down the middle of the room.

Julián didn't say much, just shook his head and glanced around. "It's . . . nice." He kicked his dirty shoes up on the table, smearing soot on the tablecloth.

She served us each a bowl of black beans. "The people around here are very nice."

"What? You thought I lived in a slum?" Julián rolled a tortilla.

I slept heavy that night, my body resting comfortably on that thin, lumpy mattress, the two of us separated from Julián by the curtain. The next morning, we rose once again and took the same route into the city with the same driver in the same truck. I hauled more wheelbarrows full of wet cement, watched the men set it into the ground, the walkways coming together little by little. That's what it was like for the next few weeks. I worked from very early until late into the afternoon.

That's how the first year went. And we were still sleeping on Julián's flimsy mattress in his little apartment in Ajusco. He and Elena learned how to live together. In a way. Mostly, they did what they could to avoid each other, only speaking when it was necessary.

There was no rudeness between them, just a polite tolerance. I was caught between my love for my wife and my loyalty to Julián. I tried maintaining the peace by always keeping us busy and distracted. The three of us strolled through parks and spent afternoons wandering around the marketplaces. On weekends we visited the museums on free days, then rented a gondola to paddle around the chinampas in Xochilmilco.

But I knew why they resented one another, that it was my attention they both vied for.

It was on a weekend afternoon in mid-September, after the Independence Day celebrations when we had watched the fireworks light up the night sky like falling stars. A day when the thunderclouds rolled into the valley of Mexico from behind the tall peaks of the ancient mountains and volcanoes ringing the city. They burst open with rain, and then evaporated, the sun coming out, its light refracted, broken up, as it danced in and out from behind the buildings and trees. The sidewalks were washed clean, and everywhere there was the smell of fresh rainwater. I sat at the table with Elena. We were sipping coffee and smoking cigarettes when Julián entered and removed his wet jacket.

"Look what I have," he said, waving a damp envelope before us. Inside there were three tickets to a lucha libre match.

Back in the campo, I had seen copies of *Box y Lucha* for sale on the shelves of the newsstand beyond the church walls. Once, while buying the daily paper, I picked up an issue, thumbed through it, studying the pictures of luchadores in threatening poses. I knew that people followed the exploits of their favorite wrestlers, like daredevils.

"I managed to get three." Julián forced a smile in Elena's direction. "Let's go."

She took a puff from her cigarette, then said, "Maybe I'll stay here. You two need time with each other, I guess."

Julián removed a strand of tangled hair from his eyes. "You should come, Elena. It's a wild time."

He was trying. I could see that, and so could Elena. After a year, Julián had finally surrendered to the fact that she would never leave me.

"Well, all right then." She rose and stabbed her cigarette in the ashtray.

We grabbed our coats and made our way to the corner bus stop without thinking or hesitating. That's how we were back then. Impulsive, young, and with enough energy to still be impulsive, even reckless.

* *

From the outside, the arena looked like any other old colonial building in the Centro Historico, all of them badly in need of refurbishing, with crumbling facades and broken concrete steps. We pushed through the crowd inside the lobby where people milled about, drinking refrescos or beers and smoking cigarettes. The stage was in a large, open stadium with seats that extended up along the walls to the very top. The ceiling was wide, reaching past the circuit of floodlights shining down on the entire spectacle. On the main floor there were more seats grouped around an elevated square ring surrounded by yet more lights. Running along the perimeter of this ring were three thick padded cords that swung and bounced around each time someone touched or brushed up against them. People filed in from all sides into the arena, swarming in like colonies of ants as they filled every seat. Everyone wandered about unhurried, some eating roasted garbanzo beans out of oily paper bags or sipping juice from clear plastic pouches with straws tied around their openings. I smelled smoke, popcorn, and coconut milk.

Julián said there would be two pre-matches before the main

event, the first a warm-up bout to get the crowd excited, the second a little more serious. By now, the place was full. Rows and rows of heads filled the whole stadium, the excitement so intense it felt as though everything around us would burst. A referee stepped into the ring, circling around inside, as the crowd quieted some. He made the announcement about the first match between Mini Tornado and Relampaguita.

"Do you know these wrestlers?" Elena asked Julián, her voice shouting over the cheers.

He shrugged his shoulders and spoke without looking at her. "I've heard of them. They are minis."

Two wrestlers stepped into the ring and ran around a few times, the crowd applauding and shouting at them.

"Children?" Elena asked.

"No." Julián sighed. "Minis are midgets. Like Samuel Avalos's daughter Trinidad back in La Peña."

They called her an "enanita," a dwarf. She'd been born with a deformity and never grew larger than a few feet tall. She would stand on a wooden crate when she helped her mother bag groceries at the store her family owned. The mini wrestlers tumbled around inside the ring, doing flips and somersaults. When the referee blew his whistle and called a foul after Relampaguita, the good guy, pinned the evil Mini Tornado to the mat, the crowd went crazy, booing and shouting obscenities at the referee from their seats.

"Cheater!" a man in a suit and tie shouted.

"Fixed! Fixed!" yelled an old lady in a rebozo and skirt.

There were screams and curses. People threw bags of nuts and popcorn at the ring. The floor was so sticky. Men with angry red faces balled up their fists and heckled the referee. The second bout featured a rudo named Hijo del Mal versus Eclipse. Eclipse strutted out from behind a satin curtain wearing a pair of white tights with red boots. Around his waist was a thick belt emblazoned with the image of a yellow sun. The mask covering his face was made of red fabric with openings cut out for both eyes, his nose, and mouth. He removed a long white cape, stood in the center of the ring, growled and flexed his muscles. A woman sitting behind us rose and ran up to the ring. She presented him with a flower, which he took, and graciously thanked her.

"Marry me!" screamed another lady a few seats over.

Eclipse was stout with thick legs and arms. His torso was wide, not lean at all, and his neck was fat, thick like a tree stump.

"What do these people see in a guy like that?" I shouted to Julián. "He's heavy. Such a chaparro."

Julián laughed. "He's got charisma."

A series of loud boos rippled through the arena as Hijo del Mal made his way into the ring. Every piece of clothing he wore was black. Black boots, black tights, a long black cape, and a black mask. I could see through the mask's slits that the areas around his eyes had been painted black. When he removed his cape, Hijo del Mal used the ring's corner buckles to climb up to the third padded cord. He balanced himself there, swaying carefully for a moment before launching himself off, doing a complete back flip, both feet landing on the ring's mat with a mighty thud.

"This one will fade into the night," he screamed, pointing to Eclipse.

A few people around us cheered el Hijo's name, shouting back to him to destroy Eclipse, to make him pay for something he'd done. Julián said theirs was an old rivalry that went back a few years.

"No one knows how it started," he explained now. "But those two really hate each other."

The referee called the fight in favor of Hijo del Mal, and Eclipse looked crushed as he was led out with the help of his trainer and a man who worked for the wrestling company. Then the next bout between El Angel and Furia began. El Angel used to be called

Demonio. He was once a rudo who fought alongside Furia. The two had been close friends for many years, tag teaming opponents and winning bouts all around the city and in other parts of the country. But then they had had a falling-out over a woman, and Demonio gave up his evil ways, became a very devout Catholic, and changed his name to El Angel. Today's match was very important because it was for caras; the winner would unmask the loser.

El Angel wore light blue tights and white boots with thick soles that made him taller than he was. The mask that covered his face was the same shade of blue as his tights and with white piping around the mouth and eyes. He wore a cape covered in white feathers. When he stepped into the ring, a few of them drifted down to the ground. Some of the boys ran up to collect them, and they forgot one, so I walked over, picked it up, and gave this to Elena, who placed it in her purse. The mood in the arena changed, though, when Furia entered, pushing past the crowd, toward the ring. He wore red stockings and boots, and his mask was decorated with flames. He stuck his tongue out a lot as he strutted around up there, shoulders back, wide chest puffed out like a cocky rooster.

"¡Tramposo cobarde!" a spectator yelled out at him, making a lewd gesture. Seeing this, Furia leapt off the stage and onto the arena floor. Several people jumped out of his way when he charged after the man, throwing chairs around. People screamed as the man ran off towards the closest exit. El Angel stood in the corner, his back to us. When the referee glanced away, Furia snuck up behind him and landed two punches into Angel's back. He fell over in agony, and Furia proceeded to kick him a few times.

"Look!" I shouted to Julián. "Did you see? And the referee's doing nothing." I stood on my chair and yelled out, "Hey, señor Angel! Behind you," as others joined me, trying in vain to get the wrestler's attention; we were too far back for him to hear us.

By the time he turned around, it was too late. Furia had stopped kicking Angel. The referee pretended not to see any of it.

"Disqualify him!" another man shouted. "That's illegal. That's a violation!"

The referee, though, did nothing as Angel got back on his feet and stumbled to his corner. Julián called the referee a chueco. He was crooked and was well known for favoring rudos, letting them cheat without disqualification. As the match began, the crowd grew progressively unruly, tossing trash at the stage and one another, shouting out obscenities at the referee or the luchadores.

¡Pinche baboso! What's wrong with you?

You fight like a maricón, Angel.

Furia, your mother must be so ashamed of you. Evil monster!

The two flew around and tumbled and kicked, and it was all colors and lights and twisting limbs as those men used their bodies to hit and punch and leap. I watched a short woman in thick stockings, her swollen purse draped over her arm, stand on her chair and make a series of gross gestures with her tongue and fingers. Then I felt it: my heart racing in my chest, thumping loud and fast. I couldn't think, I couldn't see anything else but this moment. I knew that day that this was what I had been longing for, that this was where I belonged.

* *

Lucha libre became my religion, the wrestlers were my gods. In the rudos, I saw my own doubts, those that held me back. I saw my anger towards my father and his violent ways. I felt the loss of my mother, who had given me so much adoration, who had nurtured my hopes even as my father tried molding me into someone I wasn't. There too was my longing to see my brother and my sisters again, which weighed on my shoulders, pressing me down, heavy and agonizing, as I struggled to break free. I threw myself into it, buying the magazines, attending matches on the weekends, either with Julián or Elena or by myself. Hauling wheelbarrows full of cement all day. Lifting bricks and moving rocks made me stronger, gave me a sense of confidence, perhaps a bit of arrogance, even. For the first time in my insignificant life, there was a purpose, a clear direction, a reason for having made the decision to move to the city.

I learned that a luchador could win a match by pinning an opponent down to the mat for a count of three, ousting them from the ring for a count of twenty, or forcing them to submit until the luchador gave in. Performing illegal maneuvers or ripping an opponent's mask off was cause for immediate disqualification. I learned to identify basic moves like a rana, a plancha, and a tornillo; studied the techniques; practiced them during my breaks at the construction sites with some of the other men. They'd laugh at me, lying in the shadows of the parked cement trucks, drinking refrescos from tall glass bottles with slender necks, pointing and cracking jokes.

If you're not careful you'll break your neck, Vega.
Stop fucking around and get back to work, tarudo.

I didn't care what they said or thought. It was my obsession.

Elena Vega

A whole year of living with him. Under his roof. His eyes always on me, always scrutinizing everything I did and said to my husband. I was tired of it, so I convinced Ernesto that it was time for us to find our own place. He made excuses, of course, but I was firm. We found a modest apartment not too far away from Ajusco. It had a little courtyard out back with a stone fountain, water gurgling out from the spout.

I could tell Julián wasn't happy.

He glared at me. "You can both stay as long as you need. It's not a problem."

Ernesto sensed how determined I was. He knew one year had been too much. "We're still in the city. On the other side of the university."

"I know, but—"

Ernesto interrupted him, "We can't live here with you forever, hermano," then glanced over at me, tension set in his face.

I was relieved once we were out of there and settled in our place. No Julián. My husband to myself again. Just like back in La Peña before he came along and changed Ernesto. I grew nopales and aloe and chayotes in discarded tires and buckets, anything I could fill with dirt. It felt wonderful to have my own cooking stove, our own bed. I bought cups made of glass instead of clay. I

got a sewing machine, and then up went curtains. Then embroidered pillows, coverlets for the bed, a tablecloth. I made friends
with many of the other women in the colonia. It's easy to forget
the person you were and become someone else, isn't it? Especially
when one is so young, untainted by life's misfortunes.

FREDDY VEGA

A year after our mother died, Mercy started high school and I became a senior. We walked to campus together, saying very little along the way. While my classmates got to go to the mall after school and hang out at the food court, I stayed home to watch her. She was my responsibility now, my father would remind me.

The depression first came to me in small waves. Restlessness. Agitation. Guilt because I didn't do anything to help save my mother from dying. Mornings were bad. I'd have to force myself out of bed. I didn't shower or comb my hair. At school I was dazed, unable to focus, easily distracted, as if everything around me were happening in slow motion. My limbs felt disconnected from my body. I spent lunchtime in the bathroom stall crying. It was Mike Foster who heard me that afternoon. The cafeteria was serving lasagna, and the smell of overcooked cheese and marinara sauce wafted through the windows. I forgot to latch the stall's door, and Mike opened it, the fly of his Z Cavaricci pants halfway undone. I was sitting on the toilet, my eyes red and watery. He asked if I was okay.

"Yeah, man. I'm good." I rushed to the sinks, composing myself in the mirror.

Mike finished in the stall, walked over, and started washing his hands. "It's all fucked-up. When my dad died, people gave my mom these stupid books about grieving. Pages full of dumb advice."

"Yeah," I said. "Sucks."

He dried his hands, wadded up the paper towel, tossed it in the trash, then picked at a small pimple on his right cheek. "I won't say anything, man. You know?"

I kept my gaze fixed on the graffiti scrawled on the wall. "Thanks, dude."

He was true to his word, and from that moment on, we were inseparable.

* *

I had to wait for Mercy in front of the school's main entrance. We were to stay inside all afternoon until my father came back from work. One day at school, Mike told me he scored some weed from this metalhead named Joey Stopani. High-grade stuff. It'll help with your depression, he claimed. His house was about a mile away, near South La Verne and Third Street, right by Belvedere Park Lake, where my parents used to take us to feed the ducks and pigeons when Mercy and I were younger. Mike invited me over because I needed to distract myself from "all that death shit."

He was right. I gave Mercy the number to his house. "If anything happens, call *me* first."

Mike's father had left him some money, enough for a hefty down payment on a red Toyota Tercel. We went for drive-through, ordering cheeseburgers and fries and sodas, and then headed back to his place. Once we parked, he rolled a joint, lit it, took a big hit, and handed it to me.

"Inhale," he said. "Hold it in for as long as you can, then release."

It burned my throat. I coughed, puffs of smoke sputtering out from my nose. My mouth went dry, and I knew that I was inside Mike's car, but none of it felt real. I had to touch my arms and legs to make sure I was still in my body. Mike was saying, *Relax, bro. Relax. Let it take you where it needs to.* I remember laughing at something he was talking about.

It was the first time in a while that I felt good.

Free again.

* *

My father met Hugo one random morning. He was out for a run when he stopped and saw Hugo lifting weights in his garage. My father struck up a conversation with him, and the two became fast friends. They worked out together, sparred in the boxing ring Hugo bought used from a guy who'd once been the junior weight champion of East Los Angeles but got hooked on heroin after he hurt his back in a fight. Hugo loved hearing about my father's adventures in Mexico when he'd been a luchador. The dude was a bit of a lucha libre fanatic; Hugo watched all the old movies and kept news clippings and articles of all his favorite técnicos like Santos and Blue Demon. He had no wife. There were three children from two different women. There was nothing remarkable about them. They were married with kids of their own. They had jobs. Took vacations to Cancún and Yosemite. Leased minivans and didn't visit their father nearly enough.

One Sunday, my father invited Hugo and a couple of his friends from the factory over to our house for a game of cards. There were three of them and they all addressed each other by last names. There was Rincón, who wore a striped train conductor hat and had a missing finger. There was Hernandez, who had also lost his wife, not to a disease or an accident, but to another woman. And, of course, el Hugo with his chubby fingers and muscly tattooed arms, meaty, thick necked, his face pockmarked. The guy looked like a cartoon sailor. They brought cases of beer and bottles of tequila and ordered pizza, and Mercy and I ate and watched them play poker or twenty-one, using chips from our checkers and Othello board games as currency. After they left, I was cleaning up and my father was in the bedroom changing when I lifted a beer can, still cold from the fridge and nearly full. I finished it in one swig, the icy alcohol warming my blood, lubricating my thoughts.

* *

One night, Mike and I decided to travel to the foothills. We followed a dirt road leading up the side of a hill, parked his car, and climbed out. Below were ravines where wild bushes and trees grew. Homeless people had encampments down there, and some said the area was haunted by tribes of Native Americans pissed at white people for taking their land. We came to a flat, barren hilltop at the end of the road, lit up a joint, and got stoned.

We started slowly down the hill, and Mike was handling the curves nice and steady. Clearing the base, I could see the main avenue below, the intersection's lights flashing yellow and green and red. Then he glanced away for a second to change the radio station, and a flicker of something slender and gray hobbled across the road. When he turned to avoid it, and the coyote darted off into a bush just as the car spun out of control, all I felt was the pull of gravity sending us tumbling down the sharp ravine, the wild branches whipping past us, the smell of sap invading the car as the windows broke. Our heads rammed against the windshield when we struck a tree. Then there was silence and the hiss of steam from the radiator. I was bleeding. Mike had flown through the windshield; the impact with the tree had flung him out of the car and onto the hood. Through the shards of glass, I could see his open eyes, a huge gash running across the length of his forehead, his legs twisted and mangled like rubber. I pushed open the car door and went around. Blood was dripping down my forehead and into my mouth. My arms were scraped. My left side throbbed. I leaned up against the busted car.

"Stay still," I told Mike, even though I knew he couldn't hear me. "Just don't move, man."

I got stitches on my forehead and had some bruised ribs, but that was it. They sent me home with a bottle of painkillers and pamphlets about the dangers of drugs and alcohol. Mike broke his leg. Once he was back home, I tried going over to visit him. His mother greeted me at the door, arms folded, eyes tired and sad. She said he was asleep. When I asked if I could come by later, she shook her head. "I don't think that would be wise."

A month after that, I heard that his mother decided to move to Arizona where they'd live with Mike's grandmother because, with all the hospital bills, she got behind on the mortgage, and they lost their house.

I never heard from Mike again.

* *

Once my stitches were out, my arm and bruised side completely healed, my father walked into the living room where I was sitting on the couch watching music videos. Out of nowhere, he grabbed the remote control from my hand and turned the television off.

"Get dressed," he shouted, tossing me a pair of my sweats and an old T-shirt.

A few minutes later we were pulling into Hugo's driveway. The dude was in the garage bench-pressing weights. My father reached behind his seat and pulled out a pair of red Everlast boxing gloves and threw them at me.

"What's up? Why are we here?" I asked, taking them.

"You've been fucking up, son." He turned the car off. "The drinking? The bad grades? The accident? This isn't you. This behavior. You could have been killed."

He ordered me out. Hugo smirked, shook my father's hand, and the two slapped one another's shoulders a few times. I followed my father through the side gate and towards the backyard. There was an inflatable pool underneath a lemon tree and a chicken coop next to a set of metal trash bins. A rooster scurried around a patch of wild weeds that sprouted from the dirt. The boxing ring was set up on a platform a few feet above the ground, and my father hopped up and inside in one graceful move.

"Come on," he commanded.

"Dad, I think—"

"Get your punk ass in here. Now!"

I maneuvered through the padded cords as he placed a pair of gloves on his hands and pointed to mine. "You're gonna want those."

He started by hopping around the ring, circling me, taking quick jabs at my body and face. I just stood there, watching the rooster peck the ground, my hands stuffed inside those fat, swollen gloves.

"Duck and cover," my father said, his words coming out of his mouth between short bursts of his breath. "Protect your face."

"This is dumb." I was irritated, and he was acting like a fucking freak and all I wanted to do was leave. Then the next thing I knew, he landed a one-two punch to my face and stomach. I fell to the ground, my eyes seeing bright swirls of color, a pain stretching like a hot rope across my abdomen. I lay crouched on the mat, legs tucked against my chest, squirming, my face throbbing.

"What the hell is wrong with you, huh?"

"You're asking me?" I tried standing but stumbled back down.

He leaned over, hands on his knees. "Get up, pendejo. Get the fuck up."

I didn't want to. I pressed my face against the warm mat, closed my eyes, groaning from the terrible pain. "Why are you acting like such an asshole?"

"Because I'm trying to keep you from ruining your life, menso.

You think you're tough?" he shouted. "You think getting into trouble, drinking, all that shit makes you a man?"

I stumbled and swayed, my knees buckling under the weight of my own body. He continued hopping around, moving in a circle.

"Come on, Alfredo. Hit me." He pointed to his chin with his glove.

"I don't want to."

He kept taunting me, calling me out, laughing. And the more time I spent in there with him, the angrier I found myself getting. Just one hit, I told myself. Just one hit, and I could go home. I jabbed and jabbed, first left then right. But he was too fast for me.

Then I saw it. That moment. Brief, but it felt as though it lasted an eternity. There was a pause, a break, and the timing was right, so I reached out, hurling my fist towards his face. The punch landed over his left eye, so strong that he stumbled back and leaned up against the ring's padded cords.

And that's how it began for me.

El Rey Coyote

P ay attention, mocosos y mocosas. Because I'm not going to repeat myself.

Here is the origin of what is called the Eternal Struggle, or la Lucha. Here I will speak of the spirit of the sky and water and sun called Te ' cnico, they who are both god and human, both male and female, both good and bad. Here, too, I will speak of the spirit of the land and fire and moon called R ' u ' Do, they who are both god and human, both male and female, both good and bad.

By telling it, we give it breath.

By writing it, we give it form.

So shall we learn it.

So shall we recite it.

So shall we live it.

In this time before time, the land was without form. Without valley. Without mountain. Without canyon. Without field. Without desert. Without jungle. Without forest.

Upon the surface of the earth, nothing walked. No human. No jaguar. No coyote.

In the air, nothing flew. No vulture. No hummingbird. No bee.

In the ocean, nothing swam. No shark. No whale. No barracuda.

For millennia, there was only the stillness, only the silence. Then, there came a loud crack, and the sky parted, and there emerged the spirit being called Te ' cnico. He of feathers and sky skin, with suns for eyes and seawater for blood. He looked down upon the expanse of nothingness and said, "Is there no one here to challenge me?"

There came another loud crack that shook the land; it parted and out of this came the spirit being called R ' u ' Do. He of fur and earth skin, with moons for eyes and lava for blood.

They looked upon each other and replied, "We shall fight for supremacy of this realm. We will wage battle to determine which of us is strongest."

But when Te ' cnico tried reaching down from the sky, he found his arms couldn't grab hold of R ' u ' Do.

And when R ' u ' Do tried reaching up from the land, he found his arms couldn't grab hold of Te ' cnico.

Day and night they tried, and their kicks and punches shook the land and sky and the seas parted and lakes and mountains and valleys and jungles were formed. Their sweat and blood fermented the soil, and this was how the people were formed, and there were many, and they made nations and cultures and they spoke different languages and prayed to different gods, and they forgot their creators.

Then Te ' cnico and R ' u ' Do said, "We shall make acolytes of several of these beings, and they shall fight for us."

Te ' cnico was first. He begat the Strongman called Enrique Ugartechea and bestowed upon him the power of invention and movement. Te ' cnico showed him in dreams how to combine the lanzas of Greco-Roman wrestling with the slippery moves, the pins, and the holds below the waist of Olympic-style wrestling to invent a whole new way of fighting that no one had ever witnessed. Then Te ' cnico sent Ugartechea across the nations of man where he introduced them to the style of lucha that dominates to this day. Then Te ' cnico told his disciple, "You shall establish a school devoted to training luchadores in the art and athleticism of this type of battle."

And, in this way, Enrique Ugartechea became the first teacher of lucha libre.

R ' u ' Do saw this and said, "I, too, shall beget an acolyte to help shape the struggle called lucha."

So, from a city called Colotlán, which is "the place of scorpions," R ' u ' Do breathed into being a man named Salvador Lutteroth. And, when he was still a child, Salvador and his family moved to the city called Tenochtitlán. There, he was enrolled in a school where boys like him were taught how to tame the land, how to grow crops and raise animals to feed their growing nation.

But R ' u ' Do had other plans for the boy, so he planted in him the spirits of Restlessness, Inspiration, and Adventure.

After finishing his studies, Lutteroth joined the Mexican Revolution, making it up to primer capitán. He married his querida, Armida Camou Olea, left the military service and worked in an office. He and his wife begat four children—Salvador, Hector, Enrique, and Elsa. And they moved north, to the great city called Juárez. It was while attending a match at the Liberty Hall theater in El Paso, Tejas, that Lutteroth first saw la lucha. He grew captivated by it; some would even say he became obsessed.

In a dream, R ' u ' Do told him, "You must leave Juárez and return to Tenochtitlán with your family. There you will establish a wrestling syndicate. You will build a temple. It shall be a shrine, an homage to the great struggle we call lucha libre."

They called it Arena México.

So begins the Age of Man.

Te ' cnico and R ' u ' Do said, "We shall make them cover their faces." Then Te ' cnico begat Corbin James Massey, a gabacho from Tejas best known by his wrestling name in the United States: Cyclone Mackey. This warrior wore a mask, a simple black thing stitched together with leather.

"Come," Lutteroth told him. "Wrestle with your mask on. We will call you La Maravilla Enmascarada."

Then R ' u ' Do saw this and replied, "I, too, shall create a masked luchador. And he shall be called Murciélago Velásquez."

His armor was a pair of baggy exercising trunks and a leather vest with a hood. Murciélago Velásquez would enter arenas, open his vest, and release several live bats into the air, terrifying the spectators. A fight between el luchador Octavio Gaona and Murciélago changed everything. When Murciélago lost the match, Gaona unmasked him, revealing his identity to the public.

The lucha de apuestos was born.

Then Te ' cnico proclaimed, "I shall make the greatest fighter of them all. He shall be called El Santo."

The man was born Rodolfo Guzmán Huerta in Tulancingo, Hidalgo, the fifth of seven children. He was just a boy when his family too moved to Tenochtitlán because, like always, there was nothing in the campo, only la miseria. They, like all the others before them and after them, rose, packed their belongings, and migrated away from home, away from the land that had sustained them to a place of concrete and steel, a place of endless grids of avenues intersecting like nets, to that city soaring thousands of feet above sea level and ringed by volcanoes where a new kind of might takes root inside the body.

Rodolfo's family settled in Tepito, donde se vende todo menos la dignidad. He first wrestled under many different names—Rudy Guzmán, El Hombre Rojo, El Demonio Negro. Some say Rodolfo's manager came up with three options for names—El Angel, El Diablo, and El Santo—and that Guzmán chose the last of these. Others say he thought of the name after reading the novel *The Man in the Iron Mask* by the French writer Alexandre Dumas.

El Santo begat Blue Demon, he in his cobalt mask with its silver borders, his glittering cape, blue tights, and boots with white laces. Blue Demon never lost a lucha de apuestas, so he died without his fans ever seeing his true face.

El Blue Demon begat Mil Máscaras, he who transformed the sport into an international phenomenon. He wore many masks, each distinguished by an *M* stitched into the center of the forehead. This was how he came to be known as the man of a million faces. He made his international debut at the Olympic Auditorium in Los Angeles. He took lucha to Japan, where it remains a popular sport.

So begins the Age of Heroes.

Te ' cnico was happy.

R ' u ' Do was happy.

Still there was something missing.

Then there came those called los mini estrellas. Little stars. Gran Nikolai, Pequeno Goliath, and Arturito, named for the robot R2-D2. Arturito begat Burrito who begat Kaotikos who begat Taquito who begat Baby Yoda. And so on.

Los minis begat las mujeres who next claimed the cuadrilátero as their own. It was los Americanos who first sent las luchadoras to Tenochtitlán and to the rest of the republica. They struggled, las mujeres luchadoras.

They were banned from the sport.

They couldn't organize and form collectivos like los hombres.

So they found audiences outside the major cities, in pueblitos and colonias with small populations. Asi las mujeres persisted.

Como Irma González. When she became engaged to her husband, she promised him she would take her botas off, hang up her leotard, and put away her capes and thick belts and never step foot inside the ring again.

She lied.

To hide her identity, she changed her lucha name. With the consent of El Santo, she rebranded herself La Novia del Santo and donned a silver mascara that looked exactly like his. Irma González was the only non–family member to be given permission to use this name and to wear the mask. La Novia del Santo begat Lady Araña. Lady Araña begat La Monja. La Monja begat Siouxie. And so on.

Then came those inhabiting the realm between the masculine and the feminine. They who are more than male and more than female. The first exótico was a gabacho from Houston, Tejas, called Sterling Blake Davis. Davis was brought to Tenochtitlán by Lutteroth. Sterling took the name Gardenia Davis because he tossed gardenias out to the crowds gathered as he made his way to the ring. El Catrín followed next, a tall and thin luchador with a fancy mustache, top hat, smoking jacket, and a gold monocle over his right eye.

Gardenia David and Catrín begat Adorable Rubí who begat El Bello Greco who begat Sergio el Hermoso who begat Disco Dani who begat la Boogie who begat el Angel Charlie who begat Jazzercise who begat Pimpinela Escarlata who begat Cassandro. And so on.

So begins the Age of Rebellion.

Te ' cnico was happy.

R ' u ' Do was happy.

Still there was something missing.

Now we've entered the era of Rey Misterio Sr. and his nephew, Rey Mysterio Jr., of Psycho Clown, of Kalisto, of Piñatita, of Kroniokita, of Chupacabrita, of Lady Loba, of Piratas, of la Llorona, of Marko el Narco, of Lili, of Occulta, of Lady Tata. Of those still forming. Of those yet to come.

So begins the Age of Legends.

Te ' cnico is happy.

R ' u ' Do is happy.

There is nothing missing.

Yet la lucha continues.

Now we have learned it.

Now we will recite it.

Now we will live it.

JULIAN VEGA

Today I'm restless again, edgy. If I check my email, I'll be bombarded with messages from students in the summer school courses I started teaching earlier this week. Questions about upcoming assignments, requests to meet for office hours. Pleas. So many pleas. And because summer sessions are so damn short, I already have essays to grade and assignments to plan.

I'm like a caged animal that's just been released. There's a text message in my private box of one of the apps I use called Papi—"for Latino guys and the men who lust after them." His name's Greg, and he's married to a woman. She's out for a few hours, getting her hair cut, running errands. He's home alone all morning.

Come fuck me, the message reads.

When I tell him where I live, he says he'll give me gas money.

Cool, I respond. *Let's do it.*

Fully vaccinated. You?

Yeah, I say. *Of course.*

He's over on the Westside. My phone says it'll take me fifty-five minutes to cover the thirteen-mile distance from my location to his house. I'm the little blue arrow driving down César Chávez towards downtown, passing Rowena, the Navarro's grocery store. The parking lot's packed with cars and trucks, green banners tied to light posts. *Masks no longer required indoors. El uso de máscaras no se require para patronizar adentro.* I don't know if my mother's in there, standing behind the counter and ringing up giant cans of refried beans and liter bottles of soda full of enough sugar to send someone into a diabetic coma.

Greg's the green dot near the blue smudge with the faded gray words that spell out *Pacific Ocean.* Between us there's an endless grid of streets and freeways, alleys and service roads. Some are yellow in spots, others throbbing bright red like arteries about to burst. The light turns green, and I go, zigzagging through traffic, speeding around slow-moving trucks and vans. I cut drivers off. They honk and give me the finger.

I just keep speeding along.

His neighborhood's all wide lawns with lush green grass. It has palm trees lined up along the curbs, swaying in salt-scented air, and homes decorated with Talavera-tiled arched entryways and thick wooden doors with hinges that groan when they open. I park a few feet away from his two-story house. Walking across the street, I try to act cool, like I belong. I'm in a pair of baggy basketball shorts, running shoes, and a black tank top. Shaved head. Tattooed. In broad daylight. Anyone can see me. Here, I'm a suspicious-looking character. I rehearse in my head what I'll say if a cop stops me:

I'm lost, Officer.

My car stalled, Officer.

No, I'm not carrying any weapons or drugs, Officer.

Yes, you can search my car, Officer.

I stroll up the driveway, all slow, natural. At the doorway I'm relieved to not have attracted any attention.

If you don't look anything like your picture, I bounce. No matter how horny I am, that shit better be recent. Luckily, this guy's legit. Older, a little rough around the edges, but sophisticated. A total zaddy.

He's in a dress shirt and tie when he answers, and he leads me down a long, dark hallway, its walls cool to the touch. Pictures crowd the top of a small side table: a boy holding a baseball bat; his wife with her arms around an old woman wearing a big sun hat and too much jewelry; Greg crouching next to a black Labrador. Walking past the bathroom, I hear a low, constant hiss coming from the toilet. A pair of linen curtains sway in the breeze. I smell the ocean, imagine boats bobbing along the water and try listening for the screech of seagulls drifting in the sky above.

I undress and lie down, the sheets soft against my back, the pillows perfumed by the scent of dryer sheets. He unzips his slacks and pulls them down. He keeps his dress shirt and tie on. The metal clasps of his garters scratch my thighs. Instantly, I'm hard. That's how mine works. It's automatic. Like turning the power switch on.

He straddles me, and we go at it.

Wrapping up's always the weird part, when you're wiping yourself down and reaching for your underwear, when you try making small talk with a dude whose face you'd just shoved into a pillow as you plowed him on the bed he shares with his wife. There's a pang of guilt mixed with the rush of excitement. Almost like you want to go at it again, but you're tapped out, spent, and you need a little bit of time to build up some more of the good stuff you're known for.

"Boy, I needed that," he says.

Who even says "boy" anymore? I follow him back down the hallway. "Glad to be of service."

He's leaving town for a few days. Sales convention in Houston. He's eager to fly again after working from home for so long. "A change of scenery. Yes, sir."

I'm relieved when we reach the foyer.

He slips a fifty-dollar bill in the pocket of my jeans. "I'll message you when I'm back."

"Yeah. Cool."

Outside, I pull away from the curb just as Greg's wife rolls up to their house and parks in the driveway. From the smudged rear-view mirror of my car I watch her unload some bags, then catch a glimpse of a little girl in crutches making her way to the front door I just passed through.

Fucking A, I think.

These straights. The secrets they keep.

ERNESTO VEGA

Time isn't a factor when one finds themselves in this state. I'm trying to speak, trying to say something to Alfredo and Grace, who I
make out across the haze growing more and more intense between
us. The last thing one experiences before they die is what mattered
most in life, that which one held closest, what one fought for and
sacrificed. It's present, all of it, every feeling and emotion, every
thought—both good and bad—every face, every single touch,
every conversation, every fight, every agony, every meal you ate,
every drink you took, every film you watched, every book you
read, every time you cried or laughed or raised your voice in anger
. . . it's all here. No angels or clouds or sky. No brimstone or fire or
sulfur. No God or Satan.

Please, my children.
Don't let me go.
Not yet. I have so much more to say.

* *

I didn't know how to feel about leaving Julián's. On the one hand,
it felt right. Elena was my wife, and I needed to focus on her,
on us. But it also felt like I was abandoning my friend. I made a
promise to myself to spend as much time as I could outside of the
construction job with him.

Less than half a mile from our new place, there was an empty lot where people dumped things. Julián and I started going there to exercise on the weekends. Someone left a couple of old mattresses, so I laid these flat on the ground and practiced doing tumbles and somersaults on my back. A group of children playing soccer stopped their game and walked over. I lied and said I was a luchador practicing for an upcoming match. Julián lowered his head and chuckled.

"Are you a rudo or a técnico?" a boy wearing a faded T-shirt and ripped bell-bottoms asked.

"Técnico. One of the good guys." I lifted my arms, and they cheered, then I let them take turns trying to tackle me. The following weekend more kids showed up. The weekend after that even more. It went like this for a few months. Then Julián suggested we find someone for me to fight.

"We could charge money. Something small," he said.

There was a guy from the construction site named Refugio who we talked into wrestling me. He agreed when we assured him that whatever we made we'd split evenly. Elena took two knit caps, one white, the other red, cut holes in the fabric for eyes, a mouth, and a nose. We pulled and stretched these over our faces to conceal our identities even though the children in the park already knew what I looked like.

"You be white," Refugio said. "Good guys always wear white."

It wasn't an impressive crowd, mostly children and a few of their parents grateful that we were providing a distraction for their kids. But it was a start. We made a few modest pesos. Not enough, but it convinced us that we were onto something. We held another match the following weekend. Then again and again. Word spread not just across our colonia but beyond. The people of Ajusco being who they were pitched in and helped in any way they could. Women made tortillas, aguas frescas, and toasted pumpkin seeds dusted with salt, which they sold to the spectators. Someone hung paper streamers in bright colors over the flat clearing we used as our main wrestling area.

"You need a real platform. A real mat," said a man named Gastón, who was known for being smart with tools. He and Julián and a few of the children went scavenging. Soon enough, they'd constructed a raised plank out of discarded bits of wood. Elena and some of the other women sewed strips of rags together and stuffed these with anything they could get their hands on—straw, newspaper, old fillings from abandoned couch cushions and mattresses. The mat became a patchwork of fabrics from old dresses, pants, shirts, blouses, quilts, and plastic tarps stitched and stuffed together by hand. It was by no means the most attractive.

But it worked.

Elena Vega

W hat I remember most about those days was how much time he and Julián spent with one another. Even though we were now in our own place, Ernesto saw him more than me. They were together at the construction site, then he'd come home, eat, rest, and bolt out the door again to see him.

"Julián says I have a real gift for lucha," he said one night.

"What makes him such an expert?"

"He just knows. I trust him."

I'll admit I enjoyed watching those early bouts. Ernesto was a real athlete, so charismatic and tough, all shirtless and muscled. It's difficult to put into words, but the moment he stepped out in front of the people, he was no longer the man I knew. It was something incredible to witness. And those crowds? They were small, yes, but they loved him so much. And I felt special when people found out I was his wife. The men congratulated me. The women smiled, but I could tell there was a hint of envy.

Back at home, though, it was a different matter.

When I tried being intimate with him, he made excuses. He was tired. We weren't teenagers anymore. Why was I acting this way? Couldn't I see that he had a lot on his mind? A friend of mine, a kind woman with sad, watery eyes, took me to the Botanica Tres

Caminos on Avenida Azteca. The curandero named Bembe López wore all white, and each of the fingers on both hands were adorned with thick gold rings that felt hot as iron filaments against my skin when he touched me.

"Dario," he shouted. "Venga, hijo."

A young man around our age appeared from behind a curtain. He was tall, with a waist so small it looked like a child's. His eyes squinted and he breathed in deep as Bembe whispered instructions in his ear. When Dario came around the counter separating us, I saw that his left leg was shorter than the right. As he gathered small bundles of herbs and roots, his footfalls made a rhythmic *tap, tap, tap* across the wooden floorboards.

"Give him a few minutes," Bembe said. "He'll mix up a remedio." He slid a red candle inside a cylinder with the drawing of a hummingbird etched in the glass. I was to crush the herbs inside Ernesto's food and scratch my initial across the crimson wax and keep it lit for several nights.

No matter what I did, he never touched me, never kissed me on the mouth. Only slight pecks on the cheek or forehead. As if I were a sister, a close friend he thought about now and again.

"Paciencia," Bembe said whenever I went to see him. "These things always resolve themselves in surprising ways. Las energías . . . they are very powerful. We must be patient."

I listened to him, but none of it was enough to keep them separated. Every evening. Every weekend. Any free moment he had was spent with Julián. Deep down inside I knew why. I was just afraid to admit it.

My mother raised me to have faith in those that carry us along, in those that provide for us. It made me resent men because they could make reckless decisions without suffering the consequences. We had to stay quiet and tolerate it. Men could make choices on a moment's notice without any kind of justification.

But I still held on to my opinions, my concerns, my autonomy. I wore pants and smoked cigarettes and would never be afraid to enter the world of men.

FREDDY VEGA

Around East LA in 1988, a lot of us Mexican American teenagers pretended that we weren't. We teased our hair and wore eye makeup like Robert Smith from the Cure. We listened to the Smiths and experimented with vegetarianism. Ian Curtis from Joy Division was our prophet.

We wanted to be English.

Our own culture was the static in the background. It was something to rebel against, to exorcise from the body. Who could blame us? Back then—shit, even now—everywhere we looked, everything we read, everything we heard was telling us that anything Mexican or Mexican American was bad. It meant you were a criminal, a gang member, a wetback leeching off the system.

And what about lucha libre? Forget it. Lucha wasn't anything back then. The films. The reality TV shows. The masks on craft beer labels, greeting cards, T-shirts, socks, fucking boxer briefs on sale at Target. Shit was nowhere. If you were lucky, maybe on a Saturday afternoon you could catch an old black-and-white Santo movie playing on Channel 34, our only Spanish-language television station. If you *really* wanted to have a true lucha libre experience, you hopped in the car, drove a couple hours south, and crossed the border into Tijuana. That's where it was really happening. But no one I knew ever went there for a lucha libre event. Everyone around here only visited TJ for one thing: to get drunk.

My father started taking us to Taco Macho every Saturday morning for breakfast burritos. They only had the one location, on Brooklyn between Mott and Saratoga. Sometimes Hugo would join us, pulling into the parking lot in his primered El Camino, the engine sputtering and backfiring when he turned the ignition off.

The owner of Taco Macho was Edgar Solis, and he knew Hugo from church. Edgar always had a toothpick in his mouth. Sometimes he removed it when he spoke, other times he just let it hang there. He took a liking to our family almost immediately. If it wasn't too busy, he'd sit with Hugo and my father for hours. The three would start off drinking coffee, then switch to horchata at around noon if the conversation went on past the breakfast rush. Mercy brought books to read. I got lost in the arcade games the place had set up in the restaurant's entryway near the front door. There were the classics like *Pac-Man* and *Space Invaders*, of course, but they'd also brought in some newer games with better graphics like *Hole in One* and *Mega Fighter*, where a martial artist ran around back alleys and warehouses fighting criminals and gangsters.

Edgar was a smart businessman, and when he found out my father had been a luchador, he hired him to come in on the weekends dressed in his tights, cape, and mask. As El Rey Coyote, my dad paraded around the main dining area, greeting customers, signing autographs, and showing off his moves. It brought in some foot traffic. Kids liked it, and their parents reminisced about the old lucha movies and fighters they'd remembered back in Mexico. Sometimes Mercy and I stayed behind and watched, laughing at times, annoyed at others. More often, though, Hugo drove us home and we waited for our dad there. At around five, he'd walk in, cape draped over his left arm, his right cradling bags full of food from the restaurant—asada tacos, rice, beans, fried taquitos, and something called a chimichanga.

That was dinner. And the food was delicious.

But it wasn't our mother's.

* *

Shortly after, Taco Macho opened two more locations—one in Montebello and another in Pico Rivera. Edgar decided to invest some money in advertising, but he didn't want to spend a crazy amount of cash. His son, Memo, was taking classes in film editing at the community college. Local business commercials featuring quirky and off-beat personalities were all over TV around this time. Miller's Outpost sold Levi's and sweaters with the help of two bumbling cowboys named Homer and JR. Cal Worthington and his dog, Spot, advertised used vans, boats, and trucks. Spot was never a dog but a tiger, a lion, a brown bear, a turtle, and even a whale in one commercial. Edgar told my father and Hugo one Saturday morning that he and Memo had an idea after seeing a Federated commercial.

"That insane white guy with the feathered hair?" my father asked.

"Yeah," Edgar went on, "hear me out."

Fred Rated, the spokesperson for the electronics chain, was really Shadoe Stevens. He advertised radio receivers, VCRs, cassette tapes, and boom boxes. The commercials were crazy and featured Fred Rated sporting wild costumes and hats while running around blowing shit up and screaming off the top of his head. They worked because everyone around us *knew* Fred Rated.

"We need a gimmick, a hook, something unique," Edgar continued.

Hugo took a deep breath in then out, his fleshy cheeks billowing like a blowfish. "So, you want Ernesto to light some tacos on fire?"

"No, tarudo." Edgar took his toothpick out and held it between his fingers. "We'll have El Rey Coyote in the commercials. Shoot them here with Memo's camera."

"What would I do?" my father asked.

Edgar shrugged his shoulders. "What you're already doing around here. Pose. Flex. Sell the food. We'll make it up as we go, hombre."

That's how it started.

I can't find them on the internet. We didn't record any, either. I only have my memories.

In one my father runs around the parking lot being chased by a couple of minis from Tijuana Edgar brought over and paid for one day of work. My father points at posters advertising two-for-one tacos or a free drink with the purchase of a seafood burrito. Then the luchadores tackle him to the ground, grab the bag of food he's holding, and take off running down an alley.

In another, Hugo—sporting a blue mechanics jumpsuit and a hockey mask over his face—revs a chain saw and barges into the restaurant's main dining area. A woman screams as another sitting at a nearby table clutches a boy next to her and shouts, *Dios santo. Nos va matar. ¡Soccoro! ¡Soccoro!* Hugo (as the murderous killer) places the chain saw down when El Rey Coyote appears before him, holding out a plate of tacos. *Try our new Taco Psicótico*, the voice-over says. *Three of our signature salsa bravas blended together with jalapeños and spicy shredded beef. So hot it'll drive you mad!*

In yet another, El Rey Coyote crouches down next to a table and whispers, *Al pastor. Asada. Lengua. Sabroso* as close-up images of steaming platters of tacos fade in and out of view. Then there's the voice-over: *How far would you go for a plate of our delicious Taco Macho tacos?* The camera then cuts to a little girl in pigtails and a pink dress standing across from El Rey Coyote. *Far*, she says, folding her arms and widening her stance. *¡Andale!* Rey shouts, extending both arms, hands open, waiting for her to attack. The little girl leaps forward and stomps on his foot. El Rey tumbles to the floor, moaning in pain as she steps over him to the table and grabs a taco from the platter. The close-up shows her taking a bite and smiling. *The authentic taste of Mexico*, the announcer whispers. *Taco Macho.*

Memo sketched up a logo with El Rey Coyote's face that they put on their bags and food wrappers and signs. Along with it they came up with the slogan *Challenge your appetite.* Taco Macho advertisements with his image appeared on the backs of bus benches and on billboards along Whittier Boulevard and Brooklyn Avenue.

He became a local celebrity. Something in him changed.

And something in me was ignited.

* *

My father never liked the choices he was given: work at this dead-end factory job or that dead-end factory job? You carry your home wherever you go, he said to Mercy and me one day. On this side of the border or on that side. Lucha libre was his home, his religion, the thing that gave him control. It made him happy to see his likeness plastered all over East Los Angeles, to see people starting to become interested in the sport.

One day, Hugo came over and told him about the building off Mission in Boyle Heights that was up for lease. It wasn't much. Run-down. Brick façade. A few busted windows. Inside, there was a main open area where the ring could easily fit. There was a set of those metal industrial doors, and on the weekends, they could roll it out into the parking lot, host outdoor lucha events.

Edgar invested in the operation, and my father combined that with whatever he had, but it still wasn't enough to secure the lease, so he pounded on the doors of neighbors and people we knew. He was a smooth talker. Trustworthy. Could get you to sign over your car. Five bucks here, fifty there. He kept track of every single person who loaned him money in a spiral-bound notebook Mercy bought with the cash she'd saved babysitting. The notebook had a picture of Prince on the cover. Inside, the pages were full of rows and rows of names and dollar amounts, each one carefully recorded in his crooked handwriting.

The following year, Gimnasio Eastside opened its doors, and people came by to catch a glimpse of the luchador/TV personality working out and performing moves at the weekend lucha libre matches Hugo and Edgar helped him organize and advertise. Then people bought memberships. Spread the word about the place, encouraged everyone they knew to join. It was a sight. An entire community moved like that.

Twenty years later, in 2009, Edgar Solis retired to Acapulco with his wife to spend the rest of his days combing the beach and golfing. He was almost seventy and couldn't keep up with the new food scene popping up around Los Angeles, so he handed the business over to Memo, who knew even less about the growing taste for Korean tacos, vegan tortas, and horchata lattes. Memo sold the company, took the money, and set up a production company that finances experimental short films and documentaries that are screened at international festivals.

* *

The only Taco Macho left now is the Pico Rivera location. The new owners are still at it, but they no longer use El Rey Coyote's face to sell their food. They've swapped it for the image of a man in a wide-brimmed cowboy hat and pointy mustache. His facial features are two black pricks for eyes and a narrow slit for a mouth. A bandido. It's basic. Crude. Cheap-looking.

El Rey Coyote

That was when I was born, Ernesto. Little did you know what I would become. The things we made one another do. The spirit of restlessness I'd plant inside your son and his son, how I'd change them forever and ever. Amen.

Like ripples in water fanning out.

Generation after generation. We are born, die, and are reborn anew. The story might be altered a little, but it usually stays the same.

JULIAN VEGA

If there's one thing the pandemic taught me it's this: everything's a
hustle to survive, to make it, because there's an endless barrage of
shit out there trying to lay waste to a life like mine, a queer Chicano
with a mediocre high school education who was somehow lucky
enough to end up in college and not slaving away in a factory or
strung-out on drugs or in prison. If guys like me—brown-skinned,
working-class, Mexican—get distracted, if we stop long enough
and forget, let our guard down, it's the end of us. We must work
harder, move faster, stay sharper, be smarter. When we all emerged
back out into this mess of a world, I told myself nothing was going
to consume me or kill me. I'd use whatever it took—my brains, my
determination, my personality, even my fucking body—to survive
the next disaster.

Because there'll be another one.

There's always something else looking to ruin people like us.

* *

A few hours into my grading, right about the time my eyes begin
to gloss over the pages, and I realize I haven't eaten anything, only
guzzled coffee, my stomach burning from the acid, there's a text
message from Tim.

Hola, he writes. *How are u?*

Fine, I reply. *Just getting some work done. You?*
Hang out tonight? A friend's throwing a bbq.
Can't. Too much that needs catching up.
But it's the Fourth of July.
I should really get these essays graded. Talk later.

That night, the air explodes. Multicolored specks of light rain down from above, vanishing just before they hit the ground.

* *

I've been corresponding with a slim white dude with pale skin and stringy, weaselly brown hair named Beckett who responded to my Papi profile. We agree to meet up at a wine bar near his place. *My treat*, he writes. And because I'm hungry and have nothing to eat, I say yes.

There's something about dominating a white guy that gets me going, something about the power I can exert over them, when I make them kneel before me, submit to me. The majority of the gabachos I hook up with get off on the idea of someone like me, all thuggish and badass, coming in and bossing them around. It's a specific type of guy. He's usually married or divorced and has kids. He's usually a businessman or holds a job down where he's in a position of power. Like Greg, who never got back to me after he said he would.

Beckett's a little too manicured, but he has a nice body and handsome features. He wears a striped tank top and skinny shorts and a silly-looking knit cap that reminds me of a tea cozy. We're sipping glasses of chilled chardonnay and munching on olive tapenade spread over chunks of soft bread. A guy at a piano is playing music, tunes I recognize but can't place, and Beckett's going on about how and why he became a nurse.

"It's a calling," he says. "And during the whole pandemic, that felt especially true. You would not believe the things I had to deal with."

"My mom wanted to be a nurse. But then she had me."

"Do you come from one of those big Mexican families?"

"No," I say. "It's just me."

He looks disappointed by my answer. "Anyway, let's tell stories."

"Okay," I say, not liking at all where this is going. "What do you want to hear?"

"The first time you had sex with a guy," Beckett says, chuckling.

"Huh. Okay. Well—" I begin before he cuts me off.

"For me it was summer camp."

The guy was one of those high school kids hired to supervise them, he continues. His name was Drew. Beckett caught him jerking off in the woods behind their cabin. It was a secluded spot. His shorts were pulled down around his ankles. He called Beckett over, and he went to town on him.

"I'm such a slut, I know. And you?"

I make up some bullshit story about being in high school and getting cruised while waiting for the bus to the mall. I was bored, I say. There I was, I say. Waiting at the stop when I noticed this dude circling the street. He drove a white hatchback. A rosary hung from the rearview mirror.

Beckett gasps. "Sex and Catholic imagery? Madonna would be *so* proud."

"I hate Madonna."

"What kind of a gay are you?"

"A bad one?"

We're both a little buzzed, so we leave the bar and decide to walk around the neighborhood. We window-shop and step inside a clothing store to try on stuff. Everything Beckett pulls off the rack is small and tight. Jeans so slim I wonder how guys fit into them.

When he tries on a pair and steps out of the dressing room, I tell him they might tear if he bends down.

"What's your point?" he asks, standing in front of the four-way mirror.

"They're tight. Incredibly tight. I can see your junk."

"You're supposed to be able to!"

He shrugs.

Beckett spends seventy-five dollars on the jeans. What I would do for seventy-five dollars right now. We leave the store, then head over to his place.

* *

His is a Spanish-style building with arched entryways and wrought-iron sconces emitting a dim, hypnotic glow. It's the kind of place location scouts love to use in exterior shots for movies or television shows. There's a courtyard with a gurgling fountain in the center and fragrant potted plants and a hummingbird feeder. I think about my apartment complex, the peeling stucco exterior, the rusted wrought-iron security doors, the cement courtyard with toys and bikes belonging to the children who live there but I never see.

His place is spacious. There's a leather sofa strewn with decorative throw pillows in mismatched patterns, a flat-screen television, a wood coffee table with fat, squat legs, and a round dining table next to the kitchen with stainless steel appliances. He lights scented candles.

"Take a load off," he says, directing me to the couch as he heads down the hall.

There's an alert on my phone. An email from the chair of the English Department of one of the colleges where I lecture details a litany of excuses regarding why they won't be offering me a contract to teach the two classes I normally do this coming fall. Down two means I'll be out a hefty amount each month. This late in the game also means that any available sections at the dozens of community colleges in Southern California will be taken already.

Fuck driving 120 miles south to San Diego.

Fuck driving 115 miles north to Santa Barbara.

Pick up an extra job waiting tables or bartending or standing around in a polyester vest greeting customers or flipping burgers? That's not what I went to school for. That's not why I spent hours studying Freire or Kant or Derrida.

Beckett returns, sits close to me on the couch. He pushes my pant leg up, pulls my socks down; his fingers stroke the muscles on my calves. I stand and unzip my jeans and they tumble to the ground. He removes his striped tank top, and his chest is flecked with moles, his stomach flat. He's on his knees in front of me, stroking my legs. We sip more wine. Soon our clothes are off, and then I'm easing my way inside of him.

Only temporary, I think, reaching for my phone once I leave his place.

Just until I can figure this out. Get a handle on things. I scroll through my contacts.

You can do this.

I type it without thinking: *Hi.*

Tim replies almost immediately: *Hey!!!!! Thought u ghosted me for good. LOL. S'up?*

Does that offer for work still stand?

Of course. My place. This Saturday. 7 pm. I'll get you oriented.

ERNESTO VEGA

Julián started working as my assistant. Because he was so loyal, he became more and more important to me as word about my reputation grew. Advertisements announcing upcoming fights started to spread well beyond our side of the city. Julián saw to it. Pretty soon we were pulling in spectators from all over. The extra money allowed me to buy training equipment like weights, sneakers, running suits, and headbands. Julián kept me honest, on track, by making sure I exercised in between breaks at work, when I came home, and on the weekends.

Elena tolerated it. She spent her days keeping our new place neat and clean. She was happy to be away from Julián, happy to have a new set of friends. They shopped at the Mercado La Bola together or visited the other tianguises around nearby Coyoacán. I was glad when she was distracted, when she wasn't watching my every move, when she wasn't worrying about all the time I was spending with Julián.

"People will start talking about the two of you," she said one Saturday morning when I told her I'd be meeting him at Parque Santa Ana.

"What do you mean?"

She bit the corner of her lip. "Always together. Like a pair of maricónes."

I grabbed my sweater as I headed for the door. "You and everyone else around this pinche vecindad need to stop being such metiches."

What I did with Julián was my business.

* *

One day, a man in a plaid jacket, bell-bottom jeans, and thick sideburns running down the sides of his jaw showed up to one of my matches. The soil around the dirt lot was still dimpled from the fat raindrops that had pummeled the city during a recent thunderstorm. Everything washed clean and the sun was out, turning the air muggy and thick with moisture. The man sweated through the green turtleneck he wore under his jacket. His name was Ramon Avila and he worked as a talent scout for one of the many lucha libre syndicates popping up all around, flooding the sport. New ones sprang up faster than weeds in the vacant lot where I trained, others simply vanished, and smaller collectives would join forces to compete for supremacy against the largest of them all—the Empresa Mexicana de Lucha Libre.

"Which one do you represent?" Julián asked Avila.

"The Sindicato Nacional de Mexico." He handed over a card.

Julián smirked, then glanced over at me. "The SNM is good. Kara. Nuklear. Cenisa. You've represented some good fighters."

"We made them famous." He pointed to me. "You got nice moves, Vega. You need some flash, though."

"Like a costume. A real mask," Julián replied. He smacked my arm. "What have I been saying?"

I needed something with style, Avila went on, something dramatic, not the silly-looking cap pulled over my face I still used.

Julián crossed his arms. "What's your professional opinion, then? How do we take him to the next level?"

The man glanced at me, a slight, knowing smile on his face. "Is this your—"

"Manager and business partner," Julián interjected. "That's me. Julián Tamez."

Avila told us the SNM would be holding tryouts the following week and that we should go down to let their trainers and managers look at me. We could be making a lot more money.

"Unless you and your partner here are content busting your asses for a few pesos." He looked around the lot, took in the makeshift wooden stage, the padded platform, swollen in some sections, flat and deflated in others. I'd landed hard in one of those areas, my shoulder slamming with force against the wood. Now it was sore, and I was trying hard not to wince from the pain as I stood before him.

"Well—" Julián started to say before Avila interrupted.

"If you want to stay doing this amateur shit go ahead. But I'm here to tell you that I like what I see." He jabbed his thumb into my aching shoulder. "You got star power. You're good with the audience. But you need work, need a good costume and mask and a name. If you stay here and keep wrestling like this, on that worn mat, you'll likely get injured and never recover. Then what? The SNM can help you really take off."

Without saying anything else, Avila turned to leave. We finished packing up our gear just as a handful of kids on the far side of the lot began kicking a soccer ball around.

* *

The following weekend, we went to this gym in a building situated at the very end of a wide alleyway. I was holding Avila's card, but he was nowhere to be seen when we stepped inside. The room was vast, with a high ceiling and large windows with rusty hinges.

Towards the back of the auditorium stood a wrestling ring, the padded mat covered in a bright pink tarp with a large image of the syndicate's logo—the initials *SNM* in white blocky letters resting inside an orange oval outlined in a gold border—emblazoned in the middle. A young boy stood on a rickety wooden ladder high above the ring and adjusted a pair of floodlights. He was using a rag to move the bulbs while another boy shouted at him from below.

"Eso, eso," he said to his friend above.

"Esta pinche caliente," the one on the ladder yelled back. "Necessito un guante." He pulled his hand back, took the rag and wrapped it over his palm. "Me quemé."

An older man with a purple scar running down the length of his right cheek yelled something at the boys as he approached us. "Francisco," he said. "I'm Francisco. Everyone calls me Franco. Are you both here for the tryouts?"

"Only him." Julián rubbed my shoulders. "I'm his partner and business manager."

He asked who sent us and I handed over Avila's card.

"Ah." Franco nodded. "Ramon. Very good, very good." He licked his lips and looked about. The man was squat with a wide midsection held up by a pair of legs that bowed out slightly. He wore denim overalls and repeatedly raked his fingers through the thin strands of hair clinging to his head. "This way."

We followed, our noses led by the scent of cigarette smoke and aftershave that lingered in his wake, his bowed legs chopping the perfumed air in quick, rapid movements. Through a set of doors, we found ourselves inside a smaller room with weights, a punching bag suspended from the ceiling by a thick chain, and large, flesh-colored medicine balls, their surfaces freckled with dark blotches. I removed my jacket and slipped my shoes off as several other men, all of them in sneakers and sweatpants, arrived and began stretching on the floor or against a few of the chairs grouped together around the room. The boy who'd been on the ladder rushed in, panting, his T-shirt damp with sweat. He held a clipboard and a silver pen in the same hand he'd burned, a clear ointment leaking like tree sap along the edges of a bandage. He wiped the excess on his denim pants as Franco ordered him to take down our personal information. We lined up along a mirrored wall, and the boy approached each of us asking for names, address, age, weight, height, and who to contact in case of an emergency. One man gave his abuela's name. Another simply replied *nadie* in a tone tinged with shame. I pointed, and the young boy walked over to Julián, jotting down everything he repeated.

Franco ordered us to stretch. Most injuries, he explained, happen because men don't properly warm up. After about ten minutes, he whistled then counted out as we did crunches and jumping jacks in unison. On the nearby rubber mat, we took turns, one after the other, displaying our moves—tumbles, rolls, flips, leaps from a chair. When we finished, Franco moved to a corner of the room where he paced around. The boy walked alongside him, holding the clipboard, scribbling as Franco mumbled to him. In the end, after staring at what was written for a long while, pacing back and forth, the buckles of his overalls clinking like little bells, Franco took a deep breath, turned, and walked back to where we stood waiting. Three of the six of us, including me, were invited to join the sindicato. Those who had been rejected gathered their things, thanked Franco, congratulated the rest of us, and left.

Once we were alone, the boy spoke up: "Señores, on behalf of El Sindicato Nacional de Mexico, we welcome you to our prestigious confederation. This is voluntary. As in life, there is no guarantee of success." His words rang like a chant or a prayer; I could tell he'd recited this many times before. "If you work hard, train, focus, and listen to us, you stand a good chance of making a name for yourself in this sport."

Of the three of us left, I was the only one who decided to remain. The other two shook their heads, patted me on the back, and said good luck and goodbye.

"Your training begins tomorrow," Franco explained. "Promptly at six in the evening. Bring with you a pair of gym shoes and shorts or sweatpants and a towel. You are going to be doing a lot of physical activity, so don't eat a heavy meal beforehand."

Back out on the street, I asked Julián, "Do you think I should have asked Elena?"

He lit a cigarette. "No." He flicked the match across the sidewalk. "You don't need her permission all the fucking time, do you? Besides, it's not like you quit your job. You'll still be working."

I bought a cheap pair of white gym shoes, exercise pants made from fabric that stretched when I tugged at it, and a tank top. At our kitchen table that evening, Julián told Elena all about my audition.

"He leapt from that chair and did all these wild moves. It was incredible."

Elena shrugged. "You're exaggerating."

"I'm not," he insisted. "You should have been there to see it with your own eyes. Ernesto's going to be a great luchador."

She flicked her cigarette in the ashtray, stood, and walked into the courtyard to water her plants.

Elena Vega

I can't see him, but I know that this other you is here as well, hovering around in the darkness tightening around your hospital bed. The beeping of the machine is faint, small blips punctuating your ragged breathing. You try moving your fingers. It's too hard. Your mind is slipping, isn't it? That's what makes everything difficult to recall.

—He was my hermano, you say. Julián.

—He was more than that to you. I always felt it.

—Stop, Elena. I loved you.

—I know. I nod. But there's love and then there's that.

—Then Alfredo. Our boy. Did we do the right thing?

—Solo dios sabe.

FREDDY VEGA

It was around this time, I think, late July or early August, my first summer out of high school, when I started following my father to the gym on weekends. I liked hanging out there, watching guys practice wrestling moves in the ring, checking out some of the girls who started coming in, mainly on the weekends. I'd spot for random dudes as they bench-pressed, helping them keep track of reps, sparring with them, jogging around the parking lot with them. I lost all my baby fat, the flab that had been accumulating around my midsection from eating greasy burgers and burritos when I'd get stoned with Mike.

Hugo first said it, not my father. He was holding a bunch of fliers announcing lucha libre matches between two técnicos named Cyclone and Maravilla and two rudos called Tarantula and Shockwave. He handed the stack to me to post around the neighborhood.

"You been working out?" Hugo asked as I reached for them.

"A little, I guess. Why?"

A few days later, they asked to talk with me. One of the things they told me about lucha libre was the importance of tradition, of legacy, of passing on the names and histories of former fighters.

"We want to train you," my father said. "Me and Hugo."

"Train me for what?"

"Lucha libre, dummy. You'll usher in the next generation."

"We'll design an outfit, a mask," my father said. "You'll take my name. El Rey Coyote Jr."

This wasn't presented as a choice. It wasn't up for debate.

I replied, "Yeah. Hell yeah."

Training began that fall. Basic calisthenics like sit-ups, squats, and running in place were the standard. These were done to not only help me get in shape, but they were also meant to get my body used to the constant movements typical of any athlete. There were leapfrogs, drills where I'd roll over their backs. There were laps, endless long laps where we ran around and around the perimeter of the gym. It was tiring, and I was sore most of the time those first few months. I had to watch what I ate, too. There were protein shakes, vitamin supplements, fresh fruits and vegetables, plenty of water, rest, and raw eggs, which I hated.

The main thing to remember about fighting as a luchador is this: everything is about timing. Timing is key. You must know when and how to land a punch or deliver a knee to the gut with precision so that it looks real enough to the audience, yet doesn't hurt your partner. If you're performing a fly kick from the top cord, you need to land on your side or your back in such a way to minimize injury. That takes accuracy. And there were moments during my training that I hurt myself enough to question what I was doing and whether I was committed or not. Yet, whenever I pulled a muscle or sprained my wrist or was accidentally punched by one of the other guys, my father was always there to remind me that I would be fine. The hurt is what shapes us, but we need to move past it.

* *

Back then there were three other guys who started their training the same time I did. Along with me, Gabriel Montes would be a técnico. Gabriel was a bouncer at a nightclub in Pico Rivera, one of those places where girls in miniskirts and teased-out hair would go to drink cheap, watered-down cocktails and dance around in a circle while guys in tight shirts and too much cologne watched them from the bar. Gabriel had a wife and a new baby girl, Marina. The extra cash as a luchador on the weekends would help pay for diapers and baby formula. Gabriel would be fighting under the name Dragon Steel. He was twenty-five, five foot eight, and came in weighing around two hundred pounds. He had thick thighs, fleshy arms, and a full midsection. He was a mass of meat, solidly built, with a wide back. With my thin, muscled frame and lankier body type, we were the opposite of one another. Gabriel and I had developed a couple of signature moves, including one we called "tijeras," which had him bend forward, cupping his hands on his knees, then I'd come in, roll over his back, my legs extending up and out like scissors, just before landing on the mat to deliver a kick to our opponent.

His costume consisted of a pair of neon-green leggings, silver boots with laces that matched his leggings, and a floor-length silver cape that he said was pure silk. His mask was also neon green, and the piping around the eyes, nose, and mouth was silver. The alternating colors and carefully matched accessories made Gabriel look every part the hero. It gave me comfort, even a little bit of pride, knowing he was on my side.

Then there was Esteban Cardenas and Charly Garcia, our two rudos. Esteban was a big man—weighing at least two hundred and fifty pounds. He had a prison record none of us ever asked him about. Esteban was quiet, serious, and hardly spoke, his luchador name was Sombra Negra. "La Sombra," as we referred to him among ourselves, sported a black mask with a white spiderweb design that covered the top of the forehead and extended down, outlining the eyes, mouth, and nose. The back of his cape featured an airbrushed image of a red spider with black eyes and giant fangs protruding from an open mouth.

Charly Garcia was a talkative twenty-year-old vocational student. He was originally from Arizona and had moved out to LA with his sister. He listened to David Bowie, Iggy Pop, and Adam Ant. He cursed a lot and sported a short mohawk, which he often dyed purple, green, or blue. He wore eyeliner and black lipstick and painted his nails black. He was the thinnest of our group. His wiry frame meant he was fast on his feet, though. He could springboard off the highest of the three cords around the ring with ease, then deliver fly kicks and somersaults before landing on the mat with a loud *slap*. Charly didn't wear a mask. He painted the area around his eyes and his lids a dark ash gray and streaked his cheeks with purple grease paint. He had an assortment of feathered boas, spiked vinyl chokers dotted with safety pins and buttons from some of his favorite punk rock bands—Sex Pistols, the Misfits, the Ramones, and, of course, Iggy Pop and Bowie, who had influenced him so much his lucha name was Ziggy.

* *

Hugo reached out to a woman he knew named Angelica who lived in Tijuana. She was someone he'd met during trips down there with my father to check out the lucha libre events and scout for talent. Angelica worked with a local lucha syndicate. She was their costurera, designing and putting together some of the best masks and outfits in the business.

She crossed the border and came to the gym one afternoon carrying a wicker basket with random spools of thread and a tackle box full of pins and needles and fabric swatches. She wore a lime-green turtleneck underneath an oversized brown knit sweater. She'd inappropriately paired her gray sweatpants with black high heels. Her hair was a frizzy mess, and she sported thick-framed glasses that she assured me were just for reading because her eyes were fine, and she would not be jabbing me with needles. She took a seat in the office chair, rolling back and forth, its metal wheels squeaking. Hugo leaned up against the filing cabinet, holding a slip of paper with a sketch he and my father had come up with for my outfit.

She had me stretch my arms out. She used a cloth tape measure and shouted out numbers to Hugo, who jotted them down on the scratch pad with the sketch. He held up the pencil drawing containing a mask that looked like my father's, a cape adorned with white beads along the edges, and a pair of leggings that would have white sequins running down each leg.

"Not exactly like your father's," he said as Angelica finished up and gathered her things, "but close enough."

"Yes," Angelica replied. "His outfit was made by a famous costurero in Mexico City. I can come close to matching the designs, though. It's not that hard. A wedding dress? Now, that's hard. This is easy."

"Good," Hugo continued, "because we need it fast."

Angelica shook her head and placed her hands on her hips. "No, sir. I must take my time."

"Vieja," Hugo pleaded. "Come on."

"I'll have to go back to Tijuana to do it. I have none of my tools here!" she protested. "Plus, I still need to finish up Claudia Ochoa's quinceañera dress."

"Can I go now?" I asked.

They ignored me and kept arguing.

"Just do it quick," Hugo was saying.

I stepped away from them slowly, turned, and went to the bathroom. When I came out, they were still fighting.

* *

I don't know how, but there it was one afternoon. Dangling on a wire hanger in the gym's office. The gold fabric slick and shimmering, the cape decked out with studs that gleamed in the slight breeze from the desk fan whirring in the corner. My father ran his fingers along the edges of the cape and pointed to the glass beads that had been fastened onto the stitching.

"She glued each and every one of these by hand," Hugo said.

My father shook his head and whistled.

My boots were white with thick, padded soles. They fit perfectly when I slipped them on over my tights. Hugo and my father placed the cape on my shoulders, snapped it closed with a small silver buckle.

"And here's your mask." My father pulled it out of a paper bag. "This, Alfredo, is what makes a luchador. Take a good look at it."

It was white, matching my tights and cape. Like my father's, gold vinyl outlined the mouth and the eyes, but the borders defining my features were thinner, smaller. I would breathe through a triangular cutout just above my mouth. They instructed me to sit. I leaned forward and felt my father's hands pull the mask over my face then continuing to tug the fabric towards the back of my head. He tied the laces, and Hugo stood in front of me, adjusting it so that both my eyeholes were in the center, so that my mouth and nose were free and clear of any obstructions. Stand now, they told me, leading me towards a full-length mirror nailed to the back of the office door. The person staring at me was a luchador, he was menacing. It was like I'd stepped out of my own body, and I was hovering high above, watching myself from a distance.

* *

It was a slow Saturday afternoon in early April, the weather too warm. The air inside the gym was hot and very still, and my father had asked two of the men he'd hired to help on weekends—ushering people in, selling sodas and bags of chips at the concession stand—to set up a couple of box fans around the ring to keep things circulating. I poked my head inside the auditorium to see just how big the crowd was getting as I changed that day in the office. A handful of spectators filled the room, but the place remained empty.

The first match would have Dragon Steel going up against Sombra Negra. Charly and I would follow as Ziggy battled it out with El Rey Coyote Jr. The two rudos would then challenge, in a special appearance, El Rey Coyote Sr. for the final showdown. We went over our routines. Fly kicks, choke holds, more kicks and suplexes and suicide bombs. For my bout with Ziggy, I was to swoop in from the top cord, land a solid pile drive on his chest to knock him down. He'd regain his composure, grow furious, throw glitter in my face, momentarily distracting me, tackle me down on the mat where I'd be pinned until the referee counted to three, and I'd lose the fight. El Rey Coyote Sr., watching from the sidelines, would get angry at this, accusing Ziggy of cheating, before he and Sombra would challenge my father in the final fight of the day. Ten minutes before the start, I looked out again. The auditorium was still empty. Hugo was working the room, trying to get the few people who were present all riled up.

"There's nobody out there," I announced as I returned to the office to finish dressing.

Gabriel responded, "It's this weather. They're probably all at the beach."

"Yeah," my father replied. "Don't worry, Alfredo. We'll put on a good show."

As I helped Esteban tape up his knuckles, he said, "The first time I jumped inside the ring was at an arena in Tijuana. The place was packed. The crowd was rowdy as hell. They threw bottles at me, called me all sorts of names. It was crazy."

Ziggy and I went over a couple more maneuvers while my father and the others finished getting ready. The key was to keep moving, I knew. Keep moving. Fast and quick.

Ziggy had drawn a red lightning bolt over his right cheek, and his face was powdered white. His blue eyeshadow made him appear icy, cold.

"Careful of these." He pointed to the spikes of his mohawk. "If my hair blocks you, just move out of the way like we practiced. If we stick with the script, it'll be fine."

The first bout between Dragon Steel and Sombra Negra felt as though it lasted an eternity. They put on a good show and the small crowd, especially the few kids, loved the acrobatics and the tumbles. The fight ended in a tie. Just as we had planned, Sombra Negra stomped on the ground, threatened the referee, and shouted slurs at Dragon as the crowd hissed at him. A few audience members cheered the bad guy on, pumping their fists in the air, hooting and laughing.

Hugo did the announcing of the luchadores. He tried imitating the sound and style of those I'd heard on television, which was a little funny. He stretched out his vowels, especially the Os and As, and his pitch was high, his tone rhythmic.

"Hailing from a rich and proud legacy of noble fighters," he continued. "A true son of the city of Los Angeles, a luchador with heart and valor, please welcome, making his debut here at Gimnasio Eastside, El Rey Coyote Jr."

My father stood behind me, massaging my shoulders as he followed me out, past the equipment and weight racks, stopping right at the entrance to the main room. I could hear the crowd murmuring, felt their restless feet shuffling back and forth across the faded wooden floors.

"Go," my father instructed me. "This is the real deal, Alfredo. What you've trained for all this time."

Then I stepped into the room, and the whole place ignited in cheers and applause. A handful of kids screamed and ran back and forth, their faces sticky with cotton candy and soda. There were a few hisses as Hugo introduced Ziggy and he made his way into the room and into the ring. He laughed at a guy shouting insults at him, calling him a sissy and a maricón.

"Kiss my ass, honey," Ziggy shouted across the room, turning around and smacking his thigh. "Of course, you'd probably like that."

My leggings suddenly felt too tight, my boots bulky and awkward. I was uncoordinated and grateful when the bell signaling the end of the first round rang. Hugo, now acting as my coach, beckoned me to my corner.

"This is a lot harder than I thought," I admitted.

"You're doing fine," he assured me.

In the second round, I mistimed a fly kick to Ziggy's midsection and ended up falling flat on my back, my head hitting the mat with such force that I saw spots and thought I might pass out. And, in the third round, when he lifted me up and flung me across the ring, I waited too long to rush him because I couldn't get up; my side throbbed, my legs were weak and shaky, and there was a low hum in my ears. I was disoriented, but then I looked around and saw the small crowd. They were all shouting at me to get up, get up, and fight back.

"Get him, Rey Jr.," a man in a corduroy jacket yelled at me.

"Hurry," said a short lady with pink barrettes in her hair. "Fight."

I stumbled to my feet, limbs flailing about, vision blurred by the lights and the heat and the muffled sounds. I felt nauseated, but I ignored it. I flung myself towards Ziggy, punching him over and over in the gut like we'd practiced. I pinned him down on the mat and held him there as the referee counted. Just before he shouted "three," though, Ziggy broke free, rose, and delivered a kick to my gut below the waist, pinning me down. And that was it.

The referee called the fight, and again the crowd roared and booed. Ziggy grabbed the microphone from him and began shouting to the audience, taunting them. He was all attitude, rude and arrogant. This part wasn't rehearsed: I grabbed the mic from him and shouted, "I'm not afraid of you. And I'll challenge you to a rematch anytime."

The crowd went wild. They cheered and clapped and chanted my name. *My* name. The aches, the soreness, the confusion in my head . . . it all just went away. Then Sombra Negra emerged from behind the bleachers and rushed the ring. He hopped in, took the mic from me, and began insulting my father.

"El Rey Coyote Sr. is a coward," he responded. "I wish he were here right now so that I could challenge him to a fight."

This was his cue. I pointed to the entrance. The curtains parted and then there stood my father in full costume—gold cape flowing to the ground, his tights white and shiny, boots slick and freshly polished. And, of course, he sported his mask. He walked past the audience, and some of them stopped to shake his hand or hug him. It was as though my father were a god at that moment, walking among them, patting their shoulders, lifting the babies in his arms, making them wail and cry out. He entered the ring, and I stepped aside when he took the mic from Sombra Negra.

"I accept your challenge," he replied.

What followed was a bout between him, Sombra Negra, and Ziggy. It was a dizzying spectacle of fly kicks and pile drives, leaps and body slams. In the end, my father redeemed me by winning the fight. The crowd went wild, applauding, chanting his name, congratulating me too. Afterwards, there were autographs and handshakes. A young boy came up to me and said I was his new hero. One simple match. Just one. And my whole body felt as though it had been passed through a meat grinder. On the way home, everything continued to throb. Jolts of pain shot up from my back all the way to the base of my neck and out through my arms. How did my father and the others do this day after day for so many years? With one small match, I felt done.

* *

A luchador needed to know about the power of his abilities as much as his limitations. I had to learn how to know my body, how to recognize its internal mechanism that dictated survival, and force it to get up again, to strike. It was an instinct we are all born with, my father claimed, humans and animals. We do whatever is necessary to defend ourselves, to protect those we love, those less fortunate. I needed to act without thinking. It took practice. It took learning how to rely on intuition to win a bout sometimes. Every fight was an opportunity to reevaluate what one had done incorrectly. We learned by doing. Our mistakes taught us more than our successes. It was hard letting go of the sense of hesitation that told us to *wait*, to *just wait*. We think that by waiting we'll seize the opportunity, find the right moment to do our thing. But this couldn't be further from the truth. We all possess that impulse. And we had to ignore it when it's not needed and listen to it when it felt right.

Eventually I found my style, put my own flair into the fight. My own costume, my own mask, grew on me like a shield. The crowds grew, too, and I learned how to play up the theatrics. My relationship with the sport evolved, deepened.

Participating in lucha libre isn't like playing baseball or football. It goes beyond simple contact sports. It embeds itself into the psyche, seeps into the blood and bones. It humbles a luchador in unimaginable ways.

I'd withstood it. I'd survived my first bout. I wore the scars, and the aches they'd left behind, proudly.

The fliers were printed on thin poster board, and I remember going around back then, stapling them to telephone poles around the neighborhood. My father kept one in his office, laminated in plastic. It was a side of him people hardly ever witnessed, a part of him that expressed pride, humility, and love for his children and his passions.

ESPECTACULO LUCHA LIBRE

Dragon Steel!
La Sombra Negra!
Ziggy!

EL GRAN ESTRENO DE

El Rey Coyote Jr.
Niños menor de nueve años entran gratis

(¡Acompañados con padres, por favor!)

El Rey Coyote

I'm ALWAYS here, señora. Don't be fooled. I see everything. Know everything. Somehow, I'll reveal the truth to him, your boy, and that grandson. The seeds are out there. They'll find them. Julián sees what no one else can. Alfredo's smart and resourceful.

Like his father was.

JULIAN VEGA

The evening's muggy from the flash rainstorm earlier in the afternoon that rolled in and out so quickly I nearly missed it. The trees and shrubs along Mulholland perfume the air; jasmine and eucalyptus mix with the scent of petrichor. It calms my nerves. I didn't know how to dress, so I opted for a pair of dark jeans, a tight black T-shirt, and a light jacket, but I'm already sweating from the nervousness or humidity. Probably both.

Focus, man. Focus.

The tread on my tires is worn thin since I haven't had the money to replace them, so I'm careful around the twists and bends in the road. The asphalt's always slickest from the first rains after a long dry spell. A wrong move could send me tumbling down a sharp ravine, so I grip the steering wheel, eyes steady on the taillights of the truck in front of me. Tim's house is at the end of a narrow driveway lined on either side by tall oak trees whose branches stretch across the top, forming a long and continuous arch that cuts off all lights from the city below. He'd texted, *I'll be having a few friends over. I want to introduce you to some of them.*

A Bentley, a white Tesla, and a Jaguar XJ6 are parked randomly along the circular driveway. Through the large bay windows, the whole place appears empty. After ringing the bell a few times and waiting, I open the door and step inside the foyer. To my left is a dark hallway. There's the faint sound of a ticking clock. To the right is the living room. Passing through the dining area I find a long galley-style kitchen. The counters are spotless. There's a DēLonghi stove with stubby cylindrical legs next to a Sub-Zero fridge with glass doors. A doughy white man in linen slacks and an orange collared shirt walks in through a side door. He's holding a half-empty goblet.

He bows. "El baño por favor." He wears a tan ascot around his neck and sips the remaining dregs of red wine from his glass before setting it on the counter. "Am I saying that right?"

"What?" I ask.

"You work here, don't you? You're part of the help? Now, tell me where the bathroom is." When he reaches out to place his hand on the counter, he stumbles and falls. Two other men burst through the door. A thin Asian guy in white shorts and black sandals bends down. "Emory. Oh Lord."

"Pick him up, Winston," his friend says. He glances at me. "What happened here?" He's older, white, with long gray hair wrapped in a bun resting atop his head. His skin's tan, leathery, like beef jerky, his moles and freckles the seasoning.

"Charles," Winston pleads. "Help me." They grab Emory each by an arm and lift him.

Emory is red-faced and sweating, his ascot askew. "I just came in to use the bathroom, and this young man here was—" he starts to stammer then presses his hand up to his mouth.

"Oh no. He's going to be sick," Winston shouts.

Charles looks directly over at me. "Move," he commands.

I'm standing in front of the kitchen sink. It's littered with wineglasses and tumblers, greasy forks and dirty spoons. Charles gives me a slight shove out of the way, turns the faucet on, and they lean Emory forward. Then Emory removes his hand and a torrent of vomit spews out of his mouth. Winston is massaging his back, whispering in his ear.

Charles tells him, "You need to go easy on the wine, old fella."

"It was the salmon, I think," Winston corrects him.

"Well," Charles says, "whatever it was, it's coming out in waves." He lets him go and steps away. "I need a smoke. Be right back. Just . . . hold his head up." Then he turns around and walks out of the kitchen, right past me, and towards the front door.

Emory's gagging and choking and mumbling, "Oh, Jesus. It's awful. Just awful. Winston, honey, I'm so sorry, sweetheart. I'm so very sorry."

"It's okay. It's fine." Winston catches me staring at him, gives me a knowing smile. "You're the new guy, yes?"

"I guess," I say, wincing as Emory heaves.

"Emory here's visiting us from Virginia. Aren't you?" Winston gives him a soft pat on the butt. "He likes us Asians."

At this point I'm wondering if I should leave.

"Tim's in the den," Winston replies before I can turn around and bolt. He gives a nod towards the side door Emory had first stumbled through.

"Great," I say. "Thanks a bunch." Down a short hallway beyond the doorframe the walls open, and I find myself in a spacious, sunken room. There's soft music coming from a pair of wireless speakers resting on a credenza above which hangs an oversized Rothko painting. The furniture is mid-century modern Danish, all sleek wood and brightly colored patterns. Tim's sitting on a couch, legs crossed, in a tank top. He's barefoot and nodding intently at a man in a suit and tie. The guy's burly, with the body of a bouncer. His blue dress slacks fit like leggings over his thick legs. He has a square forehead and eyes so green they look unnatural. Beside him is a woman with short blond hair, clear skin, and sharp cheekbones. She's in white jeans and chunky black boots. *Blondie* is written across the front of her T-shirt, Debbie Harry's face faded and rubbed away by too many twirls in the spin cycle. She's thin, her features those of a very handsome young man. While Tim and the man talk, she sits there, squinting at the illuminated screen on her phone, completely oblivious.

Tim sees me and smiles. "There he is. My boy, come here, come here." He rises and walks towards me, arms extended out. He grips me in a tight embrace and leads us to the couch. The man is Arno, he says, and the woman is named Vita.

"I was just telling them all about you," Tim says. He reaches for a bottle of wine and pours some for me.

I take a sip, try to steady my hand as I set the glass down.

Tim squeezes my thigh, and smirks. He's all hands and grips tonight, smoothing my leg, caressing my back, patting my pecs. "Julian here's a college professor."

"Not exactly—"

Arno sizes me up, leans forward, legs spread, hands on his knees. "That so, huh? What do you teach, eh?" He speaks with an accent that I can't quite place. *British? Australian?*

"Writing," I say, clearing my throat, hoping the perspiration gathering on my forehead isn't dripping down the sides of my face.

The woman, Vita, places her phone in her lap, wide eyes staring across the table at me, unblinking. "You writer?"

Russian, maybe? Her accent is thick, melodic.

"N-no . . ." I stammer, "I teach it. Mainly grammar and—"

"I have stories," she interjects. "About . . ." She snaps her fingers. "Fairy tales. I wrote when a little girl in Belarus."

"She's got these notebooks full of them," Arno shouts, laughing so loud it startles Tim. "She's the real deal."

"That's, that's interesting," I reply.

Tim looks towards the kitchen. "What happened to Winston and Emory? Charles? Where is everyone?"

Once he leaves the room, Arno glances over at Vita. "What are you looking at?" He points to her phone.

"The club. Is open now. I want to go." Her pale hand rakes her hair.

I finish the wine in two gulps.

Arno reaches for the bottle and pours me more. "We're going to this place. We'll all go. You too. It's gonna be wild." He winks.

A sex club, he tells me. A place called Gulch that I've heard about but have never been to. Since only men are allowed, the plan is to get Vita in by having her pose as a guy using her brother's ID. Tim and Winston return, helping guide Emory to a chair near the sliding glass doors leading out to the backyard. He's lost a shoe, and his bare foot hangs off the side of the chair like a rotting tree branch. Winston sits on the ground next to him, takes his phone out, and starts playing a game that seems to involve helping baby chicks navigate through a corn maze while being chased by an anthropomorphic dog-man in a pair of torn shorts.

Tim wiggles his feet inside a pair of leather loafers, looks around, and announces, "Time for a change of scenery, yes?"

"Oh yeah!" Vita rises, pulling up her white jeans and gyrating her slim hips.

"Let's do it." Arno claps his hands and rises.

He's bigger than I thought, massive, like a brick wall. A whole lot of man. Sex with him probably comes with a warning label: *Heavy machinery. Do not operate while intoxicated. Severe injuries may occur.* Those meaty thighs, massive pecs, that firm ass and bulky crotch make the blood rush to my head, make parts of my body twitch and quiver. Vita walks over to check on Emory. His head is thrown back, mouth open. He's snoring now, far, far gone.

She says to Winston, "You need to turn him over."

Winston doesn't look up from his game. "Everything already came up," he says. "He's fine. There's nothing left in his stomach."

"He could die," Arno says.

Winston sets his phone down and looks straight up at him, rolls his eyes, and shrugs his shoulders. "Maybe he should."

Tim laughs as he slips a jacket on over his tank top. "What a comedian."

We take two separate cars; I ride with Tim in his Jaguar, Arno and Vita following behind us in their Tesla. Tim says that Arno made a shit ton of money by investing in smart real estate decisions just when the economy tanked back in 2008. He capitalized on the misery of others, bought up a bunch of property in Venice back before all the tech companies moved in. There's a rumor that he was the one who coined the term *Silicon Beach*, but that's probably a lie.

"I have it on good authority that he's connected with the mafia." Tim takes his eyes off the road and turns to look at me. "Arno's not a guy you want to piss off. Know what I mean? He's been very good to me, to our operation. You do everything he says. He likes you a lot. You'll be paying him a visit."

"And Vita? Aren't they, like, a thing?"

"Don't worry about her," he says.

* *

Gulch is in Burbank, down an industrial street lined with nondescript warehouses. It's a white building with a bright green roof and a set of metal loading bay doors that are closed. Before we head inside, Arno helps Vita adjust her shirt and comb her short hair. They compare her face to the photo on her brother's ID.

Arno hands me the card. "That's close enough, right?"

Sergey Ivanov is twenty-four years old. His listed address is in Santa Clarita. He's thin like her. A skeletal face with gaunt cheeks and tousled blond hair stares out at the camera, neither smiling nor scowling. His face just is.

"Sure," I say. "Did you steal it? Won't your brother be mad?"

Vita shakes her head while primping herself in the car's side window, her reflection yellow and warped by the streetlights. "He's dead."

Tim and I go in first. We walk through the front door where we're greeted by a security guard in a windbreaker. He checks our IDs, then opens a second door that lets out a loud buzz. We wait inside a lobby lit by a purple fluorescent light bulb. Along the back wall there's a low counter where a guy in a leather vest sits placing condoms into a huge glass jar. He wears a surgical mask and latex gloves. Behind him, fliers posted to the wall advertise phone numbers for rapid STD testing and county safety regulations around Covid-19 and monkeypox.

Tim reads the posters, shakes his head. "Getting tired of all these diseases. Bad for business."

When the door buzzes and we see that it's them, Tim makes a show of acting real cool. At the counter, he covers my entrance fee. We place our keys and wallets inside the round trays the attendant hands us and wait for Vita and Arno to do the same. Then it's up a set of narrow wooden stairs that groan and crack under our collective weight. I'm behind Arno, those muscular thighs and plump ass just inches from my face. There's a lobby with couches and a few tables. In the corner are two vending machines selling snacks and cold drinks. Next to the bathroom entrance, there's a fold-up table where a coffeepot sits, beside it a crooked tower of Styrofoam cups and cans of sugar and powdered nondairy creamer.

Two of the giant flat-screen televisions mounted to the black walls are playing gay porn, the third one airing a baking competition. The caption at the bottom of the screen reads, *You needed to grease your pans better, Jennifer.* A man in his mid-sixties is watching intently as a woman smears chocolate frosting on a cake. He has long, stringy hair down to his shoulders and a thick mustache badly in need of a trim. He's sipping coffee from one of the foam cups. He wears a green military-style jacket, leather dress shoes, white tube socks, and no pants, just a pink lace thong, his pale ass cheeks wrinkled as deflated balloons.

"Oh wee," he's saying to another man standing beside him.

This other man, a janitor or employee, holds a plastic bucket. He's Latino, maybe about my father's age.

It might seem normal because the sex doesn't happen the minute you walk into the club's doors. It's not like you get buzzed in and, *wham*, there's a tangle of limbs and naked bodies all sweaty and raw right there and you dive in and fuck like a maniac. The interesting stuff happens down the black, narrow hallways, behind the doors, up in the balconies, inside the endless rooms that bleed into and out of one another. It's like tumbling into an M.C. Escher drawing or the Winchester Mystery House, but with slings, X-crosses, and glory holes.

"She's doing it all wrong," Arno tells the skinny white guy in the lace thong. "See how the frosting's going on all clumpy? That's because the spreader she's using's cold. She needs to run it under hot water."

The skinny guy nods. "You sound like a man who knows his way around a kitchen."

When a commercial airs, Arno takes Vita by the hand, and they turn and walk down one of the dark corridors, its floors lit up by strips of neon electrical tape. The janitor with the bucket wanders towards the bathroom, and the skinny white man in the lace thong goes over to the coffeepot, pours himself more, and heads through a door with a sign above it that reads, *Smoking patio*.

Tim kisses me on the cheek. "You think you're ready to play?"

"You tell me."

He leans in, whispers, "Welcome to the team, sport."

ERNESTO VEGA

I spent all my time doing push-ups and lifting weights, conditioning my body by eating right. Luchadores in Mexico couldn't wrestle without a license. All collectivos had to ensure their fighters were registered, otherwise they'd be in violation. I needed one before my first bout. I also couldn't go out there without a mask and a secret identity. Franco and Avila said I had to choose whether I wanted to be a rudo or a técnico.

"Sometimes it's more fun being a bad guy," Avila explained.

I found this hard to believe. "Aren't good guys better? I mean, they're the heroes, no? They get to come in and save the day. Like Superman."

"It's true, but a rudo has more of an opportunity to rile the crowd up, to get people angry and excited. A rudo's a dangerous, mysterious man," Franco went on.

But me? I was no bad guy. No. I was one of the good guys.

At least that's what I thought. How wrong I was.

* *

I developed a reputation as a técnico skilled in the art of deception in the cuadrilátero, fooling my opponents with sneak kicks and fast punches. Because of this, Franco and Avila took to calling me coyote. The Aztecas believed in a god they called Huēhuecoyōtl, a spirit named "the trickster," known for his cunning moves, for dance, and for storytelling.

Franco told me, "Coyote is short for Huēhuecoyōtl."

"What do you think of the name El Rey Coyote?" Avila asked one day.

"You both know better than I do."

I remembered the packs of coyotes roaming the cerros near my boyhood home in La Peña, remembered how the local farmers would fear them because of their vicious and predatory nature. They were grown men, seasoned farmers hardened by the land and the elements, but even they lowered their voices, spoke in soft whispers about the creatures they claimed were smart as humans and always, always watching us. It was their vigilance, the myths about their skill and power and bravery that made me think, yes, I will become him, El Rey Coyote.

Franco took me to meet a man famous for making lucha masks. His store was tucked away on a street flanked with leather shops and panaderias, the air smelling of baked bread and animal hides.

I nearly lost Franco in a crowd gathered at a bus stop. The newspaper headlines stacked in neat piles near the curbs all told of recent arrests by the Mexican government of student protestors the police claimed were communists. Independent reporters wrote of young people either being jailed or disappearing, never to be heard from again. There was an increasing sense of unease in the air, but like so many of us, I was too distracted to notice.

* *

The costurero was named Manuel. He started sewing the caras of the early luchadores when the sport was first introduced decades before. His shop was a tiny one-room space with no windows. A single sewing machine, a red Singer, sat atop a rickety table. Next to this was a wooden chair with a crocheted pillow on the seat back. There were bright-colored swaths of fabric, spools of gold and silver piping, feathers, and plastic bags full of glitter. Some of the masks Manuel had recently completed were draped across a counter and Franco walked over to examine them, nodding, his face reverent.

"¿Que onda, Franco?" The old man approached us. He wore a pair of thick-framed glasses that he adjusted, steadying himself against the display counter. Manuel winced. "This damned back of mine. Sitting in that chair, hunched over the machine day after day, it's getting harder. I'm too fucking old." He laughed and winked at me. "¿Y este joven?" The man sized me up. "New player?"

I introduced myself.

He scratched his forehead and whistled. "All these empresas and collectivos are growing and growing, adding more luchadores. I can't keep up. Shouldn't complain, though. Good for the business."

Franco reached over, patted him on the shoulder, and pointed to the masks before us. "New faces, eh?"

"We've been staying busy," Manuel replied. "Young men fleeing the campo, coming here with dreams of becoming the next Santo."

Manuel then pointed to his latest creations. The blue one with the gold design, he told us, belonged to Magic Thunder. A replacement after a particularly violent fight where his opponent ripped most of the fabric off. The green one with the red border was Rana's, and Rana did this thing where he'd eat candy that made his tongue green, and he'd hop into the ring and stick it out. The purple one was Rainbow Man's. The white one with silver feathers glued to the forehead belonged to Hummingbird 14. And that one there, the yellow thing, he went on, the one with the little black horns, that one was Demon Dog's. Each mask came with a story, he said to me, laughing as he swiped a tape measure near the

Singer. He led me to a floor-length mirror nailed to the wall and wrapped the tape measure around my neck. As he leaned in, the scent of cigarette smoke and camphor lingered on his hands and skin.

"¿Y tu?" he asked, reaching for a notebook and pencil. "What's your personaje?"

"El Rey Coyote," I replied.

Franco walked over to a rack. Several long capes hung on thin wire hooks. He studied each one, his hands stroking the smooth fabric. "How about a cape? White. With a fur collar. A coyote needs a cape. ¿Que piensas, Ernesto?"

"I don't know."

But they ignored me. Manuel set the tape measure down and scribbled in his little book. "We can do a cape, too, yes. Of course, of course."

He measured my head and neck at least ten times.

"I don't have enough for a cape," I told Franco once we were outside, clutching the receipt the old man had given me. It was a lot of money, so much so that a sour bile rose into my mouth from the back of my throat.

Franco snatched the receipt from me and shoved it in his pocket. "The sindicato will pay for it. You'll be making this back in no time. You and that nervous little friend of yours . . . always so anxious. Like flies drunk on shit buzzing about."

Then he took me to dinner. The restaurant was so fancy, like something out of a movie. There were cloth table linens and polished cutlery that gleamed under the glass chandeliers hanging above.

He ordered for us. The waiters wore red jackets with black bow ties and called me señor and jefe and promptly filled my glass whenever it was empty. When the bill came, Franco took the polished gold tray, reached into his pocket, pulled out a few bills, and tossed them on the table.

I tried not to worry. I really did. In the back of my mind, though, I knew the time would come when I'd have to answer for all these lavish things.

* *

A few days later, I brought home my outfit. Even Elena couldn't hide her appreciation of Manuel's skill. In the light of our cramped kitchen, she held the mask, her palm running over the fabric. She even brought it up to her nose and sniffed.

"Smells like new material. I'm good at sewing, but this? I could never do something of this . . . quality." Then she handed it back, removed the cape from the plastic bag, and spread it out over the table. The fur seemed to come alive in the afternoon breeze wafting in from the open window. She stood before it, arms crossed, shaking her head in disbelief. "Now, this is something."

An hour later, Julián arrived, and when I showed him, I was shocked to realize he wasn't as impressed as Elena. "It's probably the hair of some mangy dog. This is so . . . cursi, Ernesto."

"It'll be fine," I insisted.

He lit a cigarette and shook his head. "I don't like it."

I laughed. "You won't be the one wearing it. This cost us a lot of lana."

Elena uncrossed her arms. "Where did you get the money, Ernesto? How could we afford this?"

I told them what Franco mentioned, how I'd pay it all back with the earnings I'd make once I started fighting. The mask and cape were a good investment, I argued. Elena said nothing and walked into the bedroom. Julián grabbed his coat and said goodbye.

The next day, when Julián and I were at the gym, he approached Franco and Avila, who had been on the road for several weeks scouting out new talent. He asked why he wasn't consulted regarding my decision to go as El Rey Coyote.

"As his manager, I need to know these things."

Both men shrugged their shoulders.

"You should ask Ernesto," Franco replied. "Not us."

"It was my fault, mano. I'm sorry," I told him. "It will never happen again."

* *

Franco put me on a strict diet consisting of protein and fatty foods. I gulped down raw eggs and ate meals full of meats and cheeses. I needed the fats to help burn off the calories. He supplied me with protein powders and vitamin supplements that made my pee smell funny. Everything cost money that I didn't have, so he always paid for it and assured me the sindicato would handle it.

It was weeks of intense training sessions, my body sore, my limbs loose and throbbing. Elena rubbed ointment into my skin, and on Sundays, when I didn't have to work with Julián at the construction site or train at the gym with the other luchadores, we took long walks around Chapultepec Park. Just the two of us. Avila scouted around and found a few more guys, and after some time, we had assembled a pretty good, strong-looking group that formed a new stable of luchadores. Our rudos were Tormenta Roja, Neuroses, and Maloso. The técnicos were me as El Rey Coyote, Smile Boy, and Aces.

The night before my first bout, Elena made me chamomile tea sweetened with honey.

"Try to relax," she urged.

I knew she didn't approve of any of it. She swallowed her bitterness for me. I had left her no choice.

The next morning, I woke with butterflies in my stomach. And even though I was too nervous, I forced myself to eat anyway, then took a long run around the neighborhood to clear my thoughts. In the years since we'd arrived, so much had changed. Every day more people came from the rural parts of the country looking to make money, looking for a way to survive. Mostly they were single men with wives or old parents or siblings back home that needed their help.

* *

My debut fight would take place at a small arena. There was a ring on a raised platform surrounded by padded cords with bleachers arranged on all four sides, and a table. Above the ring there were spotlights shining down, giving the mat the air of prominence it demanded. Julián arrived early with me. Elena would join us later, just before the start of the event.

"Why are you so nervous, mano?" Julián asked as we boarded the crowded pesero bus and rumbled down the road. "You've done this before."

I thought about the crowds. About being in front of all those people. "I j-just . . . It's different. Before, it was like we were only playing, only fooling around. This seems real."

"You're ready," he assured me. "You're a técnico. A good guy. You can do this." He patted me on the back as we hopped off the pesero and made our way down the avenue towards the arena. People crowded the main entrance. The energy in the air was so strong, so electrifying, it took all my will and strength to resist the urge to run and hide.

The tension between Franco, Avila, and Julián had not lessened in the days leading up to the match. Julián complained about everything—the order of the fight, my opponent, the maneuvers we'd choreographed and timed. He was increasingly annoying the other men. They said he distracted me too much, that he was too bossy and demanding.

But he was my friend, my first admirer, even more than Elena. In him, I saw all the good parts of myself. He made me believe I was worthy and loved in an unspeakable way.

Elena Vega

I tried so hard to distract you. I went to the beauty salon, bought new shades of lipstick, fancy skirts, and revealing negligees to wear to bed at night.

Nothing worked, though. I was desperate, powerless.

I was becoming dangerous, a vicious, angry woman.

FREDDY VEGA

This morning, a car parks in the gym's empty lot, a few feet away, facing the entrance. In the passenger seat there's a guy in a hoodie and sunglasses. A girl with hair the color of lime sherbet and heavy eye makeup grips the steering wheel. The engine turns off, and she sits in the driver's seat, swaying, like she's dancing to a song on the radio. The guy sparks up a joint. I see the lighter's flame reflected in the dark tint of his shades. He takes a long hit and passes it to the girl. White threads of smoke drift out, and I catch a whiff, chuckling as I think about my heavy weed smoking back in the day.

* *

I still believe that herb he scored was laced with something, because my mouth went dry, and I was aware that Mike had driven me home, but none of it felt real.

"What if my dad notices?" I started panicking, staring at the front door. "Do I look okay?"

He leaned over. "Dude, you're so fucking faded."

"Shit," I said. "He's gonna know."

He reached into his pocket and pulled out a bottle of eye drops. "Here."

I squeezed some in, blinked a couple of times, and hopped out.

"Just act chill," Mike said, then he took off down the street.

Mercy was sitting at the dining table doing her homework. I strolled in casually and stood in the kitchen. "Yo," I said. I never used that word.

"Dad called." She didn't bother to look up at me.

"Oh fuck," I said. "Oh fuck." I giggled, and she glared at me. "What?"

"You're acting funny. Anyway, I said you were in your room asleep or something. He wanted to know if we had any groceries. I told him no, so he said to be ready because we'll have to go shopping."

I was still all goofed out by the time he pulled into the driveway and honked. I took the back seat because I didn't want him eyeing me funny. I remembered Mike's advice: *Act chill, act chill.*

"Hey, Dad," I said. "How was work, huh?"

He shrugged his shoulders. "Same old thing. Since when are you interested in my work?"

"I've always been. Always, always, always." I laughed at this.

My father shook his head.

Being stoned at the grocery store was fun. All those bright lights and packages. Everything felt so good in my hands—the rolls of paper towels, the waxy surfaces of melons and apples. In the frozen food aisle, I stuck my head inside the freezers, closed my eyes, and imagined myself an arctic explorer. I filled our basket with boxes of cookies and cereal, crackers and chips, and loaves of white bread. Mercy followed my father into the dairy section, and I headed for the butcher counter.

Salmon fillets were displayed inside the front case. Their pink marbled flesh glistened smooth, each garnished with a row of lemon slices.

"I want a slab of salmon," I announced to the butcher.

"Okay," he replied, unrolling a strip of parchment paper.

"No, three," I said. "One for each of us."

"That's a lot of fish," the dude replied.

I chuckled. "Yeah. But we're hungry."

"What? Are you poor or something? On food stamps?" It was slow, and there was nobody at the counter.

"Nah, man," I said. "It's just been rough." I made up a story about my father missing the ocean, hence the fish. "We won't eat it. We'll just let the aroma fill the house to remind my father of the sea, of the place where he proposed to my mother. She passed away."

He nodded. "Anything else?"

The salmon was heavy, and I cradled the package in my arms like a baby. I tossed the fillets into the cart and looked at my father, a big smile on my face.

"What's that?" he asked.

"It's fish!" I pronounced. "Salmon."

"When the hell do we eat salmon, Alfredo? How much did you get?" He looked at the weight and price. "We can't afford this. Put it back."

I took the package and shoved it inside a freezer, crammed between boxes of frozen peas and broccoli. On the car ride back home, my father stared at me through the rearview mirror. After we unloaded our groceries, I went into my room and fell asleep without eating dinner. Everything was spinning and swirling, and I was afraid to get up and go to the bathroom. It was dark. I couldn't see anything. That night, I dreamt of her. She was standing in my room in the dress we'd buried her in.

"Your father's wrong." Her tone was stern. "I loved salmon. Now that I'm on this side, I can breathe under water. I'm even growing gills." She touched the area just beneath her left earlobe.

Then she took my hand, her fingers cold, slick, and suddenly we were in front of a vast ocean, the waves lapping at our bare feet. She tightened her grip, and we dove into the water, and I was swimming with her, my mother the fish.

That was the one and only time she came to me.

ERNESTO VEGA

People began to arrive and take seats, while others clustered in small pockets. Children ran back and forth, watched from a short distance by their mothers. Men munched on bags of American-brand potato chips covered in lime juice and sprinkled with chili powder.

"Out of the way, out of the way," Julián shouted, pushing the crowd aside as he led me towards the rear of the arena. He brushed back long strands of his knotted hair, took off his jacket, and wiped away sweat using a handkerchief shoved in his pocket.

"What's with him?" Tormenta Roja said as we entered the staging area where the rest of the luchadores were dressing.

"I was using that!" Smile Boy exclaimed when Julián snagged a nearby chair and ordered me to sit.

I stood, handed it back to Smile Boy, and told Julián, "Mano, I can change myself, okay? Why don't you go outside and look for Elena and see where she's sitting." I took the bag he was holding that contained my costume and boots.

Reluctantly, he handed it over. "Fine. But I'll be back as soon as I find her."

He turned to leave; I was finally alone. There were so many pieces to tie, buckles to snap, and fabric to pull and tug over my thighs and arms. Franco helped me lace up my boots. Gently, he instructed me. Not too loose or not too tight. It made all the difference, he assured. We covered the rundown. The mini wrestlers were out there now, getting the crowd going. I could hear shouts and cheers.

"You and el Shadow are fighting the second bout. First, it's Smile Boy versus Maloso. Then you two, then Aces and Tormenta Roja. Got it?" Franco raised his thumb.

I nodded.

"How are you doing?" he asked.

"Good," I said, watching Shadow a few feet away.

"You nervous?" Shadow gripped my shoulder.

"He's fine," I heard Julián shout, rushing over to stand next to me. He reached into my bag and handed me the mask. "Elena's here. She's near the entrance."

"Was there no room up close for her?" I asked.

"Yes, but it's better she sits in the back, or she'll distract you."

The match between Smile Boy and Maloso worked the audience into a frenzy of roars and jeers. At the top of the third round, Smile Boy landed a kick to Maloso's midsection that caused him to stumble out of the ring and into the front row. The spectators seated there shouted and leapt out of the way, spilling popcorn and bottles of soda as Maloso sprang back onto the mat before the referee began his count. Maloso landed a solid tope on Smile Boy's forehead and stomped on his toe. Then he took the técnico's left arm, twisted it behind Smile Boy's back, and kicked him. This sent Smile Boy flying into the ring's cords, bouncing back, legs wobbling, stumbling around, as the whole place erupted in cheers and hollers. Coming up behind him, Maloso placed him in a choke hold, and Smile Boy fell to his knees, the rudo pressing his large body on top of Smile Boy while he struggled to break free. The referee counted to three as the bell dinged, signaling the end of the match. Maloso was crowned the winner. Score one for the rudos.

There were more shouts, more insults. The energy was strong enough to blow the roof right off and send it propelling into the sky. My pulse quickened. Every muscle in my body tightened. It was me and el Shadow up next. Behind the stage, where no one could see us, we patted each other on the back and wished each other good luck.

"Just like we practiced," Shadow told me.

"Just like we practiced," I repeated, going over the routine in my head.

El Shadow went out first. A little girl screamed at the sight of him, then turned and ran off. His presence brought about a wave of curses from the audience. They called him a good-for-nothing. They booed and lobbed profanities at him.

He squeezed through the padded cords, strutting around up there, moving in circles as the announcer watched. The more he paraded about, arrogant and exaggerated, extending his arms out, that wide barrel chest oiled and unblemished, the angrier and angrier people grew. Shadow then stomped around, growled, shouted insults back at them, laughing the entire time.

It was a riot. They hated him, and he loved it.

Then it was my turn. Julián helped me tie the cape as the announcer introduced me. Then, as if by some force of magic or mysterious energy, I pushed myself out there into that crowd, Julián trailing right behind. A spotlight fell on me. I stopped a few times, spread my arms out, imitating Shadow, and the crowd went wild. So many shouts and cheers. I felt invincible. While making my way through, shaking hands, holding babies, I glanced over to Elena and blew her a kiss. Everyone clapped and a few people whistled. All this time, el Shadow was standing in the middle of the ring, arms crossed, legs spread far apart.

Our first round consisted of simple maneuvers—rolls over one another's backs, fake kicks and punches—until the clock ran out.

In the second round, I was to take Shadow down halfway through by leaping from the top cord of the ring as I let out a loud, piercing howl before slamming into him, staying like that as he lay flat on his back, until the referee counted to three. This was my signature move. We called it *El Chillido Coyote*. Once he recovered, Shadow took the mic and called a foul and challenged me to a rematch.

"Very well." I laughed. "El Rey Coyote looks forward to extinguishing your sombra for good."

At this, the crowd burst out in roars and cheers, so much that I thought I felt the floor of the ring vibrate. I gave the mic back to the referee before bowing, jumping out, and running past the audience and back into the staging area.

* *

I was good at pretending to be good. Franco and Avila, the other luchadores, Elena, even Julián all agreed. So did the crowd, apparently.

Julián wanted to celebrate that night. I invited Elena, but she wasn't in the mood. She sat at the kitchen table, playing with a deck of cards and smoking.

"Go ahead," she replied when I insisted that Julián would not mind. She chuckled, rose, and grabbed a bottle of rum from the cabinet. "We both know how he feels about me."

"What does that mean?"

She poured herself a glass and took a few sips. "He wants you all to himself. Go. I'll just get in the way."

"Elena," I pleaded. "Stop being so . . . jealous."

She took another sip. "Leave me alone."

I did just that.

Elena Vega

I let him go that evening. I don't know why. Something told me I had to. Then he stumbled in at around one in the morning. I heard the front door open and shut, the tap of his shoes across the living room tiles.

"You smell like a cantina," I said.

"There were a lot of copas." His voice was low, scratchy.

Then came his body lying next to mine, his arms around my stomach. His touch wasn't tender, but hard and rough. I let him do to me everything that came next. It wasn't love we were making. There was no passion to it. He was far from me, removed. When we finished, I rolled over on my side and tried to sleep. Nausea mixed with rage and jealousy swelled inside my stomach.

I wanted to run, to leave that situation behind. But how? No. I would stay and change it, change him somehow. This was not the life or marriage I envisioned for myself. I would not remain stuck here. At least not like this.

Santa Maria, madre de Dios, ayúdame. I whispered this over and over that night until I fell fast asleep.

Santa Maria, madre de Dios, ayúdame.

Santa Maria, madre de Dios, ayúdame.

El Rey Coyote

They were around back in those days. Hidden in the shadows, of course. Leading secret lives because that pinche patriarchal, macho society dictates everything with the help of the church and those fucking conservative politicians!

They were known by many names, most of them slurs.

Maricónes.

Jotos.

Culeros.

Mariposas.

Homosexuales.

It's never easy, being that way. In any era. As a child, Julián was a gentle boy. He was prone to mood swings, shy, so he was teased by the others; they called him a sissy, a weakling. He developed into a quiet, withdrawn child. Entering the preparatoria, things didn't get better for him, but they didn't get worse. By then he grew a few inches, developed a strong voice, and even sang at the Noche Santa celebrations organized by the nuns at Nuestra Señora de los Milagros in La Peña. He dreamt of being a singer. His mother and sisters encouraged Julián by asking him to serenade them. His father didn't have the time or energy to entertain his son's strange fantasies.

"I want to be famous," he would say to his father. "Like Agustín Lara or Pedro Vargas."

His father laughed, shook his head as he removed his dusty hat and boots, dirt embedded underneath his fingernails, ten tiny dark crescent moons.

"Deja de esas pendejadas, mijo. There are no such destinies for men like us."

Julián understood that it wasn't his father's fault, that the pessimism he harbored was something he'd learned from his own father. They were part of a long line of men perpetually abandoned by a government that had promised to take care of them. All that desperation turns to anger, to rage, to mistrust. The men grow resentful. Their bitterness distorts them, poisons everything and everyone around them.

Pero ese Julián . . . he had Ernesto. His only friend and companion. Those two young boys, barely sixteen, were always running off into the cerro, exploring the caves and remote canyons surrounding La Peña. It was the gentle brushing of their legs beneath the water that hot afternoon, lying so close to Ernesto's bare body, the way his friend let Julián caress his thighs, his penis.

Ernesto laughed. "It feels funny."

Julián watched, though, fascinated by the sensation of it, how quickly it hardened in his smooth palm. Then Ernesto propped himself up on his elbows, leaned in, and kissed Julián on the lips the way he'd seen the male actors in the magazines at the puesto de periódicos do to their famous wives and leading ladies.

"Ernesto, why did you do that?" Julián asked, the boy's long eyelashes moist from the river water.

"No lo se," his friend replied. "Did you like it?"

Julián paused. "Si," he replied. "I . . . guess I did."

"Sale y vale. Maybe we'll do it again."

Then they lay beside each other, their skin warming under the sun, the rocks beneath them growing cool from their sweat, their foreheads pressed together.

Ernesto never felt closer to someone than he did to Julián that day and every day afterward. It was more than a friendship, more than love those two boys experienced. There was no language for what was growing between them. Just a silent understanding, a knowledge that they were different, meant for other things, meant for each other.

Then came the fight between Julián's parents, the incident with the lye, his mother's blinding, and his father's incarceration. Julián saw the state his family was in, then decided he needed to look elsewhere for work to provide for them.

And Ernesto's father? He ordered the boy to stop wasting time with school.

"You're nearly a man, pinche huevon," Rutilio Vega yelled at Ernesto. "A trabajar como un hombre, pendejo maricón."

He left school and joined Rutilio and Heriberto in the fields. He learned to tend to the animals. They raised the pigs and started selling them.

JULIAN VEGA

Arno and Vita were lost in the maze, and Tim and I sat in the lounge for a while, just talking, watching guys parade in and out. He'd asked if I wanted to go inside, but I was more comfortable with him, at ease in his presence. I hadn't felt so relaxed, so wanted since Phillip. As the night wore on, we both started fading. Soon, he patted me on the back and announced he was ready to go.

We got to his house at around two thirty in the morning. Since it was so late, he suggested I spend the night. He made it clear to me that there would be no fucking around between us.

"That's where I draw the line," he explained as we drove down the freeway, the lanes empty and smooth as ribbons of silk. In the distance the skyscrapers clustered around downtown LA looked solemn, sorrowful, threads of mist swirling around those steel edifices like scarves blowing in the humid breeze. I was a bit disappointed. I wanted to make out with him, wanted to rip his shirt off, bury my nose inside his armpits, take in that earthy man scent, spread his legs, straddle him, let him inside me. But I also understood. Sort of.

I slept in one of his many spare rooms. I chose the one next to his.

I stripped down, took care of myself, pretty sure he heard my moans and grunts. The next morning, as I showered, I purposely left the bathroom door wide open, strutted around with only a towel wrapped around my waist. He was in his office, hair tousled, stubble sprouting from his jawline and chin. I stood in the doorframe, shirtless, abs taut, chest smooth, my scalp rough and wet and fragrant as fuck.

He handed me a personal check. "Here."

There was enough to last me a few months. "What's this for?"

"Buy yourself some new clothes. Nice shoes. Don't skimp, either. Get some good stuff. High-end. You'll pay it back in no time."

I folded the check and held it in my damp hand.

"I'm going to have my salon give you a facial. Some nice skin products. Scrub and buff you clean."

Once dressed, he led me to the front door, my car coated in a sheen of morning dew.

"What's next?" I asked.

He embraced me in a tight hug and planted a big kiss on both my cheeks. "Go home. I'll be in touch in a few days."

I started my car, making my way, slowly, inch by inch, down the street, breathing nice and easy only once I was down on even ground again.

* *

Two weeks pass, and no word from Tim. I'm both disappointed and relieved. Does this mean none of his clients want me or aren't attracted to me? I text him a few times and his reply's always the same: *Nothing yet. Sit tight. I'll reach out as soon as I hear something.*

Pay day rolls around, and my check from the two summer classes plus what Tim gave me will be enough to keep me afloat until . . . until, fuck. I don't know. All this thinking makes me nervous, angry, so I bolt for the door, start my car, and peel off down the street.

* *

No sound inside the hospice today. No telephones ringing. No nurses being paged over the intercom. No coughing patients or the cracks and beeps from the security guard's walkie. I haven't seen Randy Bravo since that first time back in June. The entryway's quiet, the air just beyond the double doors warm, stifling.

Farther in, there's the sound of music playing. Walking across the main lobby towards Abuelo's room, I pass the double doors leading to the massive banquet hall. Inside, the curtains are pulled back, sunlight flooding through the tall windows along the left-side wall. A handful of old people in wheelchairs are grouped around a lady with red cat-eye glasses wearing a crisp purple dress with white bows adorning the shoulders. She's playing a piano. A melody I know. Eric Satie. "Gymnopédie No. 1."

If I would have lingered a little longer there, leaning against the doorway, listening to the recital, my gaze focused on the pillowy white heads of hair, gathered like tufts of cotton, I would have missed him altogether. I turn around, continue down the few steps and find my father sitting in the chair near Abuelo's bed. He doesn't see me at first, but eventually rises, brushes his hand across the lap of his faded jeans, then looks up, catches me standing in the doorway.

"Oh, hey," he says. "I was about to take off."

I nod. "How's he doing?" Abuelo's eyes are closed. A gummy white film covers his lips.

"The same."

The white film is petroleum jelly one of the nurses spread across his lips so that they won't chafe and dry out.

"You good?" He squints at me, asks it as if he were talking to a casual acquaintance, someone he hasn't seen in a while.

"As good as I can be. How are things down at the gym?"

It's the same, he replies. Like Abuelo's situation. Stable but not improving.

He gives me a pat on the shoulder as he passes, says, "I'm glad to see you, mijo."

"Yeah." I take his seat, reach over the hospital bed safety rail and grip Abuelo's hand.

Then my father pauses. Turns to face me. Like there's something else he wants to say.

"See you," I reply, not giving him the chance.

He walks away to the opening chords of Chopin's "Nocturne No. 9 in B Major, Opus 32, No. 1." I want desperately to understand why we do this to one another. Why are we constantly pulling away from one another? Why do we resist?

ERNESTO VEGA

Julián wanted to celebrate my gran estreno. That night, he showed up dressed in a silk shirt and blue polyester slacks, his hair washed and combed with pomade. The scent of cologne filled the entryway of the apartment.

He forced a smile towards Elena and said, "Buenas."

"Buenas." She was on her third trago of rum.

"It'll just be us tonight, hermano," I told him.

"¿Que esperamos? Let's go, then."

I didn't even kiss my wife goodbye.

Outside, the air was full of energy. Across the street, a woman sold warm tortillas from a wooden cart parked along the sidewalk. A barefooted boy in a striped T-shirt and tattered corduroy pants sat near a storefront, pleading to anyone who passed for a few pesos. A police officer wielding a slick black club in his right hand approached him.

"El dueño pide que te vayas," he told the young beggar.

"Pero es que tengo hambre," he whined, wiping snot from his nose.

"Lárgate, chamaco." The officer gripped his club.

The boy rose and scurried off.

On the street corners, women in tight skirts with long tan thighs smoked cigarettes as they waited for a local pesero to take them to the Centro Historico, to those ornate antique buildings, tangled bougainvillea vines clinging to their slender columns.

We stopped at a puesto along Calle Reyna Ixtlixóchitl because Julián needed cigarettes. We drank cold orange Mirindas and thumbed through the comic books stacked on the shelves— Memín Pinguín, Hermelinda Linda, Kalimán. I picked up a copy of ¡Alarma! The cover featured the bullet-riddled bodies of a man and woman lying in the street. ¡BAÑO DE SANGRE EN TE-POTZOTLÁN! the headline read in all capital letters.

Julián leaned over my shoulder. "Ay, hermano. Don't look at all that disgusting violence and . . . depravity." His breath carried the scent of cigarette smoke mixed with orange syrup from his refresco. "We're celebrating," he continued. "Your big estreno. ¡Vámonos!"

We ate tacos at a sidewalk puesto later that night. Then we ended up at a pool hall where he beat me three times in a row at eight-ball. Then two shots of tequila at a cantina plastered with magazine covers featuring naked women, their breasts powdery and firm. Copas of strong mezcal at another cantina. A loud table full of men with red faces and neat mustaches argued over President Gustavo Díaz Ordaz and his administration's handling of the student massacres in Tlatelolco during the 1968 Olympics.

One member of the group called Ordaz an inept tyrant.

Another raised his glass, drank, and flung it across the room where it shattered above the head of a lady in a red wig. She screamed, and the man shouted, "¡A la revolución!" and the whole room, including me and Julián, replied in unison, "¡Que viva!"

He tapped me on the shoulder and slurred, "You want to go to a real wild place, hermano?"

I wasn't thinking of Elena back home, alone, waiting up for me. It was good to be out with Julián. I'd missed his attention, his laugh, how he was always up for anything, the way he doted on me. Like I was the most important person in the world.

"I'm at your disposal," I said, finishing my trago and slamming it on the bartop.

"Eso." He clapped his hands. "Let's go, my friend. Let's go where we can really be ourselves."

I don't remember how we got there or what part of the city we were in. All I recall is an uncomfortable ride down Avenida de la Reforma on a crowded pesero where an old man in a frayed sombrero and huaraches sang an old Agustín Lara song for money.

Julián shouted over the roar of trucks and screeching brakes, "I know this one." Then he cleared his throat and joined the viejo, the two of them in perfect harmony with one another, hitting the same notes. Such a beautiful melody, and it felt like he was singing only to me. Everyone applauded, and when the old man removed his hat and passed it around, the passengers threw in what they could—coins, a few paper pesos, one lottery ticket. The viejo offered to split the profits with Julián, but he declined.

"No, señor," he told him as we exited the bus. "Gracias, pero no."

"Que dios lo bendiga," he replied, his face astonished at the level of Julián's generosity.

Down one street, then another, then another, and into an unlit alley where I nearly tripped over a drunken bum crouched next to a set of trash cans. Through a narrow wooden door and down a set of concrete steps. We were inside another cantina. To my left a set of five booths with tables along the wall. Across from this, a dance floor where lights encased in metal sconces hung from chains above the heads of the few people embracing as they swayed their hips to the sound of a man in a green sequined dress crooning on the stage. There was a bar with bottles of alcohol arranged on iron shelves. Behind the counter stood a thin man with a man-icured mustache and a pink handkerchief tied around his neck. He listened to the music, swaying to the sound of the guitar accom-panying the singer.

The bartender waved and smiled when Julián and I approached.

"Juliánito," he shouted. "Where have you been, ¿querido?" He reached across the counter and kissed him lightly on the lips. The man glanced over to me, smiled, and winked. "And who's this?" We shook hands. He caressed my palm.

I nodded. "Ernesto Vega a sus órdenes."

"¡Ay!" he replied. "Tan galán y varonil."

"This is Rogelio," Julián told me. "He runs the place. How are things?"

Rogelio looked to be about forty. His dark skin told me he had strong sangre indigena. *Maya, maybe?* He was taut, muscular, sporting an aquamarine sweater and gray polyester bell-bottoms. Around his neck dangled an oval medalla of La Virgen Milagrosa, her tiny, engraved arms outstretched, the folds of her robe glinting in gold bands under the lights.

"Aquí," Rogelio replied. "Serving bebidas y mordidas all day."

As the two talked, I glanced around. There were only men. Sitting close together in the booths or dancing under the swaying lanterns. Some wore makeup and earrings. One man a few stools over leaned against the bar. He was in a silver dress with a plunging neckline. A feathered boa was wrapped around his shoulders. He walked over.

"My name is Carlos, but here they call me Carlotta." Carlos, or Carlotta, sported long gloves that reached up to his elbows. He wore bright red lipstick, blue eyeshadow, his cheeks dusted with orange rouge.

"I'm Ernesto. It's a pleasure to meet you."

Carlotta leaned in and whispered in my ear, "How about we

go towards the back, behind the stage, yes? I'll give you the best mamada you've ever experienced."

Rogelio overheard, reached across the bar, and placed his hand on my forearm. "This macho is taken, Carlotta. ¿Verdad, Juliánito?"

Julián smirked and reached for my hand. "Yes. At least for tonight."

He led us to a booth, and we sat down.

"Where are we?" I asked.

"Look around."

Julián said he found these bars through a friend, an intimate friend, when he first arrived in the capital. Here, he felt less lonely, less of an outcast, less of a degenerate.

"Was this man your . . . ¿amanté?" I replied, unable to fathom the idea. Not because I found it unnatural or disturbing, but because I'd never seen or thought of such a thing.

Julián lit a cigarette. "He was. We used to come here a lot."

"Did you two dance? Hold hands?"

He watched the couples on the dance floor embracing one another, bodies pressed together so tight it was hard to tell when one man ended and the other began. "All of it," he replied, smiling. "We made love too."

He flicked the ash from his cigarette, and I reached for it, took a puff, imagined my lips against his again like we'd done years before on the rocks when we were teenagers. I gave it back to him and studied the silhouette of his face, his slim jaw, sharp nose, the protruding ridge of that beautiful brow.

His fingers caressed mine. "Does it make you jealous, Ernesto? Imagining me in the arms of another man?"

I laughed, tried hiding my confusion, my curiosity. "I don't know. All of this is a bit too much for me to take in, hermano."

"What about that time? Back at the rio in La Peña? I held your . . . we kissed."

"Ah." I waved my hand. "We were kids. Nothing more."

Julián leaned in close now, his face a few inches from mine. I could feel myself getting aroused, the fabric of my underwear tightening near the crotch in ways it never did when I was with Elena.

"I see you, Ernesto," he replied. "I know where your true passions lie. We belong together."

When he kissed me, I let him. I gave in without a fight.

Elena Vega

Maybe it was the spirits the curandero talked about, their uncanny way of orchestrating things, their methods, their ability to see how situations will play out far into the future. Maybe they were telling me to give up and go back home. Because I didn't need candles or teas or spirits to know I was losing, that Julián's influence, his presence, was a force stronger than any I'd ever encountered. Bembe had asked me how much I was willing to sacrifice to keep what I thought was rightfully mine.

I didn't know. But what I did know was that I would not lose this battle.

As time passed, I knew the bond between them was strengthening and growing, pushing me out. I neither resented Ernesto nor Julián, in fact. I only wish he could have understood how frustrated I was. Was he trying to abandon me again? I would die before letting that happen.

FREDDY VEGA

It was right after the whole aerobics craze of the '80s. Women were putting away the leg warmers and thick cotton headbands. The Jane Fonda shit was too slow, too gentle, I guess, and they were looking for something a little less timid, a little more aggressive. My father had been "doing recon," as he called it, going to other indie gyms and the bigger chains to see what they were up to.

He came in one day with this idea. We'd start offering classes in step aerobics and this thing called Tae Bo, a weird combination of boxing and Tae Kwon Do. I thought it was a dumb move. We were a gym. Not a fucking Weight Watchers or Jenny Craig. Hugo was on the fence about the whole idea.

"Just you wait," he told us.

When he got this way, when he was determined and carried that tone in his voice, it was impossible to talk him out of anything, no matter how fucking insane the idea. It was the same tone he used after my mother died and he announced he'd be quitting the factory job to open this place. I imagine it was the same one she heard back in the day, too, when he told her he was leaving the rancho with his friend to find work in the city. Still, I tried to discourage him. How would it look, I asked, if a bunch of women in leopard-print tights descended on this place? What would that do to our image?

He pulled a comb out of his pocket and ran it through his hair. "What pinche image?"

Hugo leaned up against the ring. The room was packed with guys bench-pressing, hitting the punching bags, doing crunches, running on the treadmills.

"Help me out here, man," I told him.

But Hugo only rolled his eyes. "I'm staying out of it."

We hired a construction company to come in and wall off a section of the main gym, dividing the large room into two smaller ones. We had to squeeze some of the weight racks and cardio equipment closer together, but it wasn't that big a deal. The ring remained where it was, smack in the middle, resting a few feet above. We lined the walls inside the new place with mirrors and installed laminated flooring that looked like wood, set up lights and mounted fans and a portable AC unit, and the space was good to go.

We advertised for instructors and got some new people to come in and teach the step aerobics classes. Tae Bo was offered four times a week and led by a woman named Chastity and her fiancé, Devin, who wore his hair in a ponytail and reeked of patchouli oil.

I had to get used to it all. The constant loud music blasting from the room, the shouts and cheers, and all those women in striped leotards and frizzy hair clutching water bottles. They were mostly middle-aged mujeres who loved, and I mean *loved*, flirting and gossiping with my father. He liked recounting his glory days back in Mexico City, exaggerating his exploits. Since he was a widower, they brought him tamales, old margarine tubs full of menudo, bags of pan dulce, giant bottles of Santa Clara brand rompope straight from Tijuana. Now and again, the daughters or nieces of some of these ladies accompanied them, and they were always nice to look at, to flirt with, to charm in my own way.

"You are just like Ernesto," they'd say. "The two of you identical."

I might have been wrong about our decision to start offering these classes. I had to admit it. This was looking like *un when-when* as Hugo would say. We were raking in more cash than we did the lucha libre bouts.

* *

Nineteen ninety-four. I had just turned twenty-three. In January, the Northridge Earthquake collapsed freeway overpasses and destroyed thousands of homes. In East LA water pipes burst, pictures fell, shelves toppled over. Mercy called from Berkeley, astonished.

In June of that year, everyone watched O.J. Simpson drive around the city in a white Ford Bronco while cops tailed him after they discovered his wife and her friend murdered. O.J. was a suspect, and his running didn't help his case one bit. In Sacramento, Governor Pete Wilson used his office to target undocumented people. There were immigration raids in and around the nearby factories and across the city. One day, a couple of police officers in a black van and tactical gear showed up at the gym and asked if we employed any "illegal aliens."

"You got a search warrant?" my father asked them as they stood at the main entrance, then proceeded to poke around, opening doors, harassing some of the guys lifting weights.

Everyone was on edge that summer. Even though the city had burned and been turned upside down a couple years prior because of the whole Rodney King verdict, there we were again, all of us brown folks walking a tightrope, our lives ruled by fear and uncertainty.

The papers called him the "Eastside Rapist." The composite sketches on the news showed a skinny white guy with a large mole just below his right eye. He wore a red baseball cap and a gray sweatshirt. He stalked community college campuses at night, sneaking up on women leaving their evening classes. He ambushed them in the school parking lots, dragged them into the bushes, and even into some of the empty bathrooms. They were beaten and raped. One of his victims, twenty-two-year-old Vanessa Delatorre, was so severely attacked she was in a coma.

He had a type: young Latinas in their early to mid-twenties, small- to medium-framed college students. We started offering self-defense classes for women where they learned basic moves that could save their lives and maybe put a stop to those sick perverts out there.

Grace Mata showed up to the gym one day in early July with two friends, all of them studying to be nurses. Another girl in their class had been recently assaulted by the "Eastside Rapist," they said. Luckily, she had a can of mace and was able to spray the guy in the eyes. The girl ran to a corner mini-mart and called the cops. Their school was doing nothing to beef up security. Areas of the campus were dark. There were no emergency phones to use in case something went down.

"It's bullshit." Grace crossed her arms and clutched her keys, their metal tips poking out of the cracks between her knuckles.

"Smart." I pointed. "Holding your keys that way. You punch someone coming at you like that, and you can do some real damage."

"It's called a hammer strike. I saw a guy on the *Phil Donahue Show* talk about it."

Her friend Denise said her brother told them about us, how we were teaching the women to rely on themselves in case anyone decided to fuck with them.

I remember their first class, all three of them sitting on the floor together with the rest of the group, cross-legged, watching the instructor we'd hired, a muscly white guy named Lee who was a Hollywood stuntman, go over basic moves—groin kicks, heel-palm strikes, and elbow strikes. Grace was in a pair of sweats and a ratty Lakers T-shirt, her long hair in a frizzy ponytail running down the middle of her back like a piece of rope.

Lee had them stand, instructed them to watch carefully, demonstrated some moves, then paired them and made them practice over and over. Then they all sat on the floor again.

Lee scanned the room. "I need a volunteer."

Everyone looked at each other.

Grace raised her hand and stood. "I'll do it."

He then glanced over in my direction. "Mr. Vega. Can I get some assistance?"

I unzipped my jacket and strolled to the center of the room. "Let's do this."

He had Grace stand a few feet away with her back to me. "I'm going to teach you how to escape from a bear-hug attack."

Next, I approached from behind, wrapping my arms around her waist. A couple of the girls giggled and rolled their eyes.

"Now get in closer," Lee instructed me. "And wrap her waist very tight." He guided my arms. "Come on, man. Don't be shy about using those muscles."

I could hear Grace's trembled breathing, felt her body shake as I squeezed her waist.

"I won't hurt you," I whispered into her right ear.

"You better not," she replied. "I'll kick your ass."

I chuckled. "Yeah, right."

"Now," Lee said, "Miss Grace, you bend forward slightly from the waist." This worked to shift one's weight, he told the class, making it harder for an attacker to pick his victim up, which he would try to do. "This also gives you better maneuverability to throw your elbows from side to side to distract him."

Next, he told her, turn and face your attacker, using either your elbow to hit him in the face or kneeing him in the groin. We practiced it a few times, Lee shouting out the commands to Grace, me pretending to get jabbed in the eye by her elbows.

"Next," Lee continued, "Miss Grace, I want you to do it alone. Without my guidance." He wore a whistle around his neck, blew it, and shouted, "Now."

I strolled up over to her, wrapped my arms around her waist once more, and held her body close. Then she bent forward, and I felt her sharp elbow jab me so hard in the eyeball that I saw stars and my head pulsed from the pain. And when I yelled out, she didn't stop. Facing me now, that young woman with her delicate arms, dug her fingernails painted neon green into my biceps, curled her leg, and jabbed me so hard in the nuts I collapsed on the floor, curling up and groaning. The women gasped. Someone shouted, *fuck*. Lee stood there, frozen, whistle still in his mouth.

"Shit, shit." Grace ran over, bent down, and tried getting me to stand. "I'm sorry! I'm so very sorry."

She was waiting for me in the parking lot with her friends. I asked her out right then and there, and she said yes. Three months later, I proposed. We were married in a small ceremony in the spring of 1996. A knee to the groin like that? Shit.

I couldn't let her go.

She was a fighter. Like me.

El Rey Coyote

There was nothing you could do. You know this. You're smart, Elena. Don't play naïve, mujer.

Ernesto was never yours.

Or Julián's.

Or even mine.

He belonged to something bigger, something we could never compete with; his own ambition and drive to break from his past, to get as far away as possible from the person he was supposed to be.

No matter the cost.

JULIAN VEGA

Phillip and I were tight, inseparable, all throughout our freshman and sophomore years of college. We studied together, took classes together, went to the gym together. Wherever one of us was, the other wasn't too far away. When he was taking a seminar on religion and philosophy and learned about the concept of dualism as represented in the yin and yang symbols, he said it was like us.

"We're two opposite sides of the same whole," he explained. "Balancing each other out."

He was right, I guess. In so many ways, we were diametrically opposed. I could wake early and go for a run, when all he'd want to do was sleep in. I always liked going out and doing things—hiking, trips to the beach, amusement parks—and he'd be perfectly content staying indoors all day, watching movies or playing video games.

It made sense then that one night, coming back from a frat party Brian had invited us to, that we found ourselves stumbling into a tattoo parlor on University Avenue, in a strip mall next to a seedy adult bookstore. Flipping through the binders full of sketches and drawings, Phillip pointed a firm finger to one.

"There," he pronounced. "We're getting this."

It was a *yin* and *yang* symbol.

We agreed he was *yin*—the dark side—because he was relaxed, nurturing, and provided spirit to things. That made me *yang*—the light half—because I was quick, restless, always on edge, and I gave form to things, breathed them into being.

"Where do you want them?" the tattoo artist asked. She was thin with jet-black hair and pale skin.

They'd go over our right shoulder blades.

Phillip gritted his teeth, winced, but he took it like a pro.

Yin and yang, he explained, was about equilibrium, about two forces in harmony. He could never be completely yin and I could never be completely yang. We would move and flow and change over time, but we would always be in balance with one another as long as we were together.

He read me a passage from the Tao Te Ching:

Be totally empty,
embrace the tranquility of peace.
Watch the workings of all creation,
observe how endings become beginnings.

* *

I grew to depend on his presence in my life, and he felt the same about me in his. But we never did anything romantic. It went on like this for two years.

This isn't to say I didn't try. There were a few times when I let my hand linger on his arm, my knee press against his a little firmer. We made out once, but he stopped me before things could get too intense. His dormmate was away for the weekend, so we were in his room cramming for exams. He was on his bed, and I was sprawled out on the floor. It was a warm evening, and the air-conditioning system in the whole building was out. We'd opened the windows and had stripped down to our boxer briefs. He was so handsome even as he glistened with sweat, the pages of his textbook sticking to his damp fingers. As he reached for the tumbler of water next to his nightstand, he caught me looking up at him. I was visibly aroused; it was difficult to hide in my underwear.

He took a long swig of water. "Someone's thinking with the wrong head."

I got up off the floor and sat on the bed, his bare legs behind me. Then I reached back, caressed them, and Phillip closed his eyes, and I could see that he too became aroused. He rested his head on a pillow, his book opened and splayed across his chest. When I leaned over, he wrapped his arms around my shoulders. It was a light kiss, nothing deep or passionate. But there was tenderness in it, the longing for more. He let go of me and rose from the bed, grabbed a pair of basketball shorts from a pile of laundry and put them on.

"We shouldn't," he said.

"Even though you want to?" I asked.

He nodded.

He was afraid. Because of his father, who'd converted to a religion that preached the evils of homosexuality. He would die if he found out.

"My mom's cool," he continued. "More understanding. But my father? Has a temper. Scared the crap out of me as a kid. This would make him lose his shit. The thought alone petrifies me."

That kind of put a damper on things. I didn't want to dump any additional anxiety on him, didn't want any awkwardness between us to develop if I pushed too hard, so I eased up.

At the beginning of our junior year, his mother was in a serious car wreck. It was painful watching him agonize over it. I did my best to help him stay focused on his classes, to distract him from feeling guilty about being so far away from her, from feeling helpless because there was really nothing he could do. One morning, during the Spring term of our junior year, she took a serious turn. I was standing in line at the coffee shop in the campus food court.

The place was crowded with everyone shuffling about—instructors and professors holding impromptu meetings with colleagues or students, staff and employees ordering drinks to take back to the office, delivery drivers unloading crates of milk and cream. I was surprised to see him because it was past ten a.m. on a Tuesday, and he was supposed to be in an anthro lecture taking a test, a test he'd been stressing over for the past couple of weeks. He was crying and didn't pull away when I took him by the hand and led him to a table. I told him to sit.

"Have you eaten anything?" I looked over at the pastry case. "Do you want a bagel? A yogurt?"

"No."

"Coffee?"

I was worried. He was almost catatonic, eyes unblinking, face emotionless.

Then he said, "I just got off the phone with my dad. He's booked a flight for me back home. I need to be by her side. I don't know what condition she's in. Man, I can't lose her."

"You won't."

I was too young back then, unfamiliar with the way the prospect of death can rattle you, can make everything around you loose and transparent, the way it can shatter the illusion we all walk around with that we're invincible. I stayed quiet. I watched the line of bored undergrads scrolling through their phones, the professors with their tired and worried looks, the coffee shop employees darting around behind the register. My parents were strong and healthy. Abuelo Ernesto was still at the gym. Nobody I knew was even close to dying.

We left the coffee shop. I skipped all my classes that day and helped him pack, then I drove him to the airport and sat with him inside my car. We listened to music, and he told me stories about his mother. How she couldn't stand figs and was afraid of the dark, how she'd saved all his elementary school art projects and kept them in a box under her bed, what she told him when he came out to her in high school. *You're my son. You will always be. I love you no matter what.* We held hands, and when it came time to check in, we went to the airport terminal and hugged. Then he turned and walked through the double doors, the same duffel bag my father had helped him carry up the stairs that day years before slung over his shoulder. He called me a few nights later to say she was hanging in there. He was crying, and there was so much pain in his sobs and words that I didn't know what to do except to stress how lonely campus was without him.

"I'm scared."

"She's going to be fine," I assured him.

He decided to take Incompletes for the rest of the term and wouldn't be returning until the fall. It made sense, I replied. He'd spend the summer there helping her recover.

"It's gonna be a long couple of months. My dad's become even more of a tyrant."

"Hang in there," I replied. "It'll be over soon, and you'll be back."

Then he said something that surprised me: "It's taken all this for me to realize how much I need you in my life."

ERNESTO VEGA

Franco placed me on heavy rotation. I was the only luchador in
our collective with a bout each weekend. The seats filled up fast.
Soon, there was enough money for an expansion of the arena. Not
a lot, but he had enough to buy the space next door. They knocked
a wall down, applied plaster, coats of paint, and soon there was
room for more bleachers, more chairs, and everyone was happier.

Julián remained by my side, acting as my coach, as my handler.
I grew to rely on him, my constant companion, because Elena just
wasn't interested in indulging my "lucha exploits."

"That's your . . . thing," she'd say.

Julián claimed she didn't understand the culture of lucha libre
the way the rest of us did, how it wasn't a sport but a way of life.
He appreciated it, respected it, understood it the way I did.

"Elena doesn't get it, and that's fine," he said "I do. I understand it. And I understand you in ways she just can't."

Elena Vega

Ernesto, there were times I hated you, hated men like you. No regard for women and the sacrifices we make for our husbands to be happy. I lean close to your dying face, your vacant mouth, your hollowed-out cheeks. All the lies and deceit are etched there in your dried-out and sour-smelling skin.

—Did you ever once consider my thoughts? My plans? No. You were so fucking selfish.

—All of it was for you, Elena.

His words come not from his mouth, but from somewhere deep inside my ghost mind.

—¡Mentiras!

There were moments, Ernesto, when I recognized something Julián and I shared, what we saw. We were fools if we thought you'd ever fully belong to either of us.

I watch now as the specter emerges from beneath your hospital bed. Gray mist like fog at first, it slowly forms into his body, your body. I hear a laugh.

—Took you long enough to figure it out, didn't it?

His faceless head shakes up and down. El Rey Coyote stands between you and me, broad shouldered, arms folded across his chest.

—To figure what out? I ask.

—That this isn't about who wins or who loses, who he loved and who he didn't. It was never about you or Julián or even your pinche familia. In the end, for us fighters, it's not about the script or about the feuds or about who the victor is. It's about the spectacle of it all. It's about the struggle. Sólo la lucha.

FREDDY VEGA

Two older cholos, veteranos, stroll in today around noon, gym bags slung over their shoulders, bandanas riding low on their foreheads.

"You open?" the shorter of the two asks. Above his left eyebrow there's a tattoo, green squiggles spelling a word I can't make out.

The other one looks around, lifts his chin like an animal trying to catch the scent of an adversary. I spent the morning mopping the floors inside the bathrooms even though nobody's used them in weeks, so the only thing I can smell around us right now is Fabuloso. And desperation.

"Open?" I say, pushing the mop bucket back against the wall. "Yeah. Barely."

"Do we gotta pay membership to use the weights?" This from the second one, still with the chin lifted, still sniffing the air.

I chuckle, and they both look at me surprised. "Nah," I say. "Just . . . go ahead."

"You sure?" The first one now. "We could pay. That's not a problem."

I wave my hand. "It's cool. Use whatever you need for as long as you need."

They point to the box of surgical masks I found earlier. "Do we need to wear masks in here?" The second one again.

"No. You're good."

They nod, bow their heads in respect, turn and head towards the racks of free weights.

It was the start of the pandemic. March 2020. Grace brought the box home after working a double shift at Navarro's. She set her purse down by the front door and sat on the living room floor. Her eyes were red.

"You crying?" I asked.

"No, baby. I'm fine."

"What happened?" I turned the television down. More news about the virus, the numbers of infected and dead—both globally and in the U.S.—hovering over the reporter's shoulder, the digits steadily ticking up.

Grace shook her head. "People are going nuts out there."

A woman bought up all the store's supply of toilet paper, and the manager on duty did nothing to stop her. When a few of the employees told her she couldn't, the woman lifted both arms up to the ceiling. *Where's it say that?* She was right, Grace said. They had to ring her up. Two customers got into a fistfight over the last bottle of hand sanitizer. A bunch of teenagers raided the liquor aisle. Just grabbed everything they could and ran off. Security was too busy keeping order to stop them. A man came in without a mask. When an employee informed him that he couldn't shop without one, the dude leaned in and coughed in her face, then stormed out.

"She takes care of her mom who's eighty and diabetic." Grace reached out to smooth back my hair but stopped herself. "I'm scared to touch you. What if I caught it and pass it?" She then pointed to the box of surgical masks on the table. Said I should take it with me to the gym.

"Nobody's coming in," I told her. "I'll be fine."

"I don't care. Take them anyway. You never know."

On the television, a nurse was being interviewed. She sobbed into the camera, "It's like a war zone in there. It's awful. So many bodies."

That day, I only took the box to put her mind at ease, to show her I was indeed taking this whole thing seriously because she thought I wasn't.

As the cholos start their workout, I pull one out. The mask's pleats stretched out to fit over my mouth. The wire guard pressed against the bridge of my nose, the smell of the fabric . . . it leads me back to the moment when Julian was born.

* *

Grace was in labor for hours, and my father and Hugo sat in the waiting room, each holding a pack of cigars in the sweaty palms of their hands. I think they were more nervous than me, in fact.

I was instructed to put on a pair of green scrubs, my callused hands stuffed inside a pair of cold latex gloves, my mouth and nose covered by a surgical mask. The delivery room was bright with intrusive lights glaring down at me and machines beeping as the doctor urged Grace to push and push. Then the head crowned, and the doctor reached inside and gently pulled and tugged and coaxed that tiny body out until there was my child. He was all puffy red skin and tiny little limbs that kicked and swatted at the air around him. The first time he squeezed my finger, I nearly melted. When I watched him yawn, I bawled like a baby myself.

He was a good kid, not fussy. Aside from the occasional cold or fever, he was healthy overall, but he was shy. Too timid. Early on, when we'd play, I tried teaching him how to be tough, to hit, to not be afraid to fall and scrape his knees. When accidents did happen, I wouldn't make a big deal about.

"It's only blood," I'd tell him. But he never got past the fear of it all.

Then the incident in the tub happened. I was right there, man. Right fucking there. I look away for one second and the next thing I know he's on the floor, screaming, blood seeping from the right side of his forehead. I lost it in the emergency room. He wouldn't stop crying, and Grace was saying it was my fault.

"You're always playing rough with him," she said.

"What the fuck, man," I shouted back, and a few of the other patients in the lobby turned to look at us. "I was with him. He was in the tub. How's that my fault?" Then the asshole security guard strolled over, acting all big and bad, and asked Grace if she needed help, glaring at me. Fucking freckle-faced redneck.

"Man," I said. Julian was writhing and squirming in my arms. "Don't even, dude."

Grace grabbed him and said to the guard, "We're good, sir. Thank you."

"Yeah. *Sir*," I replied, smirking at him. Stupid scrawny fuck.

"Freddy, don't," she commanded me. Julian had calmed down some. She clutched him, the towel pressed against his head damp and pink from his blood.

He got stitches that day. Four. That's it. Four. But Grace acted like I'd committed child abuse or some shit. From that moment on, I sensed she never trusted me with him again.

In junior high, he had few friends and preferred reading books in his room after school instead of being outside playing. He reminded me of Mercy that way. I mentioned this to her once when she stopped to visit on her way to Ecuador, where she was helping Indigenous peoples with lawsuits against companies that threatened their land.

"You're not going to be a knucklehead fighter like your father and grandfather," Mercy said, reaching out and squeezing his skinny arm. "No señor. You're going to use your brain. Like me, right?"

He smirked. "Yeah. Sure."

By the time he hit high school, his awkwardness hadn't faded away. After persuading and encouraging him, he agreed to try out for a sports team the summer before his junior year. I told myself I was doing it more for him than for me, but I knew the truth. When he started exercising and training for a spot on the wrestling team, something swelled up that was greater than pride. Like I was seeing myself in him for the very first time. I spared no expense. Got him nothing but the best—wrestling shoes, helmet, protein mixes, supplements. We spent weekends running laps. I cleared out the garage and placed some mats I'd borrowed from the gym down on the concrete where we practiced pins and takedowns. We ran drills. I taught him how to eat right. I made sure he got plenty of rest. I recorded wrestling matches on the television, and we watched them together, over and over, for hours, studying the moves.

The tryouts happened at the start of his junior year. He came home one afternoon and announced that he'd made the JV team. And I tried to hide my disappointment when I found out. Tried being proud, but I was pissed. I knew what my son was capable of. I knew he was ten times better than any of the other guys on the varsity team.

"Whose decision was that?" I asked when he told me.

He shrugged his shoulders. "Coach Valencia, I guess."

I laughed. "Gil Valencia's an idiot. What does he know? I remember that weasel. We were in the same grade. I should pay his punk ass a visit."

He sighed and slumped down on the couch. "Dad, don't. Please don't." Then he got up and stormed off down the hallway towards his room.

Things unraveled fast after that. He stopped eating, couldn't sleep. Grace and I were called into a meeting with a school psychologist. Performance anxiety, she said. Julian's nerves and fears were getting the best of him. We sat in her office, Grace with her hands clasped in her lap, Julian playing with a loose button on his shirt.

"Sometimes we place too much pressure on our kids." The psychologist had plain brown hair and a big smile. *Constanza Garfinkle*, her card read. *Family therapist.*

"Did I pressure you?" I asked Julian. "Did I make you do something you didn't want to do?"

"No, but—" he stammered before Grace stepped in.

"My husband comes from a family of athletes," she said.

"Okay, okay," Constanza Garfinkle replied, nodding, scribbling everything down in a notepad. "That might have been—"

"It's not like I forced him," I interrupted. I looked at Julian. "Did I force you? I was only trying to help."

"I know, Dad, but I'm not you."

If he wanted to quit, he could quit, I told them. Constanza Garfinkle asked Julian what he wanted to do, what he thought would be best for him. The therapist just ignored me and directed her attention to him.

"Julian, do you feel an overwhelming fear at the thought of being injured?" she asked him. "Do you start to sweat. Feel sick to your stomach?"

He looked at us before answering. "Yeah. And like my heart is beating so fast it's going to burst out of my chest.

The therapist wrote all this down, then sat back in her chair. "What you are exhibiting is what's known as *traumaphobia*. It's a fear of being injured. In your case, Julian, it's mild, but it's present."

"Does he need pills?" I asked.

Grace gripped my hand. "Whatever the treatment, we can handle it."

Constanza Garfinkle shook her head. "There's no . . . treatment for it. The only thing we suggest is exposing the patient to the stimuli causing the anxiety."

Julian asked, "So I can't quit? The cure is for me to get . . . injured?"

The therapist shook her head. "Yeah. Pretty much."

He stayed on the team, but stopped caring about it, made excuses for why he couldn't participate.

Then he just stopped altogether.

When he came out to us his senior year, I was a little surprised, yeah, maybe even bummed too. But I didn't show it. I shrugged it off, made it a point to act indifferent. When he told us he'd decided to stay in the area and attend a university on the Westside of Los Angeles, I said, "Great. You going to commute to campus then?"

"No," he told us. "I've decided to live in the dorms."

Grace started in. "You could live here, too. You father and I won't put any restrictions on you."

"Uh," Julian replied. "No offense, but I want to be independent. Experience the whole college life."

I stood. "Fine. Good. We can help pay for tuition. I mean, if that's okay with you?" I sounded a little sarcastic. I just didn't want to act in a way that made him think I was adding more pressure.

He folded his arms and glanced away. "Yeah. Yeah, that's cool. Thanks."

He was moody. Like me. Like his abuelo.

* *

During his senior year of college, Julian began getting serious with a guy named Phillip, a thin Black Panamanian with hazel eyes and curly hair. He brought the guy over one weekend. It was my birthday, and Grace had bought a cake.

"You don't remember me, do you?" The guy looked at me once they were in the house.

It took me a while, but then I pictured it. That day years before when we'd gone with Julian to help him set up his dorm room on *move-in day*. The kid was struggling to carry a duffel bag with a busted handle up the stairs, and I stopped to help him.

"Oh yeah," I said, smiling, shaking the guy's hand. "Good to see you again."

Phillip handed me a set of balloons and a bottle of tequila. He wore a pair of glasses, a striped turtleneck sweater, and dark jeans.

We'd ordered pizza from my favorite restaurant, Petro's, and Grace was in the kitchen mixing up a salad. Phillip walked around the living room, examining the baby pictures of Julian on the wall, both of them laughing. It was the first time in a while that I'd seen my son smile. He was at ease in the presence of this boy. He stood straight, rigid, his shoulders pulled back, suddenly broader. In the warm, late-afternoon sun, I realized just how tall he'd gotten, how filled-out and solid his body had become.

"Have you been working out?" I asked him.

He shrugged his shoulders. "Yeah. Some. At the gym in the rec center. We both do."

Phillip pointed to a photograph of Julian in his high school wrestling singlet and headgear. In it, he's inside the school auditorium, rows of empty bleachers behind him. He's crouches forward, arms reaching out, fingers spread.

"That was an . . . uncomfortable time," Julian replied.

Phillip turned to me. "I heard all about you and your father, Mr. V. About your lucha libre. I love lucha!"

"Really?" I asked, surprised. I grabbed three beers from the fridge and handed one to each of them. Phillip opened his and took a long swig.

"I shouldn't," Julian responded.

Phillip laughed. "Dude, it's your father's birthday. Lighten up some. Live a little!"

"Ay, he's right," I said, and we clinked the necks of our bottles together.

Julian shook his head, grabbed the bottle, and took a sip. "Happy?" He smirked at Phillip.

"Delighted," he replied.

Over salad and pizza and a few more beers, Phillip told me all about his fascination with lucha libre. He would not stop talking about it. He liked the old-school golden age fighters like Mil Mascara, Blue Demon, and, of course, El Santo.

"I didn't realize what a huge fan you were," Julian replied.

"Yeah. I love it."

We were staging a match that weekend, a fundraiser for a local homeless shelter. I had included myself in the lineup after a few weeks of not performing. When Julian was in the kitchen helping Grace with the dishes, I told Phillip they should both attend.

"My father will be there."

"I'd love that," he replied.

There were candles and birthday cake and ice cream and singing.

And my son was happy. He was whole.

* *

They were there that weekend, Phillip all excited, a big goofy smile across his face as he walked around the gym, making his way through the crowd.

"Whoa," he said when he saw me in my tights and boots and mask. "Mr. V., it's like you but not you."

Julian stood beside him, smirking. "You're such a nerd, Phil."

"Get a good spot out there. We're filling up fast."

He flipped out upon seeing my dad, snapped pictures with

him, and they sat near the ring, Phillip gesturing with his hands, Julian leaning back in his chair to talk with Grace. There were over two hundred people that day. We rolled open the back garage doors to let the air circulate, and Beto hired a DJ to come in and play some sounds as we got things ready. Everyone was in a great mood, the air electrified and pumped.

We planned on putting on a good show, and we did that day, one of our best yet. Scarlet Santos and a few of the other exoticos started us out. Kamikaze went up against a female ruda she knew who wrestled under the name Calamity. In the second round, as the fight was intensifying and the crowd was going apeshit over an illegal move by Kamikaze, Calamity executed a maneuver from the top cord of the ring and landed incorrectly, injuring her ankle. Hugo called the paramedics and the whole thing ended in a draw, upsetting the audience.

Then it was me against Volcán. We made a good team. José was one of my star pupils, having taken everything I'd taught him and put it to good use with dazzling leaps and dizzying moves that amazed everyone. He would come out the winner in this fight, leaving the door open for a rematch maybe the following week or month.

After I'd changed back into my street clothes, Julian and Phillip were in the office with Hugo. Grace had taken my father home. Phillip reached out and shook my hand.

"Mr. V. That . . . was . . . incredible!"

"Did you hear him shouting?" Julian laughed.

"You were?" I asked. "For me?"

"Hell yeah, Mr. V," he admitted. "You're my new hero."

When he was with him, Julian didn't seem to be in any kind of hurry to leave, to get away from us, me especially. He took his time, opened up, lingered, settled in. It was as if I got to know him more in those moments than I had in his entire life. We took

family trips to the beach. When I cleaned out the garage and Grace
and I held a yard sale, they came over early in the morning with
a jug of coffee and bagels and cream cheese and stayed the whole
day, until everything was sold. Phillip never missed a lucha event.
Every single weekend there was a match, he and Julian were there,
my loudest supporters. Afterwards, we'd head back to the house
and spend the evening inside, playing board games or cards and
eating pizza or burgers. Then their visits suddenly stopped almost
as quickly as they'd started. A few weeks went by without a single
visit. Finally, one day, Grace told me that they had broken up.

"Did he tell you why?" I asked.

"No. He just said they weren't dating anymore."

"Did he sound sad?"

"No, not sad. Just . . . regular, I guess. He's hard to read."

It was maybe a month after that, a slow midafternoon in late
June. Hugo took off early to spend time with one of his daughters. A few members were using the weight room, and there was a
Zumba class, so the sound of cumbia music filled the air. Beto was
running errands, picking up supplies, and José and Scarlet were
working on moves with Kamikaze in the ring. I could hear them
shouting commands over the music: *Duck; That's it, girl. Come
on; Hit, hit.* Since the air was warm and the sun bright, I'd rolled
open the back garage doors to let the breeze cut through. I was
inside the office, organizing some invoices, when I heard a light
tap on the door. I turned to see Phillip standing there.

"Hey, Mr. V," he said. "Long time, huh?"

I gave him a tight hug and we walked out to the parking lot.
A homeless man in tattered sneakers and a pair of stained shorts
picked through a bush near the rusted gate along the lot's perimeter, muttering to himself.

"That guy's always out here," I said, trying to cut the tension,
I guess.

"You're probably wondering why I stopped coming around, right?" He rubbed the sole of his shoe over the loose asphalt, the grit crunching. "Why Julian and I called it quits?"

"Yeah. I did wonder. But my wife and I didn't want to pry. Besides, I learned a long time ago that my son doesn't like me getting into his business."

The cumbia music had died down. Only the sound of jostling weights and Scarlet's and José's and Kamikaze's voices could be heard now. The homeless man kept muttering something that sounded like a nursery rhyme.

"I don't know what happened, Mr. V." He was crying, his words low and warbled. "He just . . . got so cold. What did I do?"

I reached my hand out, placed it gently on his shoulder, and kept it there. "It's okay, son. I'm sorry."

He said things were good between them. Great, in fact. He admitted that he saw himself with Julian for the long haul.

"Like the real deal, you know?" He wiped his tears and looked at me. "Is that stupid to think?"

I told him no, that when it comes to love, to true love, nothing is ever dumb or illogical. The homeless man wandered off, carrying a dirty blanket and two crushed aluminum cans in his hand. Phillip had a theory about Julian, and it was that my son was afraid of intimacy. He refused to let anyone get too close to him. He felt unworthy of letting himself be loved by another person.

"Including you, Mr. V." Phillip looked straight ahead, eyes piercing through his glasses, so razor-sharp I thought they'd melt the lenses. He was as tall as me, lean but solid, healthy. "Did you know my mother was in a bad accident some time ago?"

I didn't. Julian hadn't mentioned anything to us. "I'm sorry, son." It's the only thing I could think to say. "Is she okay?"

"Yes, thank God. My father's always been real stern, and he's only gotten worse since her accident." He shook his head. "I was hoping Julian would want to make a go of us, but it's clear he has other plans that don't include me. I have no other choice but to go back home."

I wished there was something I could do. And I knew that this was about more than just his father and my child, about the bond between people and families and the devastating things we do because we're too afraid to let ourselves experience loss and longing and even love. I let him unload. If my own son wouldn't open up to me, I could at least be here for this boy, another man's child. A stand-in. A surrogate father.

"I told Julian he was lucky to have you," he admitted. "That I would have given anything to call you my dad."

We stood there for a while, the silence interrupted only by the sound of grunts and shouts coming from inside the gym. I didn't try to break it by saying something stupid, by apologizing for Julian's behavior. *Phillip needs this*, I told myself. *The kid needs me to just stand here beside him near these tracks, below the overpass where people travel back and forth. All this movement around us. Nobody bothering to stop.*

We walked to his car, hugged, and patted each other on the back. I said to please keep in touch. He promised me he would.

* *

It's been a few years, and we send one another scattered emails here and there; sports news about MMA fighters and, of course, any updates on the latest having to do with lucha libre. It was his enthusiasm, his openness, his willingness to be vulnerable and speak from his heart that I appreciated most about Phillip. With him, I could let my guard down too, could stop pretending to be the kind of father my son makes me out to be—stubborn, indifferent, unsupportive. That's not me. Phillip could see this. Why couldn't my own damn flesh and blood?

The cholos finish their workout. Before they leave, the one with the tattoo above his face asks if I'll be open tomorrow.

I shrug. "I'll be here. Yeah."

"Cool." He nods, points to his friend lingering outside, just beyond the main doors. "Because the vatos from my car club are looking for a place to come and pump iron that isn't, like, one of those big-ass fucking chains. We need a serious gym."

I nod. "Sounds great, man."

We shake hands as I walk him to the door.

"Name's Louie," he says. "But everyone calls me Rascal. And that's Sonny."

The friend waves at me. "You got a firmé place here, dude. We'll be back with our whole fucking crew."

We're still needed, I think, as they hop into their lowrider and pull out of the lot. *This fucking fight ain't over yet.*

El Rey Coyote

It's not that Ernesto didn't care about you, señora. ¡No, claro que no!

It's that he never knew how to show love.

To you or Julián or anyone.

Chingado. Not even his children.

Just look what he put them through after you died. Quitting his job like that, opening the gym all so he could, what? Try re-creating his former glory?

Now I'm all for saying, FUCK IT, CABRONES. I'M GOING TO DO LO QUE ME DA LA CHINGADA MADRE. I'm all for following your dreams, for going out there and making the life you want.

But you gotta weigh the risks, you gotta take your time to think it through, to consider the pros and cons, as the gabachos like to say.

But Ernesto? Too impulsive. Never thinking.

And look now what Alfredo is having to do?

He's left having to pick up the pieces, to deal with all the mayhem.

¡Qué bárbaro!

JULIAN VEGA

I finally get a text from Tim. I'm to meet a client the next evening. He sends me a picture of the guy—handsome, buzzed head, white, late fifties.

He's seen you, Tim writes. *I sent him some pictures and details. He knows you're not opposed to kink. Bondage, costumes, light S&M, but nothing too rough or dangerous. He's familiar with our rules.*

Great. How do I proceed?

Make the initial contact. See how it goes. Report back. Name's Clay.

Then he texts me the address to a bar downtown.

The place is at the very top of a high-rise building, and the hostess seats me at a table with a view of the entire city below—huge gleaming towers lit up like giant circuit boards, red and white colored lines of traffic wrapping and snaking around the streets and skyscrapers, the sounds of honks and sirens in the distance, faint as a whisper.

I order water and sip it slowly, taking in the chatter from the handful of people around the bar and lounge area. Servers carry baskets of bread on trays, and the giant television bolted to the wall behind the bar is showing a soccer match, but nobody is watching. A little before seven he shows up. He's in boat shorts and leather sandals. Way too casual for this place, but it doesn't seem to faze him; he circles the place like he owns it, then notices me and walks over. We shake, and he orders a beer from the server and asks him to get me whatever I want. I order a beer too.

"Let's hear about you, Julian." He sips his lager. Clay wears a bright smile that's unnerving, his big green eyes staring at me from behind a pair of wire-rimmed glasses.

I shrug. "Not much to tell. I have a master's degree, teach English Composition. I like to read."

"Nobody reads anymore."

"I do." I scan the bar, trying my best to avert his gaze. "And you?"

He says ever since he could remember, he liked assembling things. It started with wooden blocks, then Legos, then something called an Erector Set. "My father was an architect. We used to build model airplanes and battleships together. That sort of thing, so I became an architect too. What about your folks?"

"My mother's a cashier at a grocery store. My father's a wrestler. So was my grandfather."

"Like WWE Smackdown?"

I shake my head. "No. Lucha libre."

He tilts his head.

"The guys with the masks?"

He snaps his fingers. "Oh. Like that movie *Nacho Libre*. What were they called? They all have, like, crazy names, right?"

"My grandfather was El Rey Coyote, and my father is El Rey Coyote Jr."

"Did you wrestle too?" He takes a long, slow look at my biceps. "You have a great body. Another?" he asks when the server comes to take our beer glasses away. "On me."

Before I can reply, he commands the waiter to bring us two more.

I switch the subject, ask what kind of guys he likes.

He sits back in his chair, tugs on a chain around his neck and rattles off qualities. They must be drug free. They must have some brains. "I'm not talking Einstein or anything." He laughs. "But be smart enough to hold a conversation." He's new to the whole escort service scene, but he had a few friends who've used them. "They persuaded me to give it a shot. I'm tired of trying to meet up with guys through apps. Too many weirdos. Too many partiers. Don't know what you'll catch."

Then he leans in and whispers that he has these elaborate fantasies.

"Sounds creative." I finish my beer.

"I want a guy with a gritty edge to him," he explains. "But not too gritty. I want a dangerous guy but not *too* dangerous. A homie type who dresses the part. And I like them uncut and of a certain size. Eight or above."

I nod, say nothing. Our server returns with the check, and Clay reaches for his wallet. When I hand over my last ten-dollar bill, he insists on paying. He rises and wipes his mouth with a crumpled napkin.

"It was nice meeting you, Julian. I had a lovely time. I'll be in touch."

"Cool," I say. "Yeah."

Clay turns and walks out of the bar.

That's it. No taking me back to a hotel room. No bullshit small talk before undressing and rolling around naked between the smooth, cool bedsheets.

He just gets up and goes.

* *

The next day there's a text message from Tim:

C says he had a nice time. Requesting you at his place this after-noon. 2 pm. Don't be late.

* *

All the houses in Hancock Park are massive and ornate, with exteriors as elaborate as wedding cakes. Compared to richer neighborhoods like Beverly Hills and Bel Air, it's not that big and not separated from the city by canyons or winding streets. It's right in the middle of Hollywood, just south of Melrose Avenue. Clay's street is flanked on either side by beautiful mansions secured behind large iron gates, or obscured from the street by tall, perfectly trimmed hedges. The stone trail leading up to his place is shaded on either side by a set of mature jacarandas. I come to the entrance of the house, descending a set of steps, and pass through a little courtyard towards a wooden door painted bright red. I'm about to knock when I see a note:

Julian, please come in.

I push the door open and find myself inside a large, dimly lit living room. Oversized pieces of furniture are grouped around a brick fireplace above which hangs a painting, an abstract piece composed of geometric patterns smashing against one another. I shout a few times, taking gentle, cautious steps farther inside the house. To my left is a winding staircase that curves upward to the second floor. A chandelier hangs above an arched entryway across from the living room. Just beyond this, I can make out a dining table with a centerpiece of fresh flowers. Heavy drapes decorate the windows. Somewhere there's soft music playing. Something classical. Bach's "Air on the G String."

"Clay?"

No reply.

Black khaki pants and a plaid shirt are carefully arranged on top of a coffee table. A pair of white Nike Cortezes, like the ones my father and his friends wore back in high school, sit on the floor next to some white boxers and rolled-up tube socks with red and blue stripes. I find another note with further instructions:

> *Please put this on, including the shoes, underwear, and socks.*
> *Then come upstairs.*

"Okay, dude," I say to no one in particular.

I change into the clothes, lacing up the shoes and tying them as quickly as I can. They fit perfectly. In fact, everything's right. The jeans are baggy on me, but the waist and length are fine. The shirt's a little long, but otherwise okay. On the stair's banister, there's another handwritten note:

> *Come up. Creep down the hall.*
> *Like you're an intruder robbing my house.*

"Okay," I whisper. "Coming up."

Yet another note on a small side table at the top of the staircase:

> *Pick up the bat.*

What fucking bat? I look around and, sure enough, there it is, propped up against the wall. Still another note, this one taped to the bat's neck:

> *Walk slowly down the hall towards the oil painting.*
> *Hold the bat tightly. At the end of the hall, you'll find a room.*
> *Go inside.*

I take very careful steps, walking past closed doors. I peek inside a bathroom with aquamarine tiles and an old-fashioned toilet with the septic tank above the seat and a metal chain you pull to flush. The door to the room is slightly ajar. There's a bed with two pillows, a nightstand, and an oversized lamp. I hear rustling, shifting, and walk over to a closet door. I turn the knob a few times, but it's locked. After a few more attempts, it gives. Clay stands there in a pair of white briefs and nothing more. He clutches a wad of money.

"Here. Take it. Just don't hurt me. Please." He shoves the money in my hand.

"What are you talking about? I'm not here to hurt you."

Clay rolls his eyes. "Play along."

I get it now and lift the bat. He composes himself. "The money's yours," he says now, in full character. "Take it." He steps out of the closet and removes his underwear.

I shove the money in my pocket, reach out, and pull him by the back of the head. He falls to the ground, kneeling.

I unzip my pants, and he goes to work on me. I undress and throw him down on the bed. When I start taking my socks off, he stops me, says I'm to keep them on. We play like that for a while before I push myself inside of him, shouting obscenities. He grunts and takes deep sniffs from a bottle of poppers he pulls out from underneath the pillows on the bed.

When I finish, I rise and tell him, "You better not tell anybody I was here, ese. I know where you live now, cabrón. If you call the cops, I'll fucking kill you."

Then I run downstairs, change into my own clothes, and bolt out the door without turning back.

ERNESTO VEGA

The SNM remained a solid group and grew at a steady pace. Franco and Avila said I had heart, courage, and imagination.

"All the makings of a big lucha libre star," they assured me.

At the start of 1970, a photographer and reporter from *Box y Lucha* spent a few days around the gym and the arena. He snapped photos of me suspended in the air as I performed my signature *Chillido Coyote*, as I pinned rudos down, as I stared at my masked reflection in a mirror. *El Rey Coyote*, the tagline read, *the técnico who can fly*. And below this was a quote from me: *It is my duty, my destiny, to help the less fortunate. This is what I was put here to do.*

When printed, the spread was impressive. Not only did it show me in the ring fighting off bad guys, in the gym training, or jogging through the park, but they also came to our apartment and captured images of me and Elena sitting out on the patio smoking cigarettes, lying in bed reading, her in the kitchen stirring a pot of caldo, holding the spoon up as I tasted it. Franco and Avila gave me strict orders to never remove my mask in front of the reporter or photographer.

One weekend, I convinced Elena to let me invite Julián over so we could listen to music and play cards. He took the *Box y Lucha* issue with the big article about me, slumped down in the armchair, and flipped through it with such force I thought he'd rip the pages.

"You both look good. Happy," he said.

"Thanks."

Elena sat on the couch beside me just staring at him. "¿Pero que te pico?" she asked, her tone sharp, bitter.

Julián ignored her question, though. He stopped at a page, his eyes catching something written there. "This says Franco and Avila are your managers." He slammed the magazine shut and slid it across the table to me. "You didn't even notice, did you?"

"I'm sure it's just a mistake," I explained. "Calm down. Why does it matter anyway?" I tried shrugging it off. "I'm still paying you, aren't I? All that money. It goes back to your family in La Peña, right? Who cares if the papers call them my managers and not you?"

Julián grabbed his coat, then rose from the chair. "I guess."

"Don't be irrational," I pleaded. "Sit down, mano."

Elena lit a cigarette. "Let him go." She blew a long thread of smoke across the room. "No vale la pena."

"Elena, please," I replied. Then I turned to Julián. "Mano, come on. Let's sit, have some beers and play cards, yes?"

But it was too late. He stormed out.

Elena lit another cigarette.

Elena Vega

I'll admit that I knew why he was angry. Yes, it might seem cruel that I said what I did that day, that my only reason was to drive a wedge between the two of you. But what did you expect? I was so tired of the charades, of feeling like I was sharing you with him.

I thought you'd be grateful. I thought maybe now you'd see how selfish and irrational Julián was. Instead, you were angry with me the rest of the day and into the night. You moped. You refused to eat dinner. You slept on the couch.

My own husband was starting to see me as his enemy. Resenting me.

FREDDY VEGA

Once the cholos are gone, I find myself standing in front of the case where my father's lucha outfit is displayed. We lost the key a long time ago, so I pick the lock to get inside. Even now, years after he last wore it, I handle it with the same care as I did their wedding photo Grace taped next to his bed in the hospice.

For almost three months. He's been in that condition for three fucking months. How much time does he have left?

The cape's fabric is frail, musty. Random clumps of fur are what's left of the collar's lining, balled up and spotted. A coyote with mange.

Maybe if I'd paid attention sooner, taken the warning signs a more seriously, this all could have been avoided.

* *

It started around 2016 with little things we chalked up to random shit that happens to all old people. Injuries and falls here and there. His stride became uncoordinated. He began to slur. We thought he might have had a minor stroke. One time, while trying to cut an avocado in half, he nearly sliced his finger off. He started having a hard time swallowing food. One of Grace's close friends named Alma is a nurse, and she told us we needed to start cutting up his meals. No bread or apples.

"He could choke," she explained.

"Why's this happening?" I asked.

"He's getting old. It's like a car when the electrical system starts to go. Wires get . . . crossed. Frayed. Things just short out. The same thing happened to my grandmother. I'm not a doctor, though."

The one doctor we could afford had an office sandwiched between a smoke shop and a nail salon in a run-down strip mall on Soto. He prescribed meds to help stabilize his moods, to help him sleep, but that was it. Even though he lived close to us, I'd always worry something might happen. He could climb out of bed in the middle of the night or leave the oven on.

"It's getting dangerous for him in that house by himself," Grace said.

"So, we move him in here with us? I work. You work. He'll be alone all day. Same difference."

"Alma says we should look into nursing homes."

"Fuck that," I replied. "I'm not sticking him in one of those places. We're not white folks, Grace."

I wouldn't hear of it.

Then, one day, he almost burned down the house by catching a palm tree on fire. Grace had bought a tres leches cake, and we were about to head out the door with a six-pack of beer and steaks to pop on the grill when my cell phone buzzed. It was his neighbor Tammy Bowers. I told her about the cake, said she and her little boy Caleb should come over, when she interrupted to say there was smoke coming from my father's place.

"It's probably from the grill," I told Grace as we made the short drive over. "Tammy's always been overdramatic. Ever since we were kids." I laughed, remembered her rail thin, with stringy blond hair and a mouth full of metal.

Ten minutes later we pulled into the driveway. As Grace went for the groceries and cake, I noticed puffs of smoke rising from the backyard. Tammy busted out from the side gate, arms flailing, in a pair of bright pink shorts, sandals, and a white blouse smeared with black soot.

"He caught the palm on fire! He's back there swatting at the flames with a blanket. Go help before it spreads!" She then ran across the street towards her place. "I already called the fire department."

In the backyard, charcoal briquettes were strewn across the patio. The AM/FM radio my mother used to listen to while she gardened was on with the volume turned way up, cumbia music thumping from the speakers. The screen door was wide open, giving me a clear view of the kitchen. The faucet was running, the sink overflowing. My father stood before the palm tree, dousing the trunk with water, circling the thing as if it were prey. He wore his frayed bathrobe, and his arms and face were smeared with ash. He resembled a warrior, someone about to go into battle.

"Dad?" I said over the blaring music. "What the hell happened?"

Grace set the groceries down and turned the radio off.

"I don't know," he said. "I squirted the charcoal with the lighter fluid, lit a match, then *whoosh*. Next thing I know, the whole damn thing's on fire."

The plumes of dark, acrid smoke gave way to flames climbing up the tree trunk, heading quickly towards the top. "Let's step away." I grabbed his shoulder, but he ignored me. I could hear sirens approaching.

"Ernesto," Grace said, trying to stay calm, "listen to Freddy. The firemen are coming. They'll put it out."

"I can stop it." He turned to look at me. His nose was runny, his eyes red and watery. "Your mother and I . . . we planted that palm. I can stop it."

Grace ran off towards the street, shouting at the fire crew. "Back here!" I could hear her shouting. "Back here!"

The flames were growing now. They were a rich red, and I could feel the warmth on my hands and arms. I tried not to, but I imagined my childhood home being consumed by all those flames, my family's history reduced to piles of soot. Across the lawn, Grace was leading the firemen into the yard. Behind them, two EMTs wheeled a gurney. At the sight of this, my father flipped out. I gripped his arm tight, and that was when he balled up his fist and punched me in the face. His aim was precise, and the hit landed on me with so much force that I lost balance and fell on the wet grass. On my back, I could see the spiky palm fronds above me, all lit up, roaring, brilliant and terrifying, whipping in the wind like large fiery lassos against a clear blue sky, so blue it looked iridescent, no ripples tearing across its surface. There was sky. Only sky. Vast and wide with possibility.

I knew then as I do now that men like my father, men like me . . . we aren't meant to walk in this world for very long. And if we aren't quick and alert, always with our guard up, our ends are tragic.

El Rey Coyote

I know you're shutting down now, slowly but steadily. I can hear the thumping of your heart growing fainter and fainter. I can see inside your body. This will end soon.

What will you carry with you, Ernesto, when you transition to the other realm?

These memories and realizations?

These voices that loved and complicated you?

The things you never let in?

Everything you resisted?

JULIAN VEGA

We never officially called ourselves a couple. It just happened. One moment we were close friends and the next we're making out and having sex. By senior year I thought a trip home to meet and visit my family would be good. I don't know why I did it. There was still so much apprehension I had around what was developing between us.

My father's and Abuelo's legacies as luchadores fascinated Phillip. He couldn't get enough of the stories I told him about what it was like growing up in my house surrounded by so much history. Truth be told, in some way, his obsession with their wrestling careers helped me better understand them. His interest in their work instilled in me a newfound pride.

It was my father's birthday. We brought him some cheesy balloons and paid one of Brian's frat buddies to score a bottle of Patrón for us. The whole way there, he fiddled with the bow we'd glued to the top.

"And he drinks, right?"

I rolled my eyes. "For the hundredth time, yes, Phillip."

"You don't think showing up with liquor will send, like, the wrong message? I mean, we aren't even twenty-one."

"He's no saint," I assured him as we pulled up to the house.

"It must have been so cool to be around all of this," he said that evening to me and my parents. Then he turned to my father. "Mr. Vega, luchadores are like superheroes to me."

I could still remember my dad's face, how he beamed with pride at Phillip's admiration. I wasn't jealous.

"I want to thank you properly," he told my father. "That day in the stairwell. When you helped me. I was feeling so lost and alone."

My father reached across the table and gripped his shoulder. "Anytime." Then he looked over at me. "I'm glad the two of you found each other and are happy together."

It was . . . weird. I'd never seen my father be so accepting.

In the kitchen, as we were washing the dishes and cleaning up, my mother patted me on the back, told me we made a cute couple. "He seems smart, levelheaded."

"He is," I replied as I dried the stack of plates and placed them back in the cupboard.

He was sitting at the dining table, elbows resting on the place mat, a wide smile across his face as my father told him about all the birthday parties they'd held for me at the gym, how he and the guys would dress up for my friends and stage bouts.

Philip said, "He must have been the most popular kid at school."

My father nodded, folded his arms across his chest. "Yeah. Something like that."

He was lying though.

* *

My dad had invited us to a lucha match the gym would be putting on the following weekend, Phillip informed me. "He said your abuelo will be there. I can't wait to meet him, man. A real-life legend of lucha libre."

The whole thing was billed as a fundraiser; all the proceeds would be going to help a downtown homeless shelter just a few blocks away. News vans were covering the event, and a few food vendors had set up stalls in the parking lot, grills already hot and smoking by the time we arrived. There were taco trucks and a man selling raspados and aguas frescas, another frying churros, the scent of warm cinnamon mixing with hot asphalt and car exhaust. They'd rented an inflatable bounce house in the shape of a castle. Kids jumped around inside, worried parents circling the thing like predators. A DJ was spinning tunes—mainly cumbia and norteño sounds—and a few couples were dancing around. We found my parents leaning against the hood of a red Nissan.

My mom gave us each a tight embrace and shouted over the music, "Isn't this something?"

Phillip beamed. "It's great."

He was swaying his hips, and my mother noticed. She reached her hand out to him. "Come on."

He looked at me and then my father, who replied, "Go for it. I need to head inside and start getting ready for my match."

Phillip was good on his feet, and my mother threw her head back and laughed at something he said. They zigzagged among the handful of other couples in the clearing next to the DJ. A set of large speakers rested atop a folding table, and strobe lights flashed on and off.

Before we walked into the gym, my mother told us that my grandfather wasn't in the right frame of mind. His thoughts, she went on, had started getting . . . jumbled, mixed up.

"Don't be confused if he says some strange things, okay?" she added.

We found Abuelo Ernesto standing at the entrance next to the case displaying his lucha outfit. He was talking to a reporter from one of the Spanish-language channels. The woman with auburn hair held a microphone towards Abuelo's mouth and nodded at something he was explaining as he gestured emphatically with his hands. A man stood behind the reporter, a camera perched on his shoulder, its light shining on my grandfather.

Abuelo looked good. He sported a white guayabera ironed smooth and a tan Panama hat with a black band. He removed it, fanning himself, as he finished the interview and walked over.

"That light is so hot," he said, placing the hat back on. "You look good, Julián."

He always pronounced my name the way they did in the Spanish-language novelas my parents sometimes watched. Abuelo eyed Phillip and nodded.

"Es un gran honor, señor Vega. Soy Phillip Cordova," he said. They shook hands. "El gusto es mio, joven."

My mother said to Abuelo, "They go to the same university."

"Qué bien."

"I'm from Panama," Phillip told him. "Like your hat."

"Si. But I bought this from a Cubano street vendor on Brooklyn Avenue who sets up right in front of a Vietnamese restaurant every day except Sunday."

Ever since the name was changed back in 1994, Abuelo refused to call the street Avenida César Chávez. To him and to my parents, it remained Brooklyn Avenue.

As we made our way towards the main exercise room of the gym, Phillip went on and on, talking a mile a minute to Abuelo of how he grew up watching matches when he was a boy.

Abuelo stopped abruptly, looked at us, a puzzled expression on his face, and said, "Julián? Is this the man you told me about? The one you were in love with?"

We glanced at each other, an awkward silence between us.

My mother took him by the arm. "Why don't we find a good spot, okay?"

We grabbed seats, Abuelo sandwiched between me and Phillip, my mother directly behind me.

She leaned forward and said, "He's on this new medication. It messes with his thoughts. Turns things a little foggy."

I nodded, focused on the people milling about, filling up the chairs around us, the music outside fading as the hour of the first match neared. Phillip was grinning ear to ear. Now and again, he'd lean in, whisper things to Abuelo, who would nod, say, *Yes, yes, exactly. You know a lot about lucha, eh?*

The first match featured two new exoticos my father and the rest of the crew were training. The rudo was named May Flores. May was massive, all muscle bulging out of a pair of electric-green tights, a wide chest oiled and slick as serpent skin. They wore gray boots with soles so thick they were more platforms. May strutted into the room sporting a silver tiara that rested crookedly on their head, a long mane of bright red hair bouncing and swaying. The crowd booed, and May shouted curses and obscenities at them.

Abuelo shook his head. "Ay, Julián," he said to me, chuckling. "Remember when you took me to that place in the capital? The men in the dresses dancing? Rogelio snapped our picture. You were in those tight slacks. So sexy."

My mom leaned forward. "Ernesto, calma, okay?"

The técnico who was challenging May Flores for the tiara was named Santa Monica, and they were a sight decked out in a long silver cape fashioned with gold studs that sparkled under the fluorescent lighting. May held a bouquet of white roses and tossed stems out to the crowd.

Santa stopped near us and handed a flower to my mother. "Para la señora."

"Gracias," she replied. "Ay, Victor. You are too much!"

Santa Monica's outfit beneath the long robe was a white leotard decorated with silver and white sequins, and a pair of red latex boots. Santa wore blue eyeshadow and red lipstick, mascara, thick eyeliner, and blush. Their black hair was curled and pulled back by a thick headband on which was written the word *chingona*. Seeing this, Phillip laughed and clapped his hands.

"Awesome," he shouted. "Real chingona."

In the middle of the second round, the crowd went ballistic when, holding them in a headlock, Santa Monica ripped May's wig off. Santa Monica ran around the ring with it as May chased them. Then Santa flung it out into the crowd, and a handful of children in the audience screamed and scurried away when it tumbled to the floor near them.

Santa won the fight, and there to present them with a new crown was Scarlet Santos, my godmother and the first exotico my father hired back in the years before I was born. Scarlet had instituted the competition to support and encourage a new crop of exoticos and to raise awareness of the dangers of *la homofobia* in our community. Scarlet glanced over, saw me there in the crowd sitting next to Abuelo, and blew me a kiss. They were in full drag—decked out in a red dress and high heels, a gold shawl wrapped around his shoulders.

In the second match between a rudo named Marco el Narco, a burly guy in a pair of cowboy boots and a black mask over his face, and a técnico named Danny Dodger who sported our city's baseball team colors of dark blue and white, the fight spilled out into the audience, sending some of the spectators running and shouting. As the crowd parted, I could see Marco lying on his stomach. Someone gasped as he staggered to get up, mask ripped off, revealing the left side of his face. The Spanish-language news reporter who'd been interviewing Abuelo ran up to the mayhem, the cameraman behind her. I heard her ask him, "Did you get that?"

Marco swayed back and forth, his knees buckling a few times, while Danny circled the inside of the ring, taunting him. "Come on," he shouted. "I'm just getting started, punk."

"Was that for real?" Phillip asked after the match ended in a draw.

"What do you think?" my mother responded.

He looked over at me. I shrugged my shoulders and stayed quiet, knowing that so much of it was always carefully orchestrated.

"I mean, I think I saw blood," he said, astonished. "I've only experienced this on television. Never in real life."

"They're playing up to the cameras, hombre," Abuelo insisted as the crowd calmed. "That's all. It's nothing serious."

He bent down, rolled up his left pant leg, and pointed to his shin. His leg was thin, very tan, dotted with dark moles and nubby skin tags that looked like raisins. "You see this?" He tapped my shoulder, grabbed Phillip by the forearm, and we looked to see a misshapen lump beneath his taut flesh.

"Ernesto," my mom protested, "don't do that."

Phillip whistled. "What happened?"

"Nerve damage," he said. "Messes the brain up, too." Then he shouted, "The other day, I didn't make it to the toilet in time and pissed my pants right there in the kitchen!"

A group of girls standing nearby heard this and laughed.

My mother rose, walked around, and stood before him. "Let's go outside, yeah? Get some air? It's too stuffy in here."

Abuelo glanced up at her and smiled. As my mother helped him stand, he turned to me. "Julián. I remember now. The rocks. We swam naked and kissed. I loved you more."

He reached out and caressed my face. I looked over to my mom and Phillip, confused.

"Yes," I replied. "I love you too, Abuelo."

Just as suddenly, he let me go. "I want a churro."

"Okay. Let's go find one." My mother led him away.

After they left, Phillip and I sat. "Those meds can really mess with your mind."

I just nodded.

They hadn't returned by the time the final match started. My father, as El Rey Coyote Jr., and José Madrigal, el Volcán, were going up against two rudos named Sangre Negra and Baby Satan. The best was saved for last. These two rudos moved with style and skill, leaping and kicking and somersaulting all around the ring. And my father and José were at top form, executing choke holds, cradles, pile drives, and suicides with elegant accuracy. Things got messy at the top of the final round when Sangre Negra flung my father out of the ring by executing a fly kick to his abdomen. When Volcán managed to do the same to Baby Satan, Baby Satan took one of the folding chairs leaning against the wall, lifted it over his head, and slammed it against my father's back.

"Oh, shit!" Phillip shouted, rising from his seat as we watched my father fall to the ground.

"Relax," I said. "It's okay. Sit down."

He ignored me though and remained standing, hands balled into fists as though he was about to jump into the fray and protect my dad. "He's not getting up, man."

"He will," I replied. "My father always gets up."

And he did. My father. He rose, shook the pain away, jumped back into the ring, and alongside his friend and companion, they kicked some serious ass, the crowd gasping, unmoving as they witnessed the flurry of leaps and jumps, the swirling colors and lights, those men doing such incredible things, things no mortal was ever expected to do.

ERNESTO VEGA

You get used to it quickly. Especially if you grew up with very little. The money afforded us a good life. There was new furniture, a color television set, rugs, a wooden dining table, a brand-new Impala with bucket seats and a cigarette lighter. There were suits for me and nice dresses for Elena. Whatever we couldn't immediately pay for, we purchased on credit, made payments as we went along. Trust was built. Then there was more credit. There were more loans. There were charities, too. Hospitals that helped poor children. Schools that needed books and supplies.

"They all love you," Julián said after a weekend bout where I went up against a rudo named Tacuache Rojo, a mean son of a bitch with massive legs and a lethal dropkick. My shoulder was throbbing from a pin down on the mat, and as we left the gimnasio, I was cringing from the pain, my face beaded with sweat.

"Love hurts un chingo," I replied.

Julián wanted to go out that night for drinks, but I didn't know how to tell him I was afraid Elena would be upset. The last time, after my big debut, she didn't speak to me for several days. Part of me didn't blame her. I'd come home so drunk, had acted so brutish in bed with her. It was getting tougher and tougher to keep them both happy. I was so tired from the bout, in so much pain that I couldn't think straight, so I gave in to his pleas. I'd have to face her wrath later that evening at home.

* *

Elena sat in front of the television watching the news. We'd finished our dinner, and it was still early. I stood and grabbed my jacket. "I'm going out."

"But your shoulder."

"It's better."

"Mentiroso. Tell me the truth, Ernesto."

"I'm telling you, I'm fine. Stop pestering me."

"You're seeing him again, aren't you?"

The lie came so easy because I was so exhausted bouncing back and forth between the two and their rivalry. She wouldn't know. It was only one damned night anyway. "No. Some of the other guys from the sindicato invited me out for cards and dominos. I won't be late."

* *

I let him take me wherever he wanted to go. So we went back there, to that same dark cantina with the men who danced with one another. This time it was busier. More patrons hanging around the bar, sipping rum or tequila, smoking cigarettes and gossiping.

Rogelio was there again. "Que gusto ver a los dos." He poured us two drinks, and we found a booth and sat, Julián sliding in very close to me, his thigh pressed against mine. Music was playing from the jukebox, the high-pitched voice of a woman singing in English. A song called "Angel Baby."

"We are fools, Elena and I." He laughed.

"What do you mean?"

He took a sip of his drink. "We both . . . want you. Yet we know you'll never fully be ours alone."

Then I placed my hand behind his neck, brought his face close to mine. Under the dim, smoky light of that club, I kissed him on the mouth, his warm tongue twisting against mine, the stubble from my chin rubbing over his soft cheek, his beautiful and pure and unscarred skin. We hugged and closed our eyes and kissed more, only stopping when Rogelio approached, holding what looked like a big white box. He brought it up to his eye.

"Una foto de los amantes," he said.

Julián placed his arm around my sore shoulder. I reached for his thigh underneath the table and squeezed it hard. Rogelio pushed a red button and then there was a flash and snap, then the black glossy tongue of the instant photo slid out from the narrow slit of the camera. He peeled back the silver strip of film, and beneath it there we were, embracing each other.

Present and in full color.

Rogelio handed me the Polaroid, and I placed it in the pocket of my jacket. Then Julián turned to me. "Let's leave. Just us."

Apparently, he thought it all through. We could board a bus to Tijuana and find work, save up enough to cross into the United States.

"But you said it was pointless, remember?" I replied.

"Things have changed, hermano. We could go. Tonight even. From here."

"And Elena? You think I should just . . . abandon her?"

"Tell her to go back to La Peña, to wait for you there. Then you and I will—"

"Will what?" I interjected. "Be husband and wife?" I laughed. "Listen to yourself, hermano. What do you think?" I pointed to the men dancing with one another, some in skirts and high heels, tissues padded against their chests meant to resemble breasts. "Do you think we can live like this? Two men?"

"I've heard of couples in el Norte, yes. In Los Angeles, Chicago, Nueva York."

"Julián, no. I can't. I won't."

"Why not?" he insisted.

"Because I'm not some pinche maricón like you, okay?" I shouted. A few of the couples on the dance floor heard and turned their gazes towards us. The room grew silent. Someone cleared their throat.

I rose, and he reached for my hand.

"Ernesto, stay. Forget about what I suggested," he pleaded. "I don't know. I think it was . . . the copas . . . they got to me. Stay. Andale."

But I'd already made up my mind. "It's late. I should get back to my house, back to my mujer."

I never set foot in that pit of a cantina again.

Elena Vega

You were gone a lot, Ernesto, and I was always alone. I suddenly missed La Peña. My friends. The life we'd left. I watched television, sewed, read books and newspapers. I took long strolls around the neighborhood, but I still felt empty, abandoned. Did you want me to find the photo of the two of you from that night when you lied, when you said you wouldn't be seeing him? Is that why you left it in the drawer, only half hidden beneath a pile of your underwear? It wasn't how close the two of you were sitting that got me, or the way Julián's arm was wrapped around your shoulder or even your hand resting on his thigh. It was how he stared into the camera. His eyes were fixed on something far bigger, something beyond me. My glance in photos always held something inside, always kept something back. But his glowed with adoration. Pure devotion. And it did something my vision never could: it was looking forward with promise.

I knew then that I was being erased.

FREDDY VEGA

I saw this shit coming. I ignored it because I didn't want to face the fact that the city I was living in, the streets that had shaped me, that had seeped into my blood and my bones, was changing, that it no longer needed people like me occupying so much space.

When the world started up again, I thought the worst of it was past us. I opened the gym, I rolled up my sleeves, took a deep breath, and waited for people to start coming in.

Except no one did. They'd all just . . . moved on.

Then wealthy investors started buying up the buildings and stores around here and demolished them in seconds. Soon after, signs went up. *Luxury lofts. New cafés and restaurants. Live, shop, and eat near downtown Los Angeles.*

A renaissance, the paper called it as people returned from the suburbs, from those wide streets with big-ass neighborhood parks, from those houses that look identical, all of them with their travertine tiles and granite countertops, their stucco exteriors each colored a different shade of tan. They came back to the city they'd abandoned, a city of filthy liquor stores and gas stations, carnicerias and taquerias, old warehouses with busted windows and rusty chain-link fences. They returned like triumphant heroes, bringing with them their organic grocery stores and teashops, art galleries and microbreweries.

And those of us who were here all along, those of us who had waged battles both inside and out of the ring, dodging bullets and drug dealers, hookers and civil unrest, those of us who cared enough to stay and fight, we suddenly found ourselves being pushed out. Again. There were more and more homeless people setting up encampments on freeway overpasses, median strips, under trees, behind dumpsters, in parks. Everywhere there were blue tarps strung together, shopping carts stuffed with rags and glass bottles of empty Modelo beer, dilapidated vans, and RVs with blacked-out windows stationed in empty lots.

All around us, people were hurting, had been hurting.

And these fools just fucking waltzed right back in like no time had passed, picking up right where they left off with no regard for us.

El Rey Coyote

Let me tell you what happened to him because of your actions, Ernesto. He fell apart. Wasted his days drinking at the cantinas and bars throughout the city, fornicating with strange men who only left him feeling emptier and more hopeless, men who only intensified the void you left behind when you abandoned him.

JULIAN VEGA

I spent the day at my parents' house, helping my mom rummage through the boxes of Abuelo's things my dad had brought over from the gym. There's his máscara, which I folded in tissue paper and secretly slipped in my bag. More articles. More photographs. A lot of him with Abuela. But then there he was again with that same man I'd noticed him with in other pictures. The lanky dude with the long curly hair and thick handlebar mustache. Gold chains around his neck. In one picture, they sit at a table inside a dim bar, just the two of them. He has his arm around Abuelo's shoulder. His black hair looks freshly trimmed, so neat each groove of the comb's teeth visible, so straight they look drawn on. Flecks of black stubble pepper his chin. Underneath the surface of the table. Clear as can be. Abuelo's right hand is cupping the man's inner thigh.

"Who's this?" I asked my mother.

She was sitting in front of the computer. She took the photo, examined it. "I don't know. Ask your dad."

He was out running errands, and I was doing my best to avoid him at that moment, so I used my phone to snap the image because I knew he'd be furious if I took it. There was something about it, something about Abuelo's hand, about the way that man was smiling that pulled me in, that kept me looking at it for hours after first finding it.

* *

My mind's always on all the bills I have left to pay. Clay's re-quested me a couple more times since our first meet-up. *I'm lucky*, I think, rounding a corner and watching the sun set behind the hills as I make my way through Highland Park, past shops and restaurants and vendors selling flowers and produce along the median strips.

I have a job. I have my own place. Small and shitty as it is, it's something, and I don't share it with anyone else. I'm not living in my car like so many people. The sun has sunk farther down into the sky, turning the light in my bedroom a dusty rose, and I'm drowsy. I think of Abuelo. His hand on the thigh of that strange man. How it just lingered there.

Unashamed and intentional.

Almost like he wanted someone to notice.

I take a hot shower. When I close my eyes, I imagine Clay, for some reason. These white homos playing twisted games, living out demented fantasies about guys like me, about brown bodies like mine. Their giant homes with so many rooms you could get lost. Shelves lined with books. More money than sense. I'm drying off when there's an alert on my phone. A transfer of funds into my Cashco app along with three emoticons: a smirking devil, a wad of money with a pair of wings, and a tiara.

Even though I just left, my mother messages me. She sounds worried, exhausted, pained by something. My father's direction-less, she says. When he's not clearing out stuff at the gym, he spends all his time tinkering with things in the backyard shed or on the internet, worrying about the future. *Anyway, I just wanted to tell you that you should spend more time with him, okay? It would do him so much good. Okay, I love you. Bye.*

I want to call back, tell her he needs to stop being a fucking wuss and go to therapy, but I finish drying off and move on.

* *

Later that day, while I'm out loading up on groceries, there's a text from Tim. Another job.

Remember Arno?

How could I forget that big stud?

He requested you. Tonight.

Maybe it's because I met them before, but I'm more confident this second time around as I drive over to the address Tim sent me.

8 pm, he'd written. *Be prepared to spend the night there. Whatever he wants. We need to keep Arno happy. He's an important client.*

Whatever he wants? I'd responded.

Don't worry about it. Just do everything he tells you to.

The address is to a house in Beverly Hills.

* *

I pull up to a two-story Spanish-style house on Benedict Canyon Drive. Arno greets me at the door sporting gym shorts and a tank top, his feet in a pair of slippers. He leads me into a cavernous living room with a tall ceiling. A portrait of a woman in a red dress hangs over the fireplace.

"A relative?" I ask.

"She came with the house. We call her Greta Duvet." His tone's proud. He slides into a stuffed chair upholstered in a loud leopard pattern. I take the couch across from him.

"Nice place," I say, even though it's not.

The living room is sparsely furnished, so it's a bit drafty. There's a piano pushed up against the far wall next to a set of bookcases displaying several signed footballs floating inside glass cases, signatures scrawled on their brown leather hides.

"I collect 'em," Arno says. "In my home country, football ain't so big."

I still can't place his accent.

"This house is something." I rise from the couch and walk towards the large windows looking out onto the backyard; there's a pool surrounded by low boxwood shrubs. In the distance is a small cabana. The French doors are open, and a woman in a headscarf and oversized sunglasses sits on a chair staring at a computer tablet.

"It belonged to some film star from the forties, I think." He claps his hands a few times and gets up. "Let's grab a drink."

He leads me by the arm into another room with wood-panel walls and a bar tucked away in a dark corner. The gin and tonic he mixes is strong, and just as the alcohol starts to hit me nice and smooth, Vita walks in carrying a three-ringed binder and an old laptop. She wears a thin tank top, cutoff denim shorts, and black boots missing laces, their tongues out and flopping as she marches across the room.

Arno lights a cigarette, then another for me. "Here we are," he says as Vita sits on the stool besides me and slams the binder down.

"This my book," she says. "The fairy tales I tell you about. You read and tell me how to fix these?"

"My baby's got a bestseller in her," Arno says. "And we need your help polishing it up."

"What do you mean?" I ask.

"You help," Vita says, pointing. "You make my book beautiful."

"I don't—" I stammer before Arno interrupts.

"You're a writing teacher. We'll hire you to do what those celebrities and politicians do."

"Ghostwrite?" I reply.

"That's it!" Arno snaps his finger, those large pecs of his flexing.

Maybe it's the alcohol, or maybe it's Vita looking at me with those big blue eyes of hers, all meek and vulnerable, but I reach for it and thumb through the pages. Most of them have strange sketches of animals with two heads, castles set against jagged mountains, and trees with knotty and tangled branches where owls and hawks sit perched, staring out with wide, bewildering gazes.

"You read?" Vita says, flipping the pages.

The lines are full of symbols and letters I don't recognize.

"Is this your language?" I ask.

"Yeah," Arno says. "Belarusian. I don't know. Its Greek to me."

Vita opens the laptop. "I say and you write."

Arno nods. "Ghostwrite," he says, owning the word as though he remembered it all by himself.

Vita places the computer in front of me. "Please, yes? Please?"

And this is how the next few hours go. Arno pours drinks, orders food, and watches as Vita tells me stories in her broken English that I then type out, word for word. Sentences that go something like this:

Once, in my place of birth, there was a little boy with a dog. Dog named Misha. The boy love this dog. But he bite him then this boy get sick and turn into wolf, I think? Or cat. Then the boy, he run away as wolf. Or cat. But he run away to forest and has adventures. Then he find a man. This man is older. Fat man with big belly and mean wife who hates the boy who is now wolf or cat.

She pauses a lot, stammers, snaps her fingers, paces back and forth:

The mean wife, she want to cook dog because husband craves it too much. So she sets a, umm . . .

"Trap!" Arno shouts. He's sitting on the couch, shirt stained with sauce from the take-out spaghetti he'd ordered.

"Yes," Vita says. "A trap."

My fingertips are numb. Head throbbing from having to focus, having to decipher what Vita is trying to say, what story she's hoping to tell, and why. Arno pours me another drink, and I've lost count at this point how many this makes. By midnight Arno has passed out on the couch, and Vita has finally stopped talking and says I should rest now and sleep on the recliner across from Arno and that we'll continue in the morning.

"I make us breakfast and strong coffee," she explains, going around and turning out the lights.

"I want pancakes," I slur.

"Nonsense. I make draniki. Gluten-free."

I rest my head on a giant pillow decorated with gold tassels. Arno's snores lull me to sleep, and I have vivid dreams. In one I'm a coyote running through a dark forest. The moon hangs low in the night sky, glowing soft as an ember.

ERNESTO VEGA

Sometimes a gimmick just works, just hits with the people in the right way. Call it luck or timing or something else. That's what happened with El Rey Coyote. Across those endless barrios and vecindades weaving through the nation like a network of veins, my reputation spread and rumors about me emerged, a myth created.

Have you heard of this new campéon? They say he has fangs sharp enough to rip through human flesh.

He's braver than El Santo, but one hundred times more vicious.

I heard he drinks a pint of coyote blood before each match.

Travelers kept photos of him in their wallets or purses to protect them from the dangers of the road and ward off the evil spirits roaming the countryside. On their altars, they lit candles, arranged news clippings with his image next to their multitude of saints and spirits—La Virgen de Guadalupe, Niño Fidencio, Virgen de la Bala, Nuestra Señora de la Santa Muerte. There, they arranged their fresh flowers, lit their candles, burned their copal, knelt and prayed, their voices so gentle and sibilant.

Perhaps it was *el look*, as Franco would say. Or maybe in him our people saw something more than just an escape from the toils of daily living. Maybe they saw salvation itself. In their eyes, the rudos were the real-life embodiments of the injustices they faced day after day—poverty, political corruption, hunger, death, all manner of pain. When they watched El Rey Coyote rush in there and pound an opponent's face into the mat, or pin him down and force him to submit, he was challenging their suffering and misery and winning again and again. He was crushing it so that they could live to see another day.

But behind it all, El Rey Coyote was just like them. He was a man with challenges and problems of his own. Someone longing for a man he loved but could never commit to and a wife whose adoration and devotion to him was so overpowering it both amazed and disturbed him.

* *

The sindicato kept me busy. As the collective's star fighter, I was pushed out there, flung from one corner of the republic to the other like a scrap of paper caught in the wind. It was thrilling and overwhelming at the same time. This meant that I was spending more and more time away from home, away from Elena.

They booked fights in Guadalajara, Morelia, Guanajuato, and even as far north as Tijuana and Ciudad Juarez. I had no choice in the matter, because with the rise in my popularity came something more valuable to the SNM than any one man—sponsorships. EsportsMex, Club Deportivos, Fabrex, and even American companies like Spaulding and Everlast suddenly turned their attention towards our humble collective. With sponsorships came money, a good deal of it. Franco and Avila couldn't be happier. And I was pleased for them, for all of us.

One day they pulled me aside. I was led into Franco's cramped office. Sitting on a desk was an open bottle of champagne and three glasses that Avila filled and passed around, his gold bracelet tinkling against the thin stems. We toasted and drank and had another and another until the bottle was empty.

"This is all because of you," Franco said.

Avila nodded, his cheeks ruddy. "Yes," he said. "Yes."

"Thank you, mis patrones," I told them. "I will forever be grateful to you both. For the opportunity you've given me."

Franco added, "You got star power. We can really take you to the next level, let us be your managers."

What else could I say? Only a fool would say no to so much fame and adulation, and I was no fool. Or so I thought.

Elena Vega

You were giving so much of yourself that it left very little for me, and I was your wife. I started out as your priority, the one you fought for, defended, sacrificed for (or so your claimed), and I became irrelevant. I wasn't one of your fans. I never wanted to be. All I wanted was to be your wife. But El Rey Coyote got in the way. In death, I try to understand you, but it's hard, try rationalizing why I stayed by your side, why I just didn't simply end our marriage the way the gringas did with such ease and frequency. But it's one thing to be una mujer divorciada in America and another thing in this country with its rules and expectations for women. I took a vow, and that meant something to me.

I think of Mercedes, our little girl. What I wouldn't give to hold her in my arms, tell her that I'm sorry for leaving the way I did. I want to tell her that a woman must be made of greater things to withstand and endure what our husbands, fathers, sons, and brothers put us through. I want to tell her not to be as naïve as I was back then, to be selfish and do whatever is necessary to live the way she wants to live.

So much I never got a chance to say to her.

That is the greatest tragedy here.

More than Alfredo's failures.

More than the agony your impending death is bringing.

FREDDY VEGA

Mercy calls me just as I'm returning to the facility after running out to grab some tacos for lunch. She's at the airport, about to jet off to some exotic part of the world again. She thinks I should get a dog or take up a hobby to help ground me.

"What are you talking about?" I ask. "I don't got time for hobbies, sis."

"You need to get your mind away from all that drama, bro. Remember how you loved reading and writing in high school? Maybe you should join a book club or take a poetry class?"

I can't help but laugh out loud as I imagine my old ass crammed into one of those elementary school desks, hunched over a piece of paper, a pencil in my sweaty hand, or sitting in a circle with a bunch of gabachas talking about the latest thriller by James Patterson or Michael Connelly.

"That's ridiculous." But I'm lying, I do have time. There were simply not enough people coming to the gym to justify opening every day.

She groans. In the background I hear a voice over the intercom announcing gate changes, flight departures, warnings about unattended baggage and suspicious activity. Mercy goes on, lecturing me about the importance of recognizing my own vulnerabilities, about knowing when to ask for help, how necessary it is to talk things out.

"I talk. I tell Grace how I'm feeling all the time. What worries me. Ask her."

"I mean a professional, Freddy. A therapist."

"You want me to see a shrink?"

"No, menso! A therapist. I have a friend up here in Oakland who knows people down there. I can ask him for some names."

"Nah. I'm all right."

According to her, I'm not in a good space mentally, and that our father slowly dying, the gym struggling, and the entire world basically coming unglued has fucked with my head, rewired shit in my brain. I'm not alone, though, she insists. A lot of people are hurting, not just me.

"That doesn't make me feel better," I say. "My misery doesn't need company."

"Dad kinda fucked you up emotionally. I mean . . . he taught you how to fight your way out of tricky situations in the ring, sure. But in the real world you're a pinche mess."

"What does that mean?"

I look over at him now. His breathing is labored. The tube sticking out of his throat is awkward, painful to stare at for long, so I avert my gaze.

"You avoid talking about things, avoid getting to the meat of the matter."

"That's bullshit, and you know it. Who looked after you when Mom died? Who made sure you were safe? Drove you to school? Easy for you to be lecturing me now that you're successful. Now that you've got your career, and you're traveling all over the world when I'm the one trying to honor them. I'm the one still stuck here, day after day, holding it together."

"I'm not trying to fight with you, bro. I'm saying this because I love you. Because I know you haven't been able to live up to your full potential. There's a lot you can still do to change your circumstance."

"Yeah," I reply. "Like write fucking poems. That'll change my circumstances for sure."

"Stop with the sarcasm."

Before hanging up, she says that Grace is really worried about me.

"Give Dad a kiss for me, okay?" she pleads. "Tell him I'll be there in a few days."

Then she's gone.

So easy.

* *

Beto swings by the house the next day to check in and see how I'm doing. He looks good. All clean-shaven, a healthy glow to him. And there I am, slumped in my recliner, clothes rumpled and un-washed, stubble on my chin, bags under my eyes. I pour us some coffee, try acting civilized by offering him some pan dulce Grace brought home from work last night.

"I'm good," he says. "Gotta cut back on the sugar and carbs, bro." He started a small security firm with José and a few of the reg-ulars who worked out at the gym. "We do concerts and shows," he goes on. "Hours are flexible, and the money's good, man. I could use someone like you, Freddy. What do you think?" Evidently, they're busy as hell now that things are up and running again.

"I don't know, man," I say. "What's it like? Just . . . standing around all night? Watching a bunch of mensos getting trashed and making fools of themselves?"

"Bro, why you gotta be so negative? It's fucking money. A

job." He pats me on the shoulder and urges me to join him. Just to get him off my back, I say I'll give his offer some serious thought.

How can I admit to him that I feel hopeless, unworthy, a pathetic failure? It's only a matter of time, though. I know I can't stay stuck in this rut forever without something giving.

* *

It's been a while since I thought about him then, out of nowhere, there's an email from Phillip when I check my account. Attached to the message is an article about a group of luchadores in Mexico City putting on a match for a local orphanage. He wrote:

> *Mr. V:*
>
> *Hope all's smooth. Hey, guess what? I'm moving back to the area. I landed an internship at the Museum of Natural History, and I'll be out there looking for a place. Maybe we can meet up?*
>
> *Cuidate:*
> *PC.*

I have no clue why I do it, but when he shows up later that afternoon, I tell Julian about the email. Hearing this, he tries acting real cool, but I can tell he's bothered.

A few days later, I text him Phillip's email address and the number I have in my contacts.

El Rey Coyote

She left him too. Your mujer. There she is now. A light blue feather of smoke lingering just above your bald head with its sagging, mottled skin.

—Don't you dare speak for me, she says. I have a voice. I had a name. I was someone real. You never were.

I laugh. We must stop bickering, señora. We're on the same side. We want the same thing.

—What's that? The blue feather that is her quivers. She's angry at me. I sense it.

—We want him to admit the truth. To confess to his lies and deceit.

Look at you, old man. I am El Rey Coyote, and you are nothing but a body that is all mangled and twisted. What do you have to show for yourself now?

JULIAN VEGA

Predawn. The sky outside filling with color. The ink of night re-
ceding as I struggle to open my eyes. Arno sits slumped upright
on the couch, snoring. Naked. His crotch is a thick shrub of hair,
coarse and untamed, his hard dick sprouting out, straight and
rigid as a pole. *Can it technically be called morning wood if it's
dawn? Dawn wood sounds like the name of a B-list actress from the
1970s.* The slightest shift in elevation sends throbbing pain up to
my temples and down the base of my neck. I rise, gather myself,
tiptoe out of the room, hand in pocket, keys and phone clutched.

    Quiet, I'm telling myself over the pulsing ache in my head,
pushing past the nausea building in my stomach. *Go for the door, go
for the door.* Then a sound. Dishes rattling. In the kitchen, standing in the square of light cast by the opened refrigerator, is the old
woman I'd seen out back the day before. She's in a nightgown thin
as gauze. The skin across her bare shoulders and arms is so pale
it looks gray, like uncooked shrimp. She's barefoot, her toenails
painted bright red. On her head, she wears a white plastic crown.
It takes me a moment to realize this is real and not a symptom of
my hangover or a hallucination or some sort of dream. She senses
me trying to sneak past and turns around so sharply that the plastic
crown falls to the floor.

"Sorry," I whisper.

She glares at me and says something in a language I can't place. "Te cunosc, duh rău."

"What?" I raise my hand up. "Look. I'm leaving." I point to the front door. "Going," I say.

Her lips part. She bares her teeth and whispers, "Marțolea. You are marțolea."

"I'm Julian. My name is Julian."

The old woman steps forward, braces herself against the edge of the kitchen island separating us. Her bony fingers move quick as she reaches for a knife, unsheathing it from the wooden block. The blade glows golden white in the refrigerator light.

"Okay," I whisper. "I'm going." I show her my car keys. "Me voy. Me voy."

"Ai venit după mine, nu-i așa?" She raises her voice, her words cold, sinister. "Mă omor înainte să te las să mă iei."

I back away, heart beating quick and fast, my breathing ragged, adrenaline sending bile up my throat. Bolting out of the kitchen, down the short hall, past the main room where Greta hangs above the fireplace, she's close behind, whispering over and over that same word: marțolea. *How can such a frail thing move so quickly?* I don't stop running until I reach the car, lock myself in, and start the engine. She's standing in the dark doorway, watching me. Knife held over her head, that thin gown blowing in the cold morning breeze, bare feet planted in a puddle of muddy water.

You are marțolea.

Maybe I am. Maybe I'm not.

But what I do know is that I'm glad to be as far away from that house as possible.

* *

The phone vibrating on the nightstand wakes me from a deep nap. It's Tim calling.

"You left?" He sounds pissed.

"This morning. I stayed the night."

"Why'd you go?"

"Some old lady came at me with a knife. I thought she was going to kill me."

There's an audible sigh. "That's just Ada. She has dementia." There's a long pause before he speaks again. "He'll want you back. Soon, too. Meanwhile, I have you booked every day next week. Get some rest. You're gonna need it."

Not two seconds later another vibration. This time it's a text message from my father. Contact information. Email address and phone number for him.

Phillip Cordova.

Fucking hell. Really, Dad? Really?

* *

The month is a blur of men, some I remember, others I casually forget. Antonio asks to watch me shave my head and pubic area. Nothing more. No sex or anything. Just stand in the bathroom. Here's an electric razor and scissors and a new can of shaving cream. Three rubber ducks sit in a row on the porcelain lip of the tub, their beady little eyes watching the whole time.

Mick answers the door wearing a pair of his wife's pantyhose and has me fuck him on his teenage stepson's bed.

"I deplore the little asshole," he says.

Ed is a wealthy property manager who is bashful and portly. I drive to his ranch house in Thousand Oaks. He wears black dress socks held up to his freckled calves by garters and a spiked choker around his neck. Next to his bed there's a pair of handcuffs, a whip, and a Ping-Pong paddle.

"Torture me," he commands. "I deserve it. I've been a very bad baby."

I put on a pair of leather chaps a few sizes too big, and I bend him over a dining table strewn with spreadsheets containing long columns of numbers. I spank him for a while, his frail white skin growing redder. Then I handcuff him to the bed, gag him with a pair of his underwear, and fuck him until I've had enough.

"I enjoyed my session, master," he says.

"Fuck off," I say.

"Yes, sir."

Vince only eats raw foods. Yoga, he states, is his religion. He's the "wellness expert to the stars," whatever the hell that means.

"The human body," he says, "hides so many mysteries."

There's a padded table set up in a corner of his living room. He lights candles and plays a CD called *Sounds of Nature*, asks which track I want to listen to: Rainfall, Crashing Waves, or Rushing Wind.

"Doesn't matter."

"Rainfall, then. I grew up in the Pacific Northwest. I miss rain. It never rains here in LA."

"It's always sunny, though."

"Sunshine's boring."

He wants to make love to my feet. He'd asked that I not wash them and to wear a pair of sweaty, smelly sneakers with no socks. I hop up on the table now, bare assed, and he strolls over and kneels before me, stroking my toes.

"They're not clean," I say.

"Perfect."

* *

They're only flesh. Bone and muscle and hair and sweat and fluids and nipples and mouths and tongues being pulled and stretched

and opened and slapped and pinched and tugged and electrocuted
and pierced and pounded and pounded and pounded.

Me to them.

Them to me.

Our bodies like ancient temples. Beautiful and ravaged.

ERNESTO VEGA

Stop it, both of you. Your constant fucking bickering is worse than the pain of this ugly tube jammed down my throat. Worse than the suctioning. Worse than the nurses who come in and change my soiled diapers and wipe my dirty ass.

—I give up, les digo. Just let me go.

—It's not up to us to decide when you're ready, Ernesto. This from Elena.

—Until then, you must contend with the repercussions of your actions, cobarde. The other me balls his fist up, swings at my face, but his hand passes through my skin.

—He's right, you know? Elena replies. You forgot about me. And Julián.

—But I tried finding him. I went by his apartment, but he was never there. Segundo and the construction company moved on to another site once the job was completed. The city's big. There were millions of places where he could lose himself.

—Excuses, the other me says.

—You're right, Elena agrees. I'm getting sick of him.

Now here comes another nurse. More cleaning. More wiping. More humiliation.

Elena Vega

I still believe that you purposefully looked for reasons not to be home, that you were avoiding me. I wanted to get even with you, Ernesto, to wound you the way you'd wounded me. ¿Y que? A woman isn't supposed to feel wrath or envy? A woman is just supposed to turn a blind eye and let things happen to her?

Fuck that, I say. And fuck anyone who thinks a mujer like me isn't tough, isn't capable of exacting revenge in life and beyond that. Here is what I know. You and I were bound together. We would forever be locked in this war. It wasn't about winning, about you getting your way or me getting mine.

It was about power.

* *

I woke one morning, startled, and he was the first person who came to my mind. All day as I wandered about, drinking coffee, distracting myself by tidying up or watching television, I kept thinking of Julián.

So, I left the apartment. I couldn't resist. An impulse bigger than all of us was pushing me forward. Down the corner, past the flower vendor. It was nearing fall. She had arranged cempazúchitles in large green buckets. I thought about the panteón back home. Surely people were already starting to prepare for the Day of the

Dead celebrations, constructing their altars, arranging candles and sugar skulls. The panaderos would begin baking pan de muerto. The air would be perfumed with the scent of burning copal. Maybe I could take a bus back there? Spend a few days visiting friends? I could make an altar to my mother and father.

I took a pesero down Reforma and Insurgentes with no clue as to where I was going. I just wanted to be out among people, lost in a crowd. I needed to hear voices, see others, remind myself that I was still alive, that I still moved in this world.

Off one pesero and on another. Following the shuffle of feet. The men in their suits and jackets and freshly polished shoes, the women in pleated skirts and starched blouses. I let myself get tossed about like an errant feather twirling in the wind. Nothing anchored me to the ground.

And then there. Ajusco. And then our old vecindad. The tortilla vendor. The carnicero. La Botanica Tres Caminos. To the teas and supplements that didn't work to call your attention back to me, to my body. Bembe was inside, the same white scarf wrapped around his head.

"Que milagro," he replied when I strolled in.

I glanced around, taking in the shelves crammed with statues and velas and dried herbs wrapped in tissue. "¿Y Dario?"

He whistled and flicked his wrist. "Se fue pa California. Agua Mansa. What brings you back, Elenita?"

I said nothing about my troubles. Why bother? I think the spirits knew it was a fruitless battle I was waging, that neither my husband nor I would ever get what we wanted. Instead, I bought a scapular and said goodbye to Bembe.

And then, a while later, there again. Standing before the building. It was Antonia who saw me first. She held a wet broom, its bristles frothy with aromatic floor cleaner. She was washing the steps and stopped to wipe her forehead with the corner of her pink mandil.

"¡Mira quien viene! Te desapareciste." She gave me a tight embrace. "It's good to see you again." Antonia took me in, squeezed my cheeks and waist. "Estas tan flaquita."

How could I tell her that my stomach could no longer hold food, about the sleepless nights, the anxiety and depression? No. Better to be strong. I took a deep breath and said, "Hola, amiga. I've missed you."

She led me inside her place. From the open door I could see the entrance to Julián's unit. Antonia served me coffee and we shared a piece of pan dulce that I had to force myself to chew and swallow. We gossiped about the neighborhood, about the recent police activity around the colonia, how the crooked cops were continuing to harass the residents. I sat with her for about an hour, grateful for the distraction, grateful for her humor and camaraderie, but soon it would be dark, so I said I should be going.

Then there he was, just as I was exiting the building. Julián was walking up the street, keys in his hand, jacket tossed over his shoulder.

He was as close to you as I could get. His crooked smile, that thin frame of his, that mane of long and tangled hair, the three gold chains around his neck, that jagged Adam's apple sliding up and down beneath the stubbly, rough skin of his throat. I didn't know what to say, so I remained quiet, let him see me.

He forced a smile. "Hola. What a surprise."

I smiled back, a real smile. "That's what Antonia said."

He nodded. "¿Y . . . Ernesto?"

"Cuernavaca." The chilly air smelled of woodsmoke. I buttoned up my sweater. "Big lucha event at an outdoor festival. I thought about going but decided to stay." I was nervous, talking too much. I fiddled with the strap of my purse.

"What brought you here?" He lit a cigarette.

I shrugged. "Just . . . lonely, maybe. La nostalgia. I miss him."

He nodded. "I know the feeling."

"We have that in common, don't we?"

"Yes," he replied, his voice tender, genuine.

I felt seen again. "This air, all the cempazúchitles . . . it's making me long for La Peña. I bet it's beautiful right now." I closed my eyes and imagined I was standing in the middle of the panteón serenading my father and grandparents.

"Sometimes I wish I could return."

I nodded. "Me too."

He cleared his throat, then said, "Listen, I was going to wash up and grab some tacos at the corner, maybe have a cerveza or two. I want to take advantage of the night, indulge my melancholy. Would you care to join me?"

What else could I say except yes?

That's how it started.

With tacos and beers and our two heavy hearts pining for a love we knew was impossible to ever attain.

FREDDY VEGA

I pay my mother a visit, polishing her headstone, brushing away blades and flecks of dirt until the gold surface is clean, glowing in the rusty orange sun. *He's still hanging on,* I tell her, tell the hot breeze blowing across the green cemetery lawn. *We don't know how, but he is.*

It doesn't help that his things are on a shelf out in the storage shed. It doesn't help that all I feel I can do is go out there and rifle through them, hoping there's an answer, a way for me to get unstuck, for me to revive him, to make him whole again. It doesn't help that I feel guilty when I see how tired she is when my Grace comes home from work, that all I can do is listen as she complains about rude customers, irresponsible coworkers, and Ofelia, the new manager who's always breathing down her neck.

"I swear. It's like she has it out for me," she rants today, tossing her bag on the floor. She lets out a long sigh and stretches across the couch, putting her feet up on the coffee table.

"I'm sorry, honey. I wish there was more I could do."

"Beto's wife was grocery shopping yesterday. Came into my lane. She told me he started a new company. Something about security. Said he might be able to get you some work?"

I nod. "Yeah. We talked."

"Are you gonna take him up on the offer?"

How can I make her understand the reluctance I feel? The fear? "I don't know."

She looks over at me, my wife. Her hair's unraveled, uniform wrinkled, pockets overflowing with random pens and the torn receipts of voided transactions. It's almost fall. Before we know it, the holidays will be here, she reminds me.

"I know, okay? Fuck, I know."

"You don't think I've noticed? You've been sleeping in. You hardly eat. I know you're depressed, but feeling sorry for yourself isn't going to do shit to help you, to help *us*. And we need help. Right fucking now."

"I know but—"

"We're pregnant," she interjects. "Pregnant, all right?"

The words hit me like a punch to the face. "But how?"

She laughs. "How do you think?"

"Are you sure? Have you taken a test?"

"Yeah, I have. Don't be dumb."

She was waiting to be sure before saying anything. She didn't want to alarm me or cause more worry, more stress. "Part of me was hoping it was a false alarm, honestly. But it's not. I went to the doctor last week."

"You should have told me."

Grace raises her voice, swats the couch cushion. "Well, I'm fucking telling you now."

"What are we gonna do about it?"

"I don't know."

"Can we even have another kid? Right now? With the way things are?"

"I don't want to talk." She closes her eyes.

"Well, we gotta decide on—"

"I'm not deciding shit right now, okay? I'm tired and my feet hurt and all I wanna do is rest and watch talk shows all afternoon for a change, instead of ringing up asshole customers."

"I'll give you some space." I grab my keys.

I drive around the neighborhood, not really paying attention to where I'm headed. I somehow end up cruising down First then hanging a left on Mission to the empty gym, park, sit in my truck, and try to clear my mind, try remembering the lessons my father taught me. It all scares the hell out of me, this life, these choices we're always having to make, the world raging and raging all around us. But I can't keep backing down.

I send Beto a text message.

The next day, there's a call from a number I don't recognize. When I say hello, the voice that replies sounds familiar at first, but I can't place it. It isn't until he calls me Mr. V that I know who it is. Phillip. He wants to see me.

El Rey Coyote

Franco and Avila held us up, talked to all the reporters and news outlets they could. El Rey Coyote was a talented fighter, they boasted. ¡Tiene valor! The crowds love him. He is on his way to becoming one of the most recognized luchadores in the country. Like Blue Demon and El Santo.

HIS STAR WILL CONTINUE RISING, they went on. ¡VAN A VER!

It's true. We were gifted. We were a showman, such a skilled athlete.

They wanted us to do television appearances, spots on the variety show circuit. They were talking with Raúl Velasco's people. An interview for his show, *Siempre en Domingo*, was in the works.

"Imagine the exposure, Ernesto," Franco said. "*Siempre en Domingo* is broadcast across Mexico and Latin America. Even the United States. You'd be recognized *internationally*."

How could we tell them that all we wanted was to stop and rest, that we'd lost hope? That we missed him?

Julián.

And Elena? She felt unmoored, detached from everything. That home was a shrine to us. It was like living inside a trophy case. But it existed only to present the illusion of success and happiness. Her resentment towards us was spreading, a veneno coursing through her veins. This is what happens when we choose to live a charade, when we are too cowardly to admit to ourselves what we really desire. Deceit is our demise.

—Why didn't she tell me this? Ernesto uses his last few breaths to shout. I needed to know.

—You're asking her now? On your deathbed?

—Don't speak for me, Elena's angry, her spirit pulsing red, throbbing, pummeling the inside of our head. Unlike you, I have a mouth.

—Fine, speak then, I say. Tell your truth. But stop fucking beating around the damn bush, mujer!

JULIAN VEGA

In biology class I learned about the thalamus, a large gray mass located in a subsection of the brain called the diencephalon. From here, the thalamus, equipped with hundreds of nerve fibers, sends information to the cerebral cortex. The thalamus regulates our sleep and controls our motor skills. It's where we learn to blink, comb our hair, yawn, write our own name. And when we experience pain, the thalamus unlocks to accept it, then closes when it's gone. When someone lives with unrelenting pain, though, the thalamus stays open, constantly receiving alerts that cause anxiety and discomfort. Experiencing persistent agony like that alters the chemical makeup of the brain.

Pain forever changes how we think.

The part of our mind responsible for our emotions and for the formation of our memories is called the limbic system. It's comprised of a group of structures that include the hippocampus, the amygdala, and the hypothalamus. These areas help us shape memories, help us assign meaning and emotion to each so that, over time, certain recollections will trigger feelings of love or anger or fear. The amygdala and the hippocampus aid in the formation of new memories, help us categorize, index, and make sense of them. Without these two areas of the brain, our experiences would just happen to us. We wouldn't know what to make of them, how they're connected. We would be scattered splinters of ourselves, stumbling about in a fugue state, disoriented.

* *

Something happened between us our final year together, caused a rift in our relationship, made our last moments together awkward, necessary only because we'd come to rely on each other both physically and emotionally. Phillip and I put on an act whenever we were out, when we visited my parents, spent weekends at the house playing board games and eating pizza, helping them organize a yard sale they had one time. He was only happy when he was there, around them. He was warm, funny, communicative. There was no awkwardness between us in those moments, no talk about the future, about our relationship, and how things were about to change for both of us.

"Family," he replied when I asked him why he liked hanging out at my mom and dad's.

"That's it?"

"Yeah. No, see? That's what you don't get. It's all about family."

"What do you mean?"

We were walking back to the dorm from the parking lot. In the distance, construction crews were busy setting up bleachers along the perimeter of what we called the Main Lawn in preparation for the upcoming commencement ceremonies. A makeshift stage had already been assembled. There were banners and balloons and rows of white folding chairs where we'd sit, waiting for our names to be called, waiting for the moment when we'd cross the stage to the cheers and hoots of our family members and classmates.

I was ready to move on.

"You got solid parents, man. They don't fight and hate each other."

I shook my head. "You don't know that."

"True," he said as we neared our dorm building. "But they're still together. That's special right there. Instead, you act like it's no big deal. You take them for granted."

I laughed at this. What did he expect me to do? Worship my mom and dad? Spend every waking hour with them?

"Just leave it, man," I said. "I don't want to talk about this. Not now."

"Then when?" He stopped in the middle of the quad.

It was late evening. The library was still open; they always extended their hours during finals week. I could see students darting in and out, the lights on the second and third floors illuminated, golden bands stretching from one end of the building to the other.

"You never want to talk anymore," he added.

"What's there to talk about?"

"Us. Me and you."

I didn't know how to tell him then that I couldn't see that far ahead, that I didn't even want to, that in my murky version of the future, he wasn't in it.

"I love you, Julian. Like truly love you. I want us to spend the rest of our lives together. It's obvious to everyone but you."

I knew all along, but I'd done such a good job pretending I'd fooled him and, more important, myself. "What do you want me to say?"

"You're fucking unbelievable."

He wanted to hear me say that I loved him too, that I wanted the same things he did, that I saw us renting a bungalow in Highland Park together, hosting parties and learning how to mix fancy cocktails for our bohemian friends. But all I could think about was how much those things terrified me.

ERNESTO VEGA

I wanted a break. I was too tired to fight, to keep the relentless pace of that schedule up. Bus after bus after bus. Matches across that vast and mountainous republic. Towns and villages so cut off, so remote, it felt as though I was stepping back in time.

Where was Julián? I missed his constant nagging, how he was always on me to rest, to eat right, to make sure I took enough time to recover from my injuries.

Franco and Avila made arrangements with a local film studio, one of a handful that cropped up around the capital during this time. I was contracted to do a series of short films, following in the footsteps of Santo and Blue Demon, already huge celebrities. They said it was a great PR move, and I agreed, but the budgets were low, the film producer and director told me. Still, the reels would be shown in theaters all over the republic. I would be a movie star.

"Like Anthony Quinn," Franco assured me.

"The exposure will be phenomenal," Avila explained. "This is the thing that will make the SNM as big as the Consejo Mudial de Lucha Libre. Give that cabrón Lutteroth a run for his money."

The two men hated Salvador Lutteroth and the EMLL. They claimed he'd monopolized the whole industry, controlled it like some mafioso, leaving very little for a smaller empresa like ours to succeed. Somebody had to take him down, they told us. This was why they pushed us so hard, why they wanted me out there all the time. I would be for our sindicato what El Santo was for the EMLL. This was why I had to do the films. The success of the whole operation rested on my shoulders alone.

"But I've never acted," I said.

They insisted it wouldn't matter. "You think Santo and those guys took fancy acting lessons? ¡N'ombre, güey!" Even before I agreed to it, they'd already informed the director that I'd do it. I had no choice.

* *

The storylines had me chasing bad guys on a motorcycle, thwarting bank robbers, and battling a coven of evil witches holed up in a cave as they terrorized a nearby town. The shooting schedules were long and complicated, and most of the time I found myself wandering around the sets in full costume waiting for the lighting to be perfect or a camera angle to be adjusted. Over the next several months, we shot nonstop. Late at night. Early in the morning. On weekends. Rain or shine. Empty fields. The beaches of Veracruz and Acapulco. The deserts of Chihuahua. Abandoned buildings. Empty lots and stores. In the houses of friends and relatives, even my own apartment. The director was relentless, crazy, maniacal. He yelled at me a lot and grew frustrated when I didn't deliver my lines properly. If I failed to land the right maneuver as I did flips and my signature *Chillido Coyote*, I was ordered to do it again, over and over, until he thought it was right. All this work in between matches and events and fundraisers. When the first shorts premiered, they were flops. The audiences hated them.

"With the next ones," Franco assured me, "we'll try again. It will be better. We have faith in you, son."

But the next ones came and went, and they, too, failed. The other luchadores in the collective grew resentful of the attention

Franco and Avila placed on me, poked fun of my bad acting, my clumsy maneuvers on-screen, the horrible production value of the atrocious films.

I just kept my head down, kept fighting, kept getting injured. It's all I knew.

Elena Vega

You were that distracted, Ernesto? Were you purposely being necio? Were you intentionally looking away?

In our moments of intimacy, Julián and I knew very well what we were doing and, more important, why we were doing it.

It was the only way for us to feel close to you.

Do you understand now? Even as you lay there, dying?

Tell me, my husband. Tell me you know why we did it.

Let me take us back to that day even though it's too painful for you to recall.

* *

I was sitting on the couch, hands on my knees. It was afternoon, bright and warm outside. The television set was off.

"¿Que te pasa?" you asked.

I'd gone to Condesa, I replied. I don't recall what I was buying, but it must not have been that significant. Any excuse to shop. It helped distract me.

"There were three boys. Students. Young."

I was cutting through Parque España on my way back when they darted past, running along the trail towards Avenida Sonora. At the intersection, all three of them stopped. There were sirens. Two police cars pulled up, stopping traffic in all directions. They flanked the boys on either side. Two of them moved quickly, running down an alley as a pair of police officers chased after them on foot. The third boy froze in the middle of the intersection, arms above his head. The police officer was crouched behind the squad car, gun aimed at the lone student who was shouting something at him. I couldn't hear, so I moved closer. I was standing only a few feet away. He was surrendering. That's all. Then he flinched. Ever so slightly he flinched. As though he'd felt an itch along his back. A lady working the newsstand across the street screamed at him not to move. Next to me there was an older man holding the hand of a little girl in pigtails, and when the officer fired his gun, the man pressed his hand over the girl's eyes. The shot made a loud boom that ricocheted off the buildings. Then someone behind me screamed.

"He fell," I told you. "Plop! Just like that. I watched the bullet pass through his skull. I saw the blood gather in a pool on the concrete."

That boy did nothing but surrender. And they killed him.

"His mother," I remember telling you. "That boy's poor mother."

I had nightmares in the days and weeks that followed. My nerves were frayed. So were everyone's. The shortages of money. All the upheaval in the streets. It happened so fast. The concerns about bills and savings made it hard to focus. You owed everyone so much.

And our streets? They were drenched in blood. All around us, everyone was screaming, and I just wanted the noise to stop.

FREDDY VEGA

About a month in, Grace's morning sickness is bad, worse than I remember when she was carrying Julian. Now that I'm bringing in some extra cash working security with Beto, she takes the weekends off and relaxes. She joined a prenatal Zumba class run by a coworker. They meet at Belvedere Park every Saturday at nine in the morning for an hour. Sometimes I go with her and run a few laps as she shakes her hips to Pitbull or Daddy Yankee. If I'm feeling nostalgic, I'll run south across the pedestrian bridge stretching over the 60 freeway and jog around the lake on the other side. I remember high school, hanging out with Mike Foster and getting stoned under these same trees, laughing at the ducks stumbling about. The neighborhood's changed too much now, so I can't even find his place anymore. Contractors are flipping houses left and right, gabachos invading, spreading like lethal spores, the Metro Gold, or "L" Line, as it's now called, glides straight down the middle of the avenue.

* *

We haven't seen or talked to Julian since Grace told me we were expecting.

"Does he even know about the baby?" I look over to her now, sitting in the passenger seat of my truck, waving goodbye through the windshield at the other moms in her class.

She opens her mouth, surprised. "I thought you told him."

"Nah. I thought you did."

"He never stops by. Always busy. I don't want to text him the news."

"We gotta tell him sooner or later, Gracie."

I can't recall the last time I called her that.

My Gracie. Mi querida.

* *

That night, we're working an event. Some crazy bullshit lucha libre chingadera put on by two rich hipsters. Phillip and I have been trying to meet up, but between the new gig and shuttling Grace back and forth to her doctor appointments, things are crazy. I'd mentioned this *thing* to him, said I would be working it and maybe he'd want to check it out.

I saw the write-up in the Calendar Section, he'd replied in a text. *Think I just might.*

There are half-naked ladies grinding up against stripper poles and payaso wrestlers who are all messy and uncoordinated, mistiming dropkicks and pile drives left and right. The audience is mainly white Westsiders sporting handlebar mustaches drinking craft beers, and flat-chested girls in rumpled dresses. All idiotas who know nothing about the sport.

It's infuriating. These fools actually paid for this mierda? My anger swells as the night goes on.

Beto, José, and I can't help but laugh at the absurdity of the whole thing—the gaudy lights and bad music, the sloppy wrestlers more interested in looking good in spandex, all oiled and glittery, than really fighting.

"Man," I say. "This is a fucking shit show. Who are these amateurs?"

"Not at all like us, huh?" Beto says.

"Hell no," says José. "Imagine if Scarlet was here? Kamikaze?" He shakes his head. "They'd wipe the floor with these pendejos."

As the night goes on and the crowd thins, one of the general managers, a gaunt white boy in thick glasses and an orange turtleneck, tells Beto that someone was going around trying to slip drugs into drinks. A girl was passed out in the restroom.

"Looks like Rohypnol," the guy says. "We didn't catch whoever was doing it, so I'm gonna need you and your guys to be on it tomorrow night. No standing around and playing fantasy football on their phones, okay?"

"You got it, boss," Beto replies. When the dude turns to leave, he whispers, "Pinches hipsters. Always fucking causing trouble."

As I pass through the crowd, stalking the arena like a predator as the final match starts, I catch myself thinking, *Why am I even here? What are any of us doing here?*

Beto and José stand near the bar full of spectators, all of them completely trashed, swaying and slurring their words, flicking cigarette ashes on the floor, slamming shots of bad tequila. Their faces are coated in sweat. Skin as pale as paper.

This isn't right. Maybe it's not too late.

Maybe there's enough in me to pull us all together again. After all, crazier shit's happened recently. Why not a comeback? Why not now?

El Rey Coyote

M ujer, no one can really blame you or Julián for the betrayal, though. You both loved him equally.

—We did, she says. And you did as well.

—Indeed. I loved him because, complicated as he was, Ernesto Vega was a warrior in every sense of the word. Because, even with his shortcomings, I was breathed into being because of him. Our heart and soul are one and the same. Our blood and bones, everything about us . . . it's inexorably linked. The truth is that when he goes, I will be gone from here as well.

—¿Y Julián? The old man gasps. These are his final thoughts.

—Yes, the mujer replies. What happened to him? Where did he go?

All I can do is shake my head and shed tears from eyes that are already starting to fade.

JULIAN VEGA

I breathe a sigh of relief at the email from the chair of the only department for which I'm lecturing this semester, letting me know I'm being offered an extra class in the spring. When I stop by the department before my first class, she's in her office, glued to her computer screen, dead ferns lining the window ledge. A bronze plaque with her name, Sonia Sandoval-Meeks, is pushed to the edge of her desk.

"Can you believe this?" She points to the ferns. "I can't keep these damn things alive. How are you?" she asks, turning to face me.

"Good. Thanks for the extra class next semester."

"Don't thank me. You're one of our best lecturers, Julian. Everyone around here agrees." She lowers her voice. "I'll be sending an email to the department, so look out for it, okay?"

"Sure." I grip my book bag. "Anything important?"

"Yes. The dean's office has finally granted our request to conduct a search for three full-time professors in this department. You should seriously consider applying. The competition will be tough, I won't lie, but you have a great chance."

I adjust my tie. "Really? That's . . . good to hear."

"Now," she tells me just as I'm heading out the door, "go polish up that CV, Professor Vega." Sylvia crosses her fingers. "You got this."

Passing the mailboxes on my way out, I scan the list of names. At the very top—way above my own—are the core faculty: Adams, Banerjee, Carmichael, Dodd, Eglin, Esposito, Franklin, Gray, Hsu, Kent, Mack, Murphy, Ramirez, San Angelo, Taylor, Wilson. I try imagining mine up there, sandwiched between Taylor and Wilson.

* *

My years as a graduate student without Phillip were marked by a deep loneliness punctuated by random academic achievements. I moved into my apartment close to campus, took graduate seminars, served as a TA for some of the very same professors I'd taken courses with as an undergrad, and eventually was given my own sections to teach. The rigorous schedule of literature seminars and lectures on skillful teaching pedagogy and papers and lesson planning was a lot, but I loved it.

I didn't have time to miss him.

I discovered a bathroom on campus tucked away in the basement of the science building. There, in the stalls and between the urinals, I had sexual encounters with other college students. I prowled the parks and the seedy adult bookstore next to the very shop where we'd gotten our yin and yang tattoos years before.

During the day, I was the upright, responsible graduate student. There were essays to grade. Books on Edward Said and Judith Butler to read. Then, in the evenings, I took to roaming the streets and alleys, the bookstores and public bathrooms where I'd hook up with guys, spending hours upon hours fucking, getting fucked, losing myself in the thrill, the raw energy and desire. It was like a drug I couldn't quit.

My father used to talk about the dual identities a luchador must adopt, these different personas they carry inside them and cultivate throughout their wrestling careers. How a técnico can transform into a rudo and back again depending on the evolution of their storylines. In the wake of our split, that side of me which had been lying dormant just beneath the surface of my skin emerged. Whether it was born out of loneliness or lust or insecurity or fear, I didn't know.

Did it really matter, anyway?

It was out in all its glory. I embraced it fully, let the mayhem in.

* *

The morning lingers. Outside my kitchen window, palm fronds swish back and forth between the power lines strung across the avenues and narrow streets of my neighborhood. Roaming cats wander down the alleys, climbing over garbage bins and plastic bags, meowing as they search for mice or pick through bloated bags of garbage. The air reeks of burning embers. The Santa Ana Winds have arrived. They're vengeful, maniacal. They suck all the life out of everything, even the marrow of our bones.

They're vampiric.

Sadistic and hypnotic at the same time.

My skin prickles. It's an unconditional response.

* *

Clay has a Mexican gardener fantasy. He wants to see me again.

Of course he does, I reply to Tim's text.

Wear faded jeans, he messages back. *A muscle shirt. Baseball cap. Boots. If you don't own a pair, sneakers will do. Leave your car in the alley behind his house. There'll be a truck. Take it and drive around to the front, get out, and pretend to work.*

The next afternoon, I park near a beat-up red truck with a bunch of gardening equipment in the bed—a lawn mower, a shovel, two yellow drums full of gasoline, an edger, a wooden crate, a pair of worn leather gloves. The thing's a mess, the seat cushions cracked and the coils are sticking out of the cheap upholstery. It takes a few tries before it turns and the engine roars, sputtering and backfiring as I drive around and pull up towards the front of the house. I take the edger out, hoisting the thing over my shoulder and lumbering up to the hedges near the front door. I have no idea how to turn the fucking thing on. Sweat pours down my face, stinging my neck, as I yank on the lever a few times before it finally starts up, the plastic blade whirring. It's an unwieldy piece of machinery, and grass and dust are flying up into my eyes and mouth and I'm coughing and itchy all over. It's already so fucking hot. I'm standing in the same spot, the edger hovering over a patch of yellowing grass. Completely drenched and feeling ridiculous, I glance towards the main door of the house. From the other side of the glass door, he steps out and waves. It takes me a few tries before I turn the ugly piece of equipment off and toss it on the ground. Clay smiles at me. He wears a pair of thin running shorts, and I trace the outline of his stiff cock underneath the fabric.

"It's Pedro, right?" he asks.

I know I'm supposed to play along. I nod.

His Spanish is terrible. "Habla English?"

"Si, señor," I say, my Spanish worse.

"Okay," he says to himself, reaching into the pocket of his shorts. They slip down about an inch, the elastic band barely clinging to the area just below his waist. He pulls out a five-dollar bill. "I'm going to give this to you." He places the money in my hand.

"Es not enough, Mr. Clay." I roll my eyes when he looks away. This is preposterous.

"But," he says, backing away, "it's all I have. Take it, Pedro. Take it. Por favor."

I remove my leather gloves and approach him. My hands glide over his bare chest, slip under his shorts, and I caress his hardness. "You will pay me some other way, yes?"

I lead him by the hand into the cool house. What follows is an elaborate fantasy, a moment that men like Clay all over this city have had about guys like me, rehearsing it in their minds again and again, getting the details just right so that it lasts and lingers in the way only these twisted things have the capacity to do.

ERNESTO VEGA

I thought the random hairs in the sink were my own, the foreign scent on my pillows left over from the last time I'd slept in our bed. The house no longer felt like mine. Another male presence had invaded my domain, sat in my lounge chair, watched my television, made love to my wife. I told myself it was my overactive imagination, my silly paranoia. The lack of sleep was making my mind play tricks on me. I was irritable, moody. When I tried resting, it was difficult to relax. I had no time to dwell on any of it.

* *

Because of the protests happening in Mexico, foreigners stopped investing in us. Stores closed. Construction companies halted work. The rich guarded their money. The very poor grew more desperate and streamed into the city from the countryside, looking for any kind of work. This only created tension in the streets and colonias. So many vagrants, the citizens of the capital said. They're bringing their crime and poverty and filth from the campo. Who needs them? A bitter restlessness descended over everything, tainting the water, fumigating the soil. No one wanted to name it, but we all knew what this was: desperation.

Then the summer of 1971, there came another armed conflict in the streets. University professors and students clashed with a secret military troop known as Los Halcones, a division of the Mexican army that had been trained by the American government. They called the event *El Halconazo*. Close to one hundred and twenty protestors were slaughtered. Among them was a fourteen-year-old boy.

Elena Vega

Did I know I'd die that night? Is that why my last words to Mercedes were the same ones my abuela Azucena once said to me? It was late, and she was in bed, the radio with its mesh speakers pressed up against the side of her head. "No te dejes engañar," I said.

My daughter pulled the covers back, and turned to glance at me. "What?"

She was experimenting with makeup. My old bottles of nail polish lined the windowsill inside her bedroom. Boys were starting to attract her attention; the walls were decorated with posters of Madonna and Michael Jackson. No crucifix above her bed. Instead, there hovered Prince, his eyes heavy with black liner, a rosary pressed against his bare chest.

"No te dejes engañar," I repeated.

"Mom, what are you talking about?"

I didn't respond. I turned the light off, closed the door, walked down the hallway past Alfredo's room, lay down next to my husband, and transitioned from this realm to the next.

I still talk to her beyond the veil separating us. Whether she can hear me or not, I don't know. Maybe I would have said more if I knew I wouldn't wake up the next day, knew I wouldn't get to see her develop into the woman she is now. But in a way, the strangeness of my hollow and random words to her so long ago still hold truth. So, I tell her again at this moment while she stands with her brother watching Ernesto die.

No te dejes engañar.

I see a few years from now, a band, slim as a string, glinting on her finger, a diamond cradled in a crown resting at its center. There will be a man. A gabacho named Eric, thin and pale as a weed. There will be a marriage. A miscarriage. Then the twins. Two niñas. A divorce. Another man who'll wound her spirit, make her mistrust, before she gives up on them entirely to raise the girls on her own. *Good for you, mija.*

No te dejes engañar.

I say this also to my nuera, Grace, pregnant with my next grandchild. My place here in the afterlife lets me bend space and time, allows me to see, to know that this baby will be born a girl and they'll name her Paloma.

No te dejes engañar.

I watch their fingers and toes forming, little tender beans. I see their eyes, their ears. I know I'll be forever bound to them, my skin their skin. All of us like those little Russian dolls, the skeletons of each generation nesting inside the next, one protecting and strengthening the other so that we may thrive, so that we may never be erased.

To all my comadres. Don't listen to the men who try controlling us, who expect us to follow along without questions, who think that we're only capable of watching helplessly as they get mangled and tortured by the forces dictating our lives. No. You howl and scream and scratch. You are revolutionaries. You must fight harder than them or it will all be for nothing.

No se dejen engañar by those who say you should mind your own business.

No se dejen engañar by those who call you terca, cabrona,

sinvergüenza. Tell them we are, that we are proud, and that they should go to hell. Tell them we are chingonas, guerrilleras, luchadoras. Nunca se dejen engañar, my sisters, my daughters. Don't listen to their lies. Ever.

No, mis hermanas. You rage. You resist.

FREDDY VEGA

Just before he got really bad, my father told me: *Don't let them take what's ours.* His eyes held a look that was a cross between peace and straight-up fucking terror. Then he gripped my arm and said that to me.

"It's okay, Dad. It's fine. You're good."

Except he wasn't, and we all knew it.

He did too.

* *

Mercy shows up first. She'd hauled ass from Santa Barbara where she was attending a conference at a fancy resort. She did a hundred miles an hour down the 101, she said to me and Grace as she walked into his room. Her hair was tangled and frayed, her eyes wide and watery.

"Good thing I wasn't pulled over." She squeezes my shoulder and hugs Grace.

Julian gets here next, a panicked, nervous mess. He reaches into the bag slung over his shoulder. I hear the sound of plastic rustling.

He holds out my father's old lucha libre mask. He turns to his grandfather. "Abuelo," he whispers. "I brought you something."

Then my father opens his eyes, squinting, as his pupils adjust to the shift in light, as he's called back from the edge this one last time. What must we look like to him right now? Bits of dust? Shadows, maybe? Blurred silhouettes without form, indistinguishable from the other?

Julian hands the mask to me, a peace offering, a gesture that lets me know he's forgiven my shortcomings. Even though my son will never be a luchador like me or his abuelo, I know with absolute certainty that he's watched and paid attention all these years, that he understands the importance of this legacy. He sees now why we struggle and why we let ourselves be wounded. He recognizes how we honor one another, how we must cherish the traditions passed down to us from father to son to son, all of us unwilling participants in a saga that began long before we were born and will continue long after we depart.

I place the máscara in my father's palms, my hands cupping his own, my fingers laced within his, braided like strips of uncooked dough. He's so small, wasted away, a tan smudge against the white hospital sheets.

Julian holds up his iPhone to show me an old photo of my father and a skinny man with a bright smile, eyes so recognizable, a face I know but can't place. He asks me, asks him, "Who was this man? What was his name?"

But I can't answer him. Neither can Mercy.

Was this why my father held on for so long? This photo? This man? Because the machines stop beeping. The flashing lights go out, our ragged breathing the only sound filling the cracks between us.

El Rey Coyote

When things got bad and the economy turned sour, all the work in the capital dried up. Like so many, Julián couldn't find anything and resorted to hanging around on the street corners, stealing, even begging for change.

Spending time with Elena only reminded him of us, only reinforced the longtime dream he'd harbored of running away, far away, but with you. So he started avoiding her. Whenever she came by and knocked, he pretended not to be home. He stopped frequenting the bars, cafés, and the sidewalk taqueria. As time passed he grew restless. We were everywhere at this time—on television, in the movies, our face plastered all over the magazines. It was as though, try as he might, Julián could not escape us. This sent him into a deep depression, reminded him of how close he'd been to achieving his long-cherished wish. He wept, stopped eating, even contemplated suicide. The people of Ajusco, being who they were, fed him, kept him company, tried in their own way to take care of Julián. But charity can only stretch so far before it snaps and breaks.

He started drinking to numb the pain. And his neighbors grew desperate because they had enough of their own worries to deal with, so they all pitched in for a bus ticket, one-way, back to La Peña.

The young man who returned was unrecognizable. All disheveled and bitter. The townspeople shielded their mouths with their hands, gossiping to one another when they saw him roaming the streets or aimlessly picking through piles of vegetables, as if searching for a lost item, at the outdoor mercado.

What a sad sight.

See? This is why the capital is so dangerous.

He spent hours in that same cantina where you two first met up again, drinking cheap mezcal because he couldn't afford anything good. This made him even crazier, more erratic. The police would haul him off to jail only to release him the next day, and then the whole thing would start all over again.

Just like his father, they said.

In a moment of clarity, brief as it was, he saw what he'd become, saw what his country had turned him into, and knew it wasn't good. *I deserve another chance*, he told himself. *This will not be how I live the rest of my days.* He borrowed from relatives and friends, sold what he could, took whatever job was offered no matter how menial. It was long, but he finally had enough to make the trip there. Al norte.

Thanks to the Americans and their paranoia, the frontera was heavily militarized, guarded by men in trucks with pistols tasked with curbing the streams of migrants from Central America, flocks of innocent people escaping wars and political upheaval, the bloodshed and endless violence.

He went first to Ciudad Juárez, then west to Agua Prieta where he met a man they called Kiko. There were two others with him, a short lady in a flowered skirt and a thin sweater, and her teenaged daughter, a girl with wide eyes and green ribbons in her hair. They were from Nicaragua, they told him.

"La matanza," the mother said to Julián, making the sign of the cross. "Esta tan mal. We had to sell my hija's gold chapas to afford this." The woman pointed to her daughter's lobes, the empty slits where her earrings once were.

"Lo siento," Julián replied.

"You pay me," Kiko said to Julián, "and I get you and these two mugrosas indias across. You follow my lead." He pressed his thumb against Julián's temple, jabbing it into his skin. He crouched down, his face inches away, his breath hot and stinking. "Understand?"

"Si, patron."

From the bed of his truck, he handed the woman a pair of thick stockings and told her to put them on.

"Pero, señor, tengo calor," she whined.

"If you don't cover your skin, you'll get bit or scratched." He pointed to her daughter. "You should have worn pants like your marimacha daughter."

They went at night, walking through flat, dry clearings. It must have been after midnight when they finally stopped. The cool desert breeze calmed their frayed nerves. Near the base of a palo verde tree, they huddled close together to rest. The girl with the wide eyes was hungry.

Kiko sighed. "Of course you are. Pinches morras always slow me down." He gave her an orange from a satchel slung over his shoulder and a canteen of water. "Toma, desgraciada. Now shut the fuck up and stop your chillando."

Soon they were fast asleep.

It wasn't the sting of the snakebite that woke him, but the woman shouting into the blue-black sky just as the sun was rising. The girl woke next, the green ribbons in her hair lopsided, comical.

"He left," the lady said, turning to Julián. "He left us."

He thought the pain was from the walking. When he rose and the blood flowed down to his foot, the throbbing was so bad it sent him tumbling back to the ground. The girl pointed. His exposed ankle. The two puncture marks and the swollen skin. Touching the area, Julián cried out.

"I know that," the lady said. "It happened to my uncle. Culebras."

"I'm fine," Julián insisted. He pulled his sock up, took his time rising. "It will be hot soon. We have to keep going, or we'll die."

It wasn't long, though, maybe an hour of walking through that barren landscape before the heat and headache and the numbness on the side of his face made Julián collapse against a boulder. The woman touched his forehead.

"Fiebre," she told her daughter. "Este hombre no tiene mucho tiempo."

He urged them to go on, to find help. He wanted to live, he said. "Please. I wasn't meant to end up like this."

She thought about everything they'd endured, a job and her marido waiting for them in California. She thought about raising her daughter in a country where she wouldn't be kidnapped by the guerrilleros who would descend upon the pueblos to rape the boys and girls. What would happen to them if they alerted anyone in this foreign country about the mojado with the snakebite in the desert? The woman looked at her daughter, her eyes dark as pits, her ribbons unraveling. *They'll send us back*, she thought. *We will die.*

She unwrapped a handmade scapular bearing the image of Santo Domingo de Guzmán, the patron saint of Nicaragua, the cloth necklace damp with her sweat as she placed this on him. "I'm sorry." She kissed Julián's scorched forehead and parched lips. "Que dios este contigo."

They never found his body.

JULIAN VEGA

We start with dinner. This time at a sports bar with giant television screens bolted to the walls and staff in team jerseys. They're advertising a "game night," so our server wears a baseball cap, black smudges under each eye. As he rattles off the specials, he keeps stopping to tug his mask down.

"Sorry," he says. "This stuff's a mess."

"Eye black," I say to Clay once he scurries off.

"What?" He tears a piece of bread in half and takes a bite.

"The smudges. It's called eye black. Supposed to reduce glare."

"You think he knows that? He's just some loser waiter working a dead-end job."

For someone who likes to be tied up, pissed on, and humiliated, Clay can be a pompous asshole.

The place is half-empty. Busboys go around vigorously wiping down every surface with disinfectant. Everyone's in costume. Playing dress-up. I'm no different. The server brings our order. Clay drones on and on throughout most of the meal, whining about the service, the "tacky" clientele, the watered-down drinks.

I can't resist, so I ask, "Why did you bring me here then?"

He replies, his tone haughty, caustic, "I thought you'd finally relax."

* *

Maybe it's because I'm Mexican American that he thinks I'd enjoy this? We're heading out for something different, he says.

"It's this thing I read about in the paper," he explains as we leave the bar. He removes his jacket before we hop inside his car. I'd never say it to him, but Clay looks sexy tonight, all trim and muscled in his black T-shirt and tight jeans. He's gorgeous in this light, such a handsome specimen. Face all chiseled and smooth. He could be a runway model. And yet it's hard to believe the things he's capable of doing in bed.

What's harder to believe is that I find myself enjoying it the more he does it to me. Like I crave it, expect it. The sting from the paddle. The tightness of the cords around my wrists and ankles. The taste of the vinyl ball gag. The blindfolds and hoods and harnesses. There's the fear and, of course, the pain, the climax that comes from it, then the afterward. The slow release and the bliss that follows as my body is flooded with endorphins.

He's turned me into a junkie. I find myself hating him the more time we spend together, even when the tables are turned, when I'm the one on top, when I'm the one with the whip in hand.

"What is it?" I ask now as he starts the engine, and we pull away from the curb.

"Lucha libre burlesque," he announces with pride.

On my phone, I find the article. Apparently it's a big hit with the white hipster crowds of Highland Park, Silver Lake, Echo Park, and the Westside. Held inside a converted theater that used to show old Mexican movies back in the '50s and '60s. Two white dudes, tech entrepreneurs from Venice Beach, poured buckets of money into renovating the space. They hired DJs, exotic dancers, party promoters, and, of course, luchadores. They added nipple pasties, stripper poles, disco balls, glitter, and a ton of other tacky shit, threw it all together, and vomited this atrocity up.

"Should be fun," he adds.

"Yep," I reply, resisting the urge to roll my eyes at him.

We're driving through the dark streets of downtown now. Past city hall and Pershing Square, the main branch of the LA public library, floodlights illuminating its façade, unblemished, smooth and creamy as butter. Tarps, random shopping carts crammed with blankets, dirty jackets, stuffed animals, a rusted birdcage, crushed aluminum cans and glass bottles fill the sidewalks and overpasses. Since the pandemic, more and more people have been pushed out of their homes, unable to afford rent. They have no other place to go but the street. We stop at an intersection, waiting for the light to turn. Two RVs—one a Jamboree, the other a Winnebago—are parked alongside a silver trailer hitched to a red truck. The windows on all the vehicles are either covered with aluminum foil or scraps of cardboard.

"This fucking homeless problem is getting worse and worse," Clay says as the light turns green, and we go. "I get it and all, but find a fucking job."

"Unhoused," I reply.

"Huh?"

"They're not homeless. They're unhoused. You should refer to them as unhoused. I lectured on the power of words the other day. We talked about the connotative difference between homeless and unhoused."

Clay chuckles. "Whatever it's called, it's a problem, and I'm sick of seeing all this depravity." He shakes his head, reaches across, caresses my thigh. "What's with you tonight?"

"I dunno." I brush his hand away, stare out the window, nostalgic and sad for something that eludes me.

"Cheer the fuck up, will you?" he demands. "Or do I have to stop this car, throw you over my lap and spank that tight brown ass of yours?"

I know how I'm supposed to respond when his tone of voice changes like this.

"No, sir," I say.

"What?" He cups his hand to his ear. "What was that?"

"No, sir," I repeat.

He slaps my cheek, not hard, but enough that it stings. "I didn't hear."

"No, sir," I repeat again, this time more forceful.

"That's it." He smiles. "That's a good boy. Now, stop your fucking moping and let's have fun."

We park in a dark lot, pay the attendant in a bright red vest and bow tie. He hands Clay a ticket, glances over at me and nods.

"Buenas noches," he says.

I don't reply.

As we cross the street towards the theater, Clay asks, "That guy a relative or something?"

"No. He was just being friendly, all right?"

He stops in the middle of the empty street, grabs me by the arm, and says, "Would you please just lighten the fuck up, Julian? Whatever's crawled up your ass and died, get rid of it. I want to enjoy myself, okay?"

"Sorry," I say. "I dunno, I just . . ."

We reach the front entrance of the theater and stand in a short line behind guys in skinny jeans and wrinkled shirts. The girls sport pink hair and hold sad, indifferent postures. They fidget with the fringes on their dresses, pick at their chipped fingernail polish, slow, careless. Clay and I stick out among the crowd of sallow-colored faces, the thin bodies, the uncombed hair, the rumpled and distressed secondhand clothing. They're like rubber bands stretched to their limit, about to snap with the slightest tug. We reach the ticket window where a shirtless guy with a hairy chest sporting a frosted white wig in a pixie cut greets us. He dons silver lipstick, white eyeshadow, and there are gems glued to his cheeks. Proof of vaccination is required. We take our phones out, show him our e-verifications from the county health department. He nods at this and smiles.

"Enjoy the show, gentlemen," he says, then hands Clay his change.

Before we can enter the building, two beefy security guards take turns patting us down, their rough hands slapping our chests, stomachs, and thighs with callous indifference.

Inside the lobby, the atmosphere is different, festive and loud. Large color posters of vintage Mexican films are framed and hanging along the walls and over what used to be the concession stand. There's an old-fashioned popcorn maker, and behind the counter, two people serve cocktails and craft beers on tap. The female bartender is topless, tasseled nipple pasties suctioned to her breasts, and they twirl each time she moves. The male bartender is blond with a military-style haircut. He's shirtless and wears a white jockstrap.

"That's a very nice view," Clay says when the guy bends down to pick up a dollar bill that's floated to the ground.

There's music blasting, and we walk through a set of gold curtains into the main theater. The seats have been ripped up, the floor painted dark black. The ring is positioned in the center of the cavernous room next to a stage bathed in light. Stripper poles are bolted to the floor and rise up and into the ceiling. Above the tracks and catwalk is the original tiled roof, adorned in gold scrolls and etchings in an art deco style.

The audience mills around the stage and ring, drinking cocktails and beer out of plastic cups, smoking cigarettes, flicking ashes all over the floor. The scent of pot and cloves mix with the aroma of sweat and bodies. Some wear face masks, some don't. Others have purchased cheap replicas of lucha libre máscaras from a man wandering through the audience.

"Pay cash or app," he shouts, lugging a recycled blue Ikea bag around. He stops, fishes around inside, pulls out a Blue Demon mask and hands it to a short guy in dark sunglasses. An announcer in a tuxedo jacket and top hat appears onstage as the room dims. To get the crowd warmed up before the main attractions, a group of buxom female burlesque dancers join him. They're decked out in lace lingerie and boas. As the music starts, a bawdy tune with trumpets and piano riffs, the women strut around and the crowd cheers. The striptease that follows is artful but slow, lumbering. It gets tiring fast, even when they remove their tops, exposing pale breasts and tender red nipples. Then here come little people wrestlers with names like Taquito, Mini Chupacabra, Baby Yoda, and Lannisterito, named for a *Game of Thrones* character, Clay tells me.

"You've never watched it?" he asks.

I shake my head.

"It's brilliant. We'll screen some of the episodes next time."

"Great." I suddenly can't stomach another second with him.

The minis continue tackling and pinning each other down as the crowd laughs and mocks them.

One girl in a canary-yellow knit sweater turns to her friend and shouts, "Am I the only one who finds this politically incorrect?"

The friend shakes her head. Strands of oily brown hair caress her cheeks. "I heard them say today's, like, Mexican Independence Day, but isn't that, you know, Cinco de Mayo?"

The first girl screams, "I have no clue. I'm terrible when it comes to history or whatever."

Jesus Christ.

The minis finish, and more stripteases by women and male exotic dancers in jockstraps follow. We can't see their faces because they all sport lucha masks, wrestlers I can't identify when Clay asks me who is who.

"I thought you were raised on this," he shouts over the music.

"I don't know what the hell this shit is," I say.

During the intermission, we watch a guy dressed as a clown make balloon animals. In the lobby a woman sits at a table offering tarot card readings, and up in the balcony, a bearded lady in leggings and a neon-orange leotard is lip-syncing ABBA songs.

Things get rowdy during the main lucha brawl, so a handful of security guards appear from behind a service exit. They stand between the crowd of spectators and the ring. Wrestlers with names like Handsome Dandy, Salvaje, Shark Boy, and Edge, some in lucha masks, some not, duke it out in and out of the ring. They throw chairs, insult the crowd, act vulgar and crass. At least I can recognize the exoticos in their pink leotards and feathered hair, their tiaras and platform boots. I think about Scarlet Santos, my godmother. The last time I saw her was years ago, at the fundraiser event when Phillip and I were together. Abuelo was fading. Fading, but he was still with us.

We're standing a few feet away when a técnico named Bobby Thunder lands a fly kick to the abdomen of the rudo he's battling, a guy called Dick Dirkledge, sending him careening into the audience. Hipsters scatter and Dick lands flat on his back. A couple of the security guards make their way past us, and because they're wearing black face masks and it's too dark for me to make out their features, I don't recognize him at first. It isn't until he turns back that I'm sure of who it is. Before I have a chance to glance away, to avoid his line of sight, my father spots me, reaches out, and grabs my arm. Intermission. The lights are back on. I squint, try focusing. He wears black pants and a black polo shirt, black boots and a belt with a walkie-talkie clipped to the buckle.

"Dad," I say.

He looks at me, then at Clay. "Julian." He laughs uncomfortably underneath his face covering. "What are you doing here?"

"Just . . . checking it out. And you?"

"Working. Security," he says.

Clay smiles and reaches out to introduce himself.

"Yeah," I say. "He's . . . he's my friend."

My father nods, looks at me, then over at Clay. "I better head back to my post," he says. "This crowd ain't so big, but Beto still wants us to be alert. Last time a guy smuggled in some GHB and was going around slipping it into drinks. A couple of the attendees were assaulted in the bathrooms and the alley out back."

"Got it," I say.

Before he turns and leaves, he says, "Call your mom, okay? She has some news to share."

As we make our way out after the finale, I glance over to where my father stands, arms crossed, stance wide as he scans the room. He notices me as I wave goodbye, nods, removes his mask and mouths *call your mom* as I turn and follow the crowd.

"So that's your old man, huh?" Clay says once we're in the lobby.

"Yeah."

"He's not doing his wrestling thing?"

"Nah. He can't keep the gym open so he's . . . doing other stuff."

"That's too bad. About the gym closing."

It's his sincerity, his pity that does it. The tone of his voice. Something red, hot, acrid lodges itself in the pit of my stomach, and I want to hit the last few remaining hipsters, push and shove them out of the way, and just run. Clay sees the mask vendor standing by the door, his bag nearly empty. He approaches him, and I follow.

"Do you think he has your grandfather's mask?" he asks.

"No, I'm not—"

Before I can finish, he turns and asks me, "What did you say his name was? Coyote something, right?" He looks to the man. "Coyote?"

"Ah, El Rey Coyote?" the man replies. "¿Si, si, como no?" He rifles though the Ikea bag and a few seconds later fishes out a cheap-looking replica of Abuelo's mask.

"Un-fucking believable," I say.

Clay pays him, and we head out the door.

On the street, waiting to cross, I hear a voice, far away, mixing with the shuffling feet and the chatter of people vacating the auditorium. My name. Someone's calling out to me. I turn and see him standing there.

Phillip.

There's that same face, a little more mature now, a little more seasoned, refined maybe. Still that tall physique, lean. His hair's grown out and he's dyed it, curly strands of honey brown tucked behind ears that are now pierced. His penny-colored eyes now behind a pair of silver-framed glasses.

"Holy shit" is all I can manage to muster.

"I saw you inside." He points over his shoulder. "I didn't want to, you know?" He reaches out to Clay, and they shake hands. "I'm Phillip. We were in college together."

Clay says, "Nice to meet you."

He points to the mask Clay's holding. "No way. Is that your abuelo's máscara? El Rey Coyote?" He takes it from him.

I nod.

Clay leaves to retrieve the car.

"You look good," he tells me when we're alone.

"You too," I say.

"So . . ." he stammers. "You out on a date?" He bobs on the balls of his feet.

"Sort of. I hear you're . . . moving back here?"

"Looks like it. Finding a place before my gig at the museum starts. Your dad mentioned this thing was going on. Thought I'd check it out. Something to do. Is it just me or was that—"

"Wild?" I interject. "Disorganized?"

"Yeah." He nods. "And, I dunno, kind of disrespecting the whole, like, tradition? Doesn't even compare to what your abuelo and dad did. I heard about don Ernesto. I'm real sorry."

"Thanks." There's a honk across the street. I see Clay's car, the tailpipe spurting out white puffs. "I should go."

"Maybe I'll see you around sometime," he tells me.

"Yeah. Maybe. Welcome back." I give him an awkward hug, taking the mask.

As I stroll towards Clay's car, I remember what he told me so long ago: *it's taken all of this for me to realize just how much you mean to me.*

* *

"I'm pregnant," my mother tells me over the phone the next morning. It's early, before seven, the neon wristband from last night's show still wrapped around my wrist, Phillip still there when I squeeze my eyes as I yawn.

It's not at all what I was expecting to hear when my father implored me to call her. *Divorce,* I thought.

"Are you keeping it?" I ask.

"Well, yeah," she admits.

I'm not sure how to respond, so I ask, "Is Dad excited?"

"At first he wasn't. I think he was scared. But life goes on, you know? People are getting married, buying houses, starting new jobs, having babies. We can't stay stuck forever. We'll figure it out. Like we always have."

You're going to be a big brother, she says, snapping me out of my daze, and I laugh a little at the thought. What kind of responsibilities will this bring? What will I have to learn? How to burp a baby? Change diapers? Feeding cycles? Maybe I'll babysit so they can go out to dinner and a movie. Teach my baby sibling how to drive when they're old enough, navigate college when they're ready.

Then my mother says, "Wait, hang on. Your dad's here. He wants me to put you on speaker."

His voice is low, quivering. "The nurse called. Your abuelo's dying."

It didn't make sense, but I asked, "When?"

"Right now. How far away are you?"

In my head, I map the distance from my place to the hospice. In my head, I imagine a network of streets illuminated in bright green, a pattern of intersecting lines separating me from the room where he is.

"I'm on my way," I tell them.

"Hurry. We'll see you there."

I hang up and go to my dresser for a clean shirt where I see Abuelo's máscara, which I'd placed in my tote the last time I was at the house. Wallet, keys, phone. I don't immediately go to my car, I open up the albums on my iPhone and scroll, stopping when I get to the photo I saved of Abuelo and that man. I realize why now, why after all this time, it called to me. That stranger. His face. The way he looks into the camera. It's the same stare Phillip had on his face the day I took him to the airport after his mother's accident, the same look he had last night when he saw me.

It's love. The purest kind.

* *

My father's numb, doesn't look me in the eye. Doesn't hug me when I walk into the room. My mom's sitting down, eyes watery, hair a tangled mess, a balled-up tissue pressed to her nose. I lean down to hug her.

Machines beep all around him. Red numbers and green dots flashing off and on.

I take the mask out of my bag and give it to my father, who places it on his chest.

Tía Mercy reaches out and strokes Abuelo's cheeks and kisses his forehead. She points to the photo I'm showing them on my phone. I ask my father, ask her who the man is, if they know his name, why he looks so familiar. They glance at each other, shrug their shoulders. *We don't know*, they both reply.

"He must have been someone special for Ernesto to have kept it." My mother rises from her chair and peers at the screen. "A friend maybe." From the side table's drawer, she pulls out a plastic box full of photos she brought from home. "I was planning on putting up more for him, but I got busy and, well, we don't want to lose them. I knew I saw it, here's the original."

As she sticks the faded Polaroid to the wall next to the wedding image of Abuelo and Abuela, his eyes flutter open, almost following her hands.

"Who was he?" I ask my grandfather.

My father says he's too far gone, that he doesn't understand. But he's wrong. I know he does. At five fifteen in the afternoon, he takes his final breath. A nurse comes in, marks the time of death and the date. Two orderlies wheel him away on a gurney. All that's left is his mask, a face hollowed out, empty, and the photos stuck to the wall, faded and incomplete. But I take a careful look at my father's face and know. I can see it now.

What my blood is made of.

* *

No costume the next time. No elaborate scenario. A week after Abuelo's passing, I drive up to his house, park, and walk through the front door and into the foyer.

"In the bedroom," he shouts.

Up the newly varnished stairs, gripping the top banister with a sweaty palm. Down the long hall, my footsteps muffled by the padding underneath the Persian runner. He sits in a club chair next to the bed, a drink and a lit cigarette on the table beside him. He wears blue sweatpants with white drawstrings and no shirt.

"What's this?" I ask. "Father and son? The thug again?"

"No." He smiles. Clay pulls his sweatpants down. His dick curves to the right, and I've never really considered the fact that it's both alluring and whimsical at the same time.

I smirk, and he notices.

"What?" he asks, taking a sip of his drink.

"Nothing," I say.

He reaches down and, from behind the chair's pillow, he pulls out the mask he bought that night at the lucha burlesque show. He tosses it to me and tells me to put it on.

"Wear it, then kneel before me, open your mouth, and get to work," he commands.

I stretch the fabric between my hands. My two abuelos. My father. All of us like cars careening down the same highway. Going forward, going backwards. Going east, going west. Going south, going north. Always following the same fucking paths.

"What are you waiting for?" he asks.

And that's when I hear myself speak for the first time. The real me living inside this one perfect body. I take it, that cheap replica, and toss it back to him. "Nah. I'm good."

Clay pulls his sweats up, stands, and shakes his head. "Julian, come on."

He reaches for my arm, but I shove him, and he falls on the floor. Hard. "Don't get up, Clay. Stay down because I'll hurt you. Don't fuck with me anymore."

Then I leave and know I'll never see him again.

* *

I ignore Tim's text messages for a few days before finally responding:

I'm out.

J, come on. Let's talk about it.

Thanks for the opportunity. Goodbye, Tim.

There's an email in my box later that day. Amid all the mayhem, I'd forgotten about my conversation with Sonia Sandoval-Meeks, forgotten that I'd applied to one of the full-time English instructor positions she'd mentioned at the start of the semester. The search committee was impressed with my file and they want to interview me. It's not a guarantee, but it's a good first step, a glimmer of hope, a move towards stability. I send a text, my fingers shaky but sure, nervous in a way I haven't been in a long time.

Hey. How are you?

Phillip replies, *Good to hear from you. What's up?*

Not much. You find a place?

I did!

I tell him about the interview.

Awesome, he writes. *Hey, if you need help prepping, let me know. We can practice on the phone before I head back there to settle in.*

That'd be great.

* *

I need in on this, I tell my father two weeks after Abuelo passes. I must help him carry on the legacy, must help revive the gimnasio. It's not much, but I take what I've saved from the hustling gigs and hand him a check, sliding it across the kitchen table.

His eyes widen. "Where'd you get all this?"

"You don't need to know."

My mom hovers over his shoulder, my baby brother or sister growing inside, becoming part of this, all of it. We'll take out a loan, I go on. Both of us. We'll reopen the gym, give those hipster organizers and their burlesque bullshit a run for their money.

"So . . . you're committed?" he replies.

"Hell yeah," I tell him.

He calls Beto and José, Kamikaze, and my nina Scarlet. We sketch ideas, stage a comeback.

It'll work because we are together, we are us, and we can never go back to the way things used to be. We all know this now. We are rebels, every single one of us. All our bodies whole again. Born and reborn in the presence of this mayhem, beautiful and terrifying at once.

ERNESTO VEGA

She caught me off guard. I was home, stretched out on our bed. My muscles were sore. (When were they not?) My skin stung from the slaps of my opponents and the bare-chested falls to the mat. My knees and arms were bruised and battered. The taste of iron was always on my tongue from the endless busted lips. Outside, a light rain was falling. Thick drops clung to the electrical wires like swollen tears. Elena moved around the bed, folding things, sighing, clutching her stomach. Reporters on the television explained the economy was good. Jobs were expected to grow. The government had a plan. The protests were calming.

But these were lies. We all knew it.

She reached for the knob and turned the set off, then walked over to my side of the bed, took my hand—sore from a sprained finger—and placed it in her own. When she told me she was pregnant, that it wasn't mine, I wasn't surprised or angry. The hairs in the sink. That scent on my pillows. I hadn't imagined any of it.

"Julián?" I said it like a question. My face felt hot. My heartbeat quickened. I closed my eyes, but it didn't help. "It's Julián's, isn't it?"

She nodded, then said, "He's vanished. What are we going to do?"

* *

369

I looked for him in the months that followed. I went around the construction sites but there was nothing. I sent word to his family in the pueblo, but they hadn't seen him either.

Julián had disappeared, and I was left with my wife, pregnant and carrying the child of the man who'd loved me, a man I had loved more than her.

What choice did I have but the obvious? *Raise the boy as my own. Give him the first name of my father, Alfredo, and the middle name of his real father, Julián.*

We took very little—some clothes, money, passports, the cardboard box with the clippings and articles. Here, too, was my lucha costume. I carried my mask in the front pocket of my jacket the whole way there.

Proof, I told myself. *This is proof.*

We packed up the car, filled the gas tank at the Pemex station before merging onto the Anillo Periférico. When you asked where, Elena, I pointed towards a vague cluster of hills in the horizon.

"Al norte. We won't stop until we reach the frontera."

* *

Only for a while, we thought. Just time away. A moment to breathe, to come up with another plan. But we knew what had been done. We knew there was now a reason to survive that was bigger than both of us.

The child wouldn't grow up here. This life deserved a fresh start in a new place, new soil. In that moment, nothing mattered. Only this: *Protect the family. Go immediately. Before it's too late.*

* *

They're all here now. My ghost wife, the other me, Alfredo, Mercedes, Grace, my grandson Julián. They watch, intention scored into their shadowed faces, as I die and am transformed. Alfredo takes my cara and shrouds my face with the hospital sheet. And I know with absolute certainty who I have been and who I will be as I push away so soft, so easy, taking this battle with me as I go. Outside, tree branches sway in the cool air. I imagine an eagle circling in the dark sky, a pack of coyotes gathering near the edge of a creek high up in the mountains of my boyhood home. They lick their paws. They sniff the air around them and howl in unison. *Come,* they beckon me. *Come weep with us.* Then I'm beside my wife and my lover's neglected bones. I'm with the memories of my son, the legacy of hurt and struggle I left him with. I'm with my daughter, watching her marvel at the curve of the earth as the airplane she travels in tips its wings towards us. I'm with my grandson, with the skin of his body, with the origins of his desires that I know are also my own.

My spirit will stay tethered to theirs, refusing to let go, even though I've failed each of them in countless ways. But I can only leave this behind, the shell of an insignificant man. And I want to tell them: listen, my children, listen. This is how we leave the world, and this is how we enter it.

Fighting. Always, always fighting.

ACKNOWLEDGMENTS

This book was born out of a random conversation with my husband one sweltering summer afternoon in Fresno, California, nearly a decade ago. Thus began an epic journey that led me down the crowded callejones and packed arenas of Mexico City, to lucha libre matches in swap meet parking lots and inside television studios, and to the neon-washed streets of West Hollywood and downtown Los Angeles. I remain eternally humbled and grateful to all those who helped guide me along the way.

Thank you to the many artists and scholars whose work inspired me, especially Lourdes Grobet, Heather Levi, and Fabián Chairez, to name but a few. Thank you to MacDowell for providing me the space and serenity to complete a significant draft; to Dean Daryle Williams and the College of Humanities, Arts, and Social Sciences at the University of California, Riverside; to my colleagues in the Department of Creative Writing and the Palm Desert Low-Residency MFA program, the Community of Writers; and to Concepción Rivera and the Tomás Rivera Endowment for the generous research support.

To my friends and colleagues across the state, across the country, across the world, and across the various universities where I taught during this process. Thank you to Tod Goldberg, Michael Jaime-Becerra, David Ulin, Gabriela Jauregui, Brett Hall Jones, Lisa Alvarez, Michelle Latiolais, Libby Flores, Grace Ebron, Alejandra Marchevsky, Dionne Espinoza, Beth Baker-Cristales, Jason Elias, Patrick Sharp, José Anguiano, Michelle Hawley, Maria Karafilis,

ACKNOWLEDGMENTS

Linda Greenberg, David Olsen, Pablo Baler, Larissa Mercado-López, Cristina Herrera, Saúl Jiménez-Sandoval, Shane Moreman, Honora Chapman, William E. Skuban, Blain Roberts, Ethan Kytle, Analola Santana, Adela Santana (QEPD), Andrew Winer, Sara Borjas, Gabriel Ibarra, Macarena Hernandez, Carlin and Jim Naify, John Rechy, Maret Orliss, Denise Hamilton, William "Memo" Nericcio, Jonathan Alexander, Josh Kun, Ruben Quesada, Armando García, Ricky Rodriguez, Luis Alberto Urrea, and Xochitl Julisa-Bermejo. You picked up when I called, invited me to lunch, gifted me figurines and cards of wrestlers to keep me motivated, wrote letters of support for me, taught my work in your classes, accompanied me on wild lucha libre excursions, and always had my back. Thank you especially to the ever-gracious Janet Fitch, who read a rough version during the COVID-19 lockdowns and sat with me (six feet apart) on her deck to talk through some necessary revisions. Also, special bendiciones infinitas y agradecimiento to Susan Straight for consistently providing praise and sound bits of advice no matter how many times she read it.

To my wonderful agent, Eleanor Jackson, for her enthusiasm and trust in me and my vision and for consistently asking me the right questions. To Olivia Taylor Smith—dear friend and brilliant editor—who championed this book from the very beginning and helped me see it in new, daring ways. To the entire team at Simon & Schuster for the warm welcome. Special thanks to Brittany Adames for providing vital input. Every writer should be so lucky to have such advocates in their corner.

To el Santo, Blue Demon, Mil Máscaras, Rey Misterio, El Hijo de Rey Misterio, Rey Misterio Jr., Lady Maldad, Adorable Rubí, Chabela Romero, Irma González, Arturito, Pequeño Goliath, and Cassandro. Their artistry, athleticism, and contribution to the sport provided boundless inspiration and entertainment. And lastly, to Kyle Behen, my favorite tecnico and the one who matters most. This one especially is for you, my love.

ABOUT THE AUTHOR

Alex Espinoza was born in Tijuana, Mexico, and raised in Southern California. His debut novel, *Still Water Saints*, was published to wide critical acclaim. His second novel, *The Five Acts of Diego León*, was the winner of a 2014 American Book Award from the Before Columbus Foundation. Other awards include fellowships from the Bread Loaf Writers' Conference, the National Endowment for the Arts, and MacDowell. He is the author of the nonfiction book *Cruising: An Intimate History of a Radical Pastime* and has written essays, reviews, and stories for the *New York Times Magazine*, *Virginia Quarterly Review*, *Los Angeles Times*, *Lit Hub*, and NPR. His short story "Detainment" was selected for inclusion in the 2022 *Best American Mystery and Suspense Stories*. Alex lives in Los Angeles with his husband, Kyle, and teaches at the University of California, Riverside, where he serves as the Tomás Rivera Endowed Chair and professor of creative writing.